Watch Me Burn

SHARON BAYLISS

Watch Me Burn: Book Two of The December People series

Published October 2019 by Animus Ferrum Publishing
Mishawaka, Indiana
http://www.animusferrum.com/

ANIMUS FERRUM
PUBLISHING

978-1-948661-60-7 - paperback
978-1-948661-59-1 - ebook

Format design graphics by Curiosity Quills Press

For my husband, who shines bright enough for the both of us.

What is to give light, must endure burning.
-Viktor E. Frankl

CHAPTER ONE

David Vandergraff could smell magic in the air, as clearly as he could smell the motor oil and burned coffee. When the news report began, the volume on the television became much louder, and the screen glowed as if demons would claw their way out at any minute. However, none of the other patrons in the waiting room of the mechanic's shop noticed anything different. They continued staring at their phones, looking pale and sick in the fluorescent light and excessive air conditioning. Before David had known he was a wizard, he dismissed such oddities as "just one of those things you can't explain." But now, he knew better.

The image of the missing girl on the screen shined so intensely, he could see her outline burned into the blackness behind his eyelids when he blinked. The girl posed in her volleyball uniform, displaying a radiant, white-toothed smile. She looked about fourteen or fifteen. She had blonde hair and golden skin and a strange radiating quality, as if the pixels in the television gave her an extra glow.

David shook his head. Since he had learned he was a wizard, anytime he noticed anything strange, from bad weather to a headache, he feared magic was involved. His daughter

Emmy was blonde, around the girl's same age, and played volleyball. So, the missing girl reminded him of Emmy—and of course, that would upset him. Besides, his heart always raced when he saw a missing child. Two of his own children had been missing for a long time. And even though they were now safe at home, the fear and grief would never leave him.

He tried to turn his attention back to scanning job listings on his tablet, but he couldn't focus his eyes on anything except the television report and all the other sounds turned into a whirring buzz.

David usually dreaded hearing "Vandergraff" called over the loudspeaker, because that meant he would be asked to pay a large bill with money he didn't have. But this time, he appreciated getting away from the television. The report about the missing girl had played three more times while he'd waited.

He had memorized every word. Julie Prescott, age fourteen, 5'3", 120 pounds, blonde hair, green eyes, last seen on July 22 in Sugar Land, Texas.

He stood at the counter and thumbed through credit cards, trying to remember which one he hadn't maxed out yet. Their SUV had broken down three times this year, and the truck, four times. He believed all the dark, and therefore destructive, magic floating around his house caused their vehicles to self-destruct. And the water heater, and the AC unit, and the dishwasher. Either dark magic was at work, or the rental home they had moved into was a piece of crap...probably both.

As David had suspected, or at least hoped, practicing dark magic hadn't turned them all into raving lunatics or given him a Voldemort-esque snake face. However, the destructive power of dark magic, even unintentional dark magic, should not be trifled with. In any case, dark magic had many limits. For example…he couldn't fix the transmission. He had to rack up more credit card debt and leave it at the mechanic's for days while they puzzled over it and ordered the wrong parts, just like a Mundane.

Reveling in the smoothly-running engine of the fixed Expedition, he pulled out of the service center and Julie's face assaulted him once again. A billboard. He idly wondered how much money her parents dropped to get her face on a billboard. Whatever they had to pay, they did it at least twice, because he saw another billboard as he pulled into Fuzzy's to grab a bag of tacos for his kids.

While he waited for his order, he saw Julie's face again….on a bulletin board flyer, and no longer found it surprising. Her face had permeated his world. He didn't know why, but he could no longer comfort himself with the thought that he might be overreacting. Magic was in play. Julie Prescott was following him.

As he got out of the Expedition at home, he noticed something white on the ground. He plucked a missing person flyer off his shoe. She had followed him home. Julie Prescott with David's footprint on her pretty, smiling face. He half-folded, half-crumpled the flyer and stuffed it into the pocket of his cargo shorts.

"Hello?" David opened the door to a too-quiet house. He shivered in the aggressive air conditioning. If they were spending this much electricity on the AC, they better at least be home.

In some ways, he didn't mind that the house was small. That meant he could keep track of the kids. They had nowhere to go. The backyard consisted of nothing but a tiny square of dead lawn marred with a large stump. This also meant Xavier and Patrick shared a room, and Evangeline and Emmy shared a room, which felt cruel and unusual, but he couldn't think of a better alternative.

David looked through the rooms and only found Patrick, in his bedroom playing a video game.

"Hey," David said. "Where is everybody?"

"I don't know," Patrick replied, not taking his eyes off the game. "Did you check the living room slash kitchen?"

"Of course..." When Patrick didn't say anything else, David continued. "The Expedition is fixed."

"Okay."

"You could show a little more enthusiasm. You've been complaining about sharing your car all week."

Patrick shrugged, still not looking away from his game.

"I brought lunch." David held out his bag of tacos.

"Okay. Thanks. You can leave it."

"Is everything okay?" David asked.

Patrick paused his game and turned to scowl at David. Patrick was the only one in the family who wasn't a winter wizard. His magic fell in the Fall, perhaps as warm as September. But when he wanted, Patrick could give a glare as deadly as the other Vandergraffs.

Patrick always glared when asked if he was okay. David knew Patrick heard the unspoken question—*are you turning dark like Jude?* Before Jude had surrendered to the darkness, he had been withdrawn, depressed, and different from his usual self...much how Patrick had been lately. Patrick seemed to sense and loathe the comparison. David understood why, but he had to keep asking. He didn't know what else to do. He had no intention of ignoring it and letting his children fall to darkness one by one.

Amanda had put it quite sensibly when she said, "He may not be likely to surrender to darkness, but he can still be a depressed teenager. That's bad enough."

The front door opened, so David had an excuse to escape Patrick's oppressive glowering, and walk back into the living room slash kitchen.

Amanda and Emmy came in the front door, looking wilted

"Have you seen this?" David asked.

The moment they had stuffed the last partially-melted food item safely in the freezer, David handed Amanda the crumpled flyer with his footprint on it.

Amanda examined the photo. "Should I? Do we know this girl?"

"Not that I know of. But I've been seeing her everywhere today. More than should be normal. I'm thinking, maybe…there is some magic in play. What do you think?"

"I think she's a cute little blonde girl from a family with money, and that's why you've seen her picture everywhere."

"Have you seen her picture before now?"

Amanda squinted at the photo. "She looks familiar… maybe. But I haven't seen this flyer before."

"Well, I've seen it five times in the past hour."

"Okay. So?" Amanda

"I thought we agreed to stop pretending magic doesn't exist. You really don't think it's odd?"

"I think you're bored."

He didn't know if he wanted Amanda to be right or wrong. If right, he could go on with life as normal. He could feel scared and horrified that another child in the world was missing—in danger…maybe even dead. But he could move on.

If she was wrong and he reacted to a spell, then that meant he had some part to play in this girl's story. Someone had cast a spell to protect her or bring her home, and somehow David was a part of that. That was how magic worked. If someone wanted to find her, they couldn't cast a spell to levitate her back home. Magic worked within the bounds of normal reality. Magic could twist fate to its will, but it couldn't do the physically impossible. He had learned the hard way you could never fully anticipate how a spell would work. The means might not be worth the ends. However, someway, somehow, the magic needed to use David to save the girl—a frightening, but also warming prospect. He would like to be the hero. He wanted to save a child after she'd been missing for days…instead of twelve years.

"Huh," Amanda said.

"What?"

"Nothing."

She looked closely at the photo.

"Seriously, what?" David asked, again.

"Well, she *is* a witch."

David looked over her shoulder at the photo. In person, he could sense another wizard, but didn't get the same "pull" from a photo.

"How can you tell?"

"Look." She pointed to a charm bracelet on the girl's wrist and chuckled. "She *really* wants people to know she's a summer witch."

"You can tell that from her bracelet?"

"Oh, yes. This circle shape with lines, that's the sun. I've definitely seen this one before."

David thought he had too. He remembered that symbol on the badges of the summer wizards who had almost taken Samantha away.

"And this one," Amanda continued, "This triangle shaped thing, that is the elemental symbol for fire."

"Fire?"

"Sure, summer wizards worship the light. The sun. Fire. Anything that can burn the crap out of you. Light isn't always warm fuzzy goodness, sometimes it's just hot."

"So, I'm not crazy."

"Mmm…I think the jury's still out on that one."

"Think about it, if her rich wizard parents put up posters everywhere, *billboards* even, to find her, you think they would have also cast a spell to bring her home."

"Maybe, if they thought it was worth the risk. You know a spell like that is dangerous. You never know *how* you're going to get what you want, or if you'll still want it when you do."

"Are you listening to yourself? To save their kid? Hell yeah, that's worth the risk."

"You're probably right. But I don't think you should get involved. It's not our concern. You never know how the spell wants to use you. It might not be what you think. In fact, it's almost never what you think."

"I don't know what I think."

"If the spell is working through you, what do you think it wants you do to?"

"I don't know yet. I figure I'd stay open to it, and see where it leads me."

Amanda opened the freezer and stared into it, letting the expensive cold air spill out into the kitchen, and closed it again without taking anything.

"You know, if it were the other way around, they wouldn't help you," Amanda said. "And if you did somehow find this girl and bring her home, they would probably attack you on sight. A winter wizard anywhere near this girl would be considered automatically guilty."

"Yeah well, I'm better than that. I'm not going to go out of my way not to help save a little girl, just because she's a summer wizard."

"That's sweet. Also, naïve and stupid."

"You know, you're basing this on what happens when a dark wizard casts a spell. Since our magic is destructive, bad things seem to happen no matter what our intention. With summer wizards, it would be different, right? Their magic is good. Good magic with good intentions wouldn't leave a wake of destruction in its path. If we assume it's the opposite, then it would leave a wake of good fortune in its path."

"I honestly know as much about summer magic as I do about theoretical physics," Amanda said. "I don't know how it works, or what it does. But I don't want you thinking summer wizards are good wizards. If winter wizards aren't bad wizards, then summer wizards aren't good wizards."

David scoffed. "I think as a group, anyway, we're bad enough."

Amanda shrugged, and now opened the refrigerator and stood in the cool air for a while before finally grabbing the gallon of sweet tea she had bought.

"I'm going to take this photo and start asking around about her," David said. "Maybe I'll find something."

Amanda shook her head. "Can you at least wait until I get paid next? I might need money to bail you out of jail."

CHAPTER TWO

David couldn't focus on anything the next day—not that his current state of unemployment required much focus. Or, as Amanda said, he was not unemployed—he was a stay-at-home dad—always with a hint of a smirk. She missed the money, but she also liked being the breadwinner. She loved having that power over him. She had worked in the public relations department of an oil company for years, and specialized in saying "we're sorry about the oil spill" in as many ways as possible. She made a decent salary, at least enough to pay for bills, groceries, and rent on their dramatic downsize in Missouri City.

In principle, he didn't mind the idea of stay-at-home dad. He hadn't been the best dad so far, and now he could spend all his energy making it right. However, staying home with the kids had not turned out as Father's-Day-card-perfect as he'd hoped. He sucked at housework, and he had trouble interacting with his kids without buying them things or taking them on expensive vacations. He didn't bring in money and didn't do anything else useful either. He didn't know how much longer he would stay sane living like this.

But today even watching television with his kids and doing laundry took too much attention. He felt unsettled, as if he had forgotten something important. Or perhaps…hadn't forgotten something. He kept thinking about the missing girl. The more he tried to distract himself, the brighter her image burned in his mind.

He knew magic was in play. The spell reminded him of white noise—somehow loud and silent at the same time. A low hum that didn't exist before he had seen the girl on the television at the mechanic's. The hum ignited his nerves and he knew he couldn't focus on anything else until the spell had run its course.

With Amanda at work, he could do research on the missing girl without her looking over his shoulder and disapproving. He pulled out his tablet and did a search for "Julie Prescott missing." The search turned up lots of hits. Mostly news sites. All of the news sites said the same thing. She was last seen a week ago. Her older brother picked her up from volleyball camp at Sam Houston State. David's stomach tightened when he read this. Emmy had attended the exact same volleyball camp for the past two summers. She would have attended this summer too if they had been able to afford it. Had the girls met before?

On the way home from the camp, the brother and sister stopped at a Gas N' Go near Sam Houston National Forest. The brother went inside the mini-mart and when he came back, Julie was gone. The story sounded strange, even far-fetched. This happened within the space of a few minutes, in the middle of the day, but nobody saw anything, and the alleged abduction was not caught on video. The car was parked out of range of any cameras, but the cops had footage of the brother entering the mini-mart as he said he did. Perhaps that could be called an alibi, but since the brother was the last one with her, and the one who told this far-fetched tale, David wrote down his name. *Nathaniel Prescott.* He was, as they say on crime dramas, a person of interest.

David found another site that could be more useful—

www.bringjuliehome.com. This site had been created and maintained by Julie's friends and admirers, of which she had plenty. The message board had over two hundred personal messages to Julie. Most of the photos featured Julie with large groups of smiling friends—pictures at school, at church, at the beach, at camp, at Disney World, the Grand Canyon, and several other vacation spots. In any case, Julie seemed to have a glorious life.

After looking at the site for a while, David considered abandoning his quest, magic or no magic. Anger bubbled in his stomach at the sight of every smiling face. Julie had plenty of people looking for her, plenty of people who loved her and missed her. The news stations loved talking about her. People had created websites devoted to her. When his children went missing, he'd been alone. No one had cared. He had little help, even from the police. And wizards of Julie's kind thought the children of dark wizards weren't worth looking for. She didn't need or deserve his help.

David let his tablet sit idle on the bed for a few minutes. He let himself be angry. But after he let the anger soak him, he decided to let it go. He knew he couldn't stop out of spite. The magic wouldn't let him anyway. And he'd rather make it his choice, instead of magic compelling him to act. He was a good person—a person who helped others even if they wouldn't do the same for him. Even if he wouldn't be rewarded for his efforts. He didn't know if that was true, but he preferred that version of the story over the one where a spell forced him to do things against his will.

He picked the tablet back up. So many people showed up in these pictures and had left messages, David didn't know where to begin. He found a tab devoted to her volleyball photos. Her teammates showed up in many of the pictures. Last year, Julie had been captain of her school's 8th grade volleyball team. Just like Emmy.

CHAPTER THREE

Emmy Vandergraff hated the summer. She hated the way every day was the same. Only empty sky and empty days—over and over and over. She hated the way the hot air felt thick and heavy. She hated the dead lawns. She hated having to save water and electricity. She hated the chemical-laden sunscreen that clogged her pores. Her list went on and on.

However, this particular summer, she complained less. Not because she hated it less, but because this summer she knew she was a winter witch. And now, she also *hated* that she hated summer. It was just so expected and cliché. But since she hadn't known she was a witch for the first thirteen years of her life, she couldn't rebel against it. And now she had turned into the perfect example of a winter witch, except perhaps for better hygiene and her fondness for her cell phone.

But when Emmy first met Julie Prescott last summer at volleyball camp, she hadn't known about witches. She hadn't known she was a winter witch, and Julie was a summer witch. If she had, she would have avoided being so *obvious* and *predictable*. But since Emmy didn't know any better, she did the obvious thing. She *loathed* Julie Prescott. With no knowledge of magic, Emmy hated Julie on sight. Looking at Julie gave her a headache, and if she got close enough to smell her, she wanted to throw up. Not that she smelled bad…the smell reminded her of maple syrup. But the fragrance could wrap around her like a snake, coating Emmy's nostrils and lungs until she suffocated.

Emmy had no reason to hate Julie at first, no *good* reason anyway, but Julie did turn out to be a bitch. Well, not to everyone else. Everyone loved her. Emmy could hear her bubbly voice everywhere she went. She smiled constantly. Fortunately, Emmy couldn't get close to Julie even if she wanted to, because a circle of girls constantly surrounded Julie, following her as moths fly around a light.

However, on a few occasions, the coaches placed them in stations together or on the same scrimmage team. Half the time, when this happened, Julie would suddenly have to leave practice to use the bathroom or see the trainer. The other times, she pretended Emmy didn't exist. She chatted and smiled with every other person she met, but not Emmy.

On movie night, Julie came in late, and the only seat left was next to Emmy. Julie gave the seat one look and then turned around and left. So, yeah, she was a bitch. If Emmy had known what they were at the time, she might have at least understood. But last summer, when witches still all lived at Hogwarts, she had hated Julie for nonmagical reasons, or so she had thought.

Later that fall, they met again. And this time Emmy knew all about wizards. It was right before she went to the hospital…the second time…and so she hadn't yet been put out of commission for the season. They played Sugar Land in an away game, so no one else in Emmy's family attended. Not that any of them had cared about her volleyball games that fall anyway.

She remembered the whole gym blinded her, as if the fluorescent lights above might burst any minute. She had the inexplicable sense of danger, and wanted to run. Some of

Julie's family members may have attended, which may have been why the whole gym felt like a battlefield. She had felt so surrounded. This time, when Emmy saw Julie warming up with her team on the other side of the gym, the truth was obvious. Julie Prescott *burned* her retinas. She was a witch. And later, when the summer wizards came to save…or, not save…Samantha, her guess had been confirmed. Julie was a *summer* witch.

They were both captains of their team, so at the beginning of the game, they had to meet at the net for the coin toss. The ref asked them to shake hands, but they didn't. Julie stared at her, looking as if she chewed on Styrofoam. Emmy stared her scariest, meanest stare. She wanted to make Julie cry, or pee in her pants. She deserved it for being so rude. But Julie looked like a deer in headlights—shoulders tensed, eyes barely blinking, like prey staying still to hide from a predator. Who knows what the ref thought of all this, but he knew what was good for him, because he didn't ask them to shake a second time.

Emmy rifled through a tangle of clothes. Her possessions had become hopelessly intertwined with those of her half-sister Evangeline. Not that Evangeline had many possessions, but they still crowded the room somehow. Evangeline refused to buy anything new, but did enjoy picking out the most ridiculous clothes she could find at consignment stores. Right now she wore an old Little League T-shirt, and a poofy purple skirt. Evangeline didn't care much about her appearance, and probably washed her hair with a mixture of herbs and lamb's blood, but her long dark hair stayed shiny and straight. She must look like her mother, because she looked nothing like Emmy, except for the fact that they both looked mean.

Evangeline lounged on her bed reading her latest in an endless stream of random used books. From the cover, she currently read an Amish Romance. That girl would read anything. She had no specific tastes whatsoever.

"Stop it," Emmy said.

Evangeline cocked one eyebrow but didn't take her eyes off the page.

"I know what you're doing," Emmy said.

"What is that?"

"You're casting a confusion spell on me so I can't find my shoes."

"I am not."

"Some sort of concealment spell, then? Don't act all innocent."

Emmy stared at her and cast a spell of her own. Real spells were different from what Emmy had read in books. Wizards didn't practice fancy wand-work or spew long chants in Latin. They didn't collect strange ingredients for potions to throw in a cauldron. Magic turned out to be both simpler and more complicated than that.

To cast a spell, you had to visualize what you wanted, and then really, really want it. The second part was hard to explain; you had to tap into something deep inside you—the magic, she guessed—and let that power flow out of you. Once you got the hang of the basics, no one needed to teach you spells. You just wanted something, and made it happen. The trick was knowing what you wanted and how to make it happen. That part was not as simple as it sounded.

Evangeline put her book down and sat up. "Stop that," she said.

"Oh, what? Having trouble reading? Letters swimming around the page in meaningless patterns?"

"I don't know what you think you're doing, but it hurts. Stop." Evangeline had her eyes shut tight and rubbed her temples.

Once the magic went out to do its thing, you just had to watch it go. At least, Emmy hadn't mastered the art of "undoing" as Evangeline called it. But Emmy knew if she turned her attention away from her minor confusion spell...or whatever she ended up casting...the effects of the spell would fade.

Emmy heard a knock on her door. "Are you dressed?" Dad asked.

"Yes," she said.

Dad opened the door.

"I didn't say you could come in, though," Emmy said.

"You don't get to decide that. It's my room. I just let you sleep in it."

"Mmmm...actually I think it's Mom's room since she pays the rent for this crap hole."

Despite his big talk about it being his room, he stayed in the doorway.

"Evangeline is casting spells on me," Emmy said. "But you know, that's not even what pisses me off. She won't own up to it. She pretends I'm the crazy one."

Evangeline stayed on the bed rubbing her forehead. "You *are* the crazy one. *She's* the one casting spells on me. Just because she can't find her shoes. She's crazy."

"Maybe you could find your shoes if you didn't shove all your stuff in your closet or under the bed when we ask you to clean your room," Dad said.

"You always take her side," Emmy said, and collapsed onto her own bed.

"Emmy, is there a summer witch on the Sugar Land volleyball team?" Dad asked.

Emmy sat up, and stared at him.

"What? Why?"

Dad took a crumpled looking flyer out of his pocket, unfolded it, and handed it to Emmy. Emmy's stomach squeezed. She had truly hated Julie. But now, she was on a missing child flyer. Emmy didn't know if that made her feel sad, but it felt *wrong*. She thought those things didn't happen to the good wizards.

"What happened to her?"

"She's missing," Dad explained, unhelpfully.

"But why do you have her photo? Do you know her?"

"I got this off the bulletin board at the gas station. I saw that she played volleyball, and I thought you might know her."

Emmy stared at her knees.

Dad came in and sat next to her on the bed. "Are you okay?"

"Yeah," she said.

"You do know her?"

"No. Well, yes. I mean, I've never talked to her. But we were at camp the same time last year. And I've seen her at games."

"Your mother thinks she's a summer witch because of the bracelet she's wearing in the photo. Do you think she is?"

"Definitely."

Evangeline sat on Emmy's other side, surrounding her. Evangeline took the flyer from Dad.

"I've never met a summer witch," Evangeline said.

"Do yourself a favor and keep it that way," Emmy said.

Evangeline handed the flyer to Emmy and she passed it back to Dad quickly, not wanting to look again.

"It can't be that bad, right? Can bad things happen to summer witches?" she asked, echoing Emmy's own thoughts.

"Bad things almost happened to her when I met her," Emmy said. "She's got this warm, fuzzy vibe about her that makes everyone fall in love. All the Mundanes, anyway. Not me. I hated her on sight. I don't know how summer wizards aren't extinct. You'd think if they crossed paths with any winter wizard who was even slightly messed up in the head, they'd get slaughtered. Why are you asking me about her? I don't understand what's happening."

"No reason, I thought you might know something useful."

"So, you think I kidnapped her?" Emmy was joking, but not completely. If anyone knew how much Emmy had hated Julie, it might make sense to accuse her.

"Of course not."

"Well, good. Because I didn't. It's not like there is room to store her in here anyway. Check the closet if you want, but there isn't even room for my clothes in there."

"Was there anyone who had a problem with her? Any jerk boyfriends? Or other weird stuff? Anyone not like her?"

Emmy smirked. *You mean, other than me?* "No, Dad. Everybody in the world loves her. Like I said, we're not friends. I don't know anything about boyfriends or anything like that. If you want to know who would want to hurt her, I would say, all dark wizards. Just being around her made me want to claw off my skin, or her skin."

Dad's face turned green at this.

"Jesus, Dad. I'm just saying. I didn't claw off her skin."

David's discussion with Emmy made the humming of the spell grow louder. David excelled at reading people, and not only in the Mundane sense. He couldn't read minds, but one of his magical skills was understanding people's intentions and whether people told him the truth. And Emmy had told the truth. About all of it. She knew Julie. She hated Julie. But learning Julie had gone missing surprised her, and upset her. He doubted she knew anything else—at least he didn't suspect she was hiding anything. And as suspected, Evangeline had no more than a detached curiosity about Julie. She had lived outside of society for the first twelve years of her life, and aside from attending a small progressive, private school the second half of last school year, she still hadn't joined society in any meaningful way.

So, David didn't know why the spell had intensified. The girls didn't know anything useful. But the magic pushed at his knees and coursed through his body like extra adrenaline. The spell seemed…excited?

He could ask the boys, but they probably wouldn't have any useful information. Xavier was more detached from the world than his sister. Through years of trauma he had found a way to use magic to numb himself into a state of near non-existence. He barely seemed to recognize his own family, let alone strangers. Patrick had never been social, and had become even less so lately. He had stopped going out to visit the few friends he had. The only time he left the house was for his summer job as a lifeguard at the neighborhood pool.

Therefore, David doubted that either of his sons would know Julie. But David appreciated any excuse to engage his sons in conversation. His daughters bickered and cast frivolous spells on each other, but he could handle that. In fact, he had trouble stopping himself from smiling when he saw them fighting. They may not have gotten along, but they acted like sisters, and that made his heart swell.

The boys got along fine, but he'd rather they fight. If they fought, he could see the life in them. At least shouting was communication. David wanted Xavier to feel something, anything—a selfish wish perhaps, because he knew Xavier needed a way to protect himself. If he started to feel things, some of it would be painful. But David feared what would happen if he kept fading. Could he fade away completely? Snuff out his soul altogether? Would David one day wake up to find nothing behind his eyes?

The boys had left the door open, so David walked in. They played Grand Theft Auto with glazed eyes. They hadn't known each other for most of their lives, but they still looked right as brothers. In looks at least, as they reminded David of himself and his own brother, James. Xavier looked like David…almost exactly like David. They both had hair and eyes a bland color of brown, and eyebrows that made them look serious all the time. Patrick looked similar, but warmer in every way. In the right light, his brown eyes had hints of red and gold.

"Can you pause?" David asked.

The game paused, but they didn't stop looking at the screen.

"And can you also turn around, and look at me while I'm talking to you?" David added.

They did…slowly.

"This will just take a second." David held the photo of the girl out for them to see. "I don't know if you've seen on the news…"

David stopped. He felt a deep chill that made his skull tingle. Patrick's eyes sparked to life, all sign of boredom or apathy squelched. He stared at the photo. He didn't appear to breathe or blink. His face paled, as if David had shown him a picture of a demon or rotting corpse, and not a sweet, happy girl in a volleyball uniform.

Xavier glanced at the photo, but then turned his attention toward Patrick, a rare flicker of life in his eyes. But David could tell he was just reacting to Patrick. He didn't look twice at the picture of the girl.

A long moment passed. "What?" Patrick asked.

"What?" David echoed in the same confused, ghostly whisper.

"I'm sorry. Did you ask me something?" Patrick asked. "I didn't hear you."

"I…didn't ask anything yet. I planned to ask if you had seen her before."

"I…" Patrick looked at the photo again, swallowed hard, and then looked away. "No. I haven't seen her before."

Now it was David's turn to stare for ten seconds. His mouth felt dry and he didn't know if his tongue would work if he used it. Finally he said, "Okay…thanks," and left the room.

CHAPTER FOUR

The only times Patrick had felt happy since finding out he was a wizard were with Samantha. Or the times with Samantha *before* his brother had raped her and she had left for New Orleans to live with some crazy aunt. Since then, he could think of only one happy day. The Fourth of July. On that day, things still sucked, of course. Unthinkable horrors filled the past, present, and future. But his family had fun that day. *Fun*—something winter wizards rarely experienced, and certainly not the Vandergraffs.

On the Fourth of July, they played with fire. And not in the controlled way they had on the solstice. They just played. Even though his parents no longer forbid magic, Patrick equated it with other dangerous activities such as drinking, driving, or sex—weighed down with rules and warnings. And Mom and Dad never let them forget it. "Approved" magic reminded Patrick of commercials for prescription drugs. The narrator talked pleasantly about all the nice things the drug could do for about five seconds, then the for the next thirty seconds they read the FDA warnings about all the horrible side effects. But on the Fourth of July, Mom had said, "If the Mundane kids can play with fireworks, I don't see why you can't too…for once, magic is probably less dangerous."

They went to a small park close to their house with a playscape and a few picnic tables. They chose a place far away from the city fireworks. Dad grilled burgers and Mom set out a spread of other picnic stuff, such as potato salad and iced tea. That would have all seemed super normal, even idyllic, if it hadn't been ten-o-clock at night, in a poorly lit park. But they wanted space to play with fire.

They set up a repelling spell around the area so no one would disturb them. Even though no one in the family, save for maybe Xavier and Evangeline, were good at magic, they found if they all agreed on one spell and cast it together, they could get the job done without much problem. Of course, agreeing on a spell was easier said than done. In most ways, trying to do magic felt like trying to survive in a foreign land when you only knew about ten words of the language.

But simple spells like repelling were so easy it was stupid. They just had to want it. Patrick would picture a bubble of darkness around them, not a scary darkness, but a safe darkness—one that could hide you from danger. He couldn't say for sure whether his visualization did any good or not, since they all cast the spell. He could sense the magic radiating off the others. It seeped into him, making him feel more powerful. Their dark energy filled the air, little demons floating around them as dark bodyguards. When he cast his spell, the already-circling demons stopped being wisps of smoke, and formed one solid impenetrable mass around them.

After he cast his spell, he turned toward the beckoning food on the table and saw Evangeline looking at him. *Looking* was the best way to describe it. She didn't glare, or a stare, or a gape. Evangeline's face didn't betray any emotion. She just *looked*, and he never quite knew why. But when she looked at him, Patrick knew she planned to cast a spell on him sometime soon. For his first predictions, he'd only been able to see big stuff that would happen seconds later, but his skills had improved.

Evangeline stopped looking at him then, but he kept close watch on her for the rest of the night, trying to avoid having his back to her…not as if that made any difference. He couldn't imagine why she would want to cast a spell on him, but that made it more nerve-wracking. Maybe this premonition came early enough that whatever he did to piss her off hadn't happened yet. He didn't get the sense she meant to harm him—her magic always looked dark, because she was a dark witch. That didn't always mean she had malicious intentions. Patrick could see the spell following her around as a black cloud ready to dive toward him at any minute.

Patrick didn't play with fire too much himself. Compared to everyone else, his fall magic was boring. He ate chips and salsa, while Dad filled the bubble with the smell of sizzling burgers and charcoal, and his siblings filled the bubble with light. Emmy and Evangeline engaged in a fireworks battle. Xavier kept to himself, drawing patterns of light in the air, occasionally spouting a shower of sparks at Evangeline or Emmy if they got too close. The girls ran around the perimeter of the playscape, their shoes crunching in the gravel, and flung light from their fingers at each other in a good-natured-to-the-death showdown. They excelled at creating sparks, but they also could throw gleaming balls, and release glowing currents, like slow moving-lightning. And the light didn't dissipate right away. Leftover light scattered through the park like fireflies. He hadn't seen Emmy play like that in a long time, and he had never seen Evangeline *play*. Before that night, he had almost forgotten Evangeline had barely turned thirteen. She was still a kid—or at least, she was supposed to be a kid.

All the while, even though Evangeline ignored him, Patrick saw her spell waiting for him. A dark cloud sucking up the fireflies.

Patrick watched the cloud hover for a week. Occasionally it would fade, or disappear briefly, most often when Evangeline had her nose in a book. That made Patrick wonder if his predictions could change. Perhaps the cloud faded if Evangeline changed her mind, or forgot about it for a while, like while she read. He wanted to see proof that the future could change, despite his prophecies.

However, the cloud still looked strong a week later, and he had grown tired of pretending he didn't know about it. Or…he was just having a bad day. The temperature had reached over one hundred degrees, and he had texted Samantha five days earlier and still hadn't heard back. And Evangeline walked past him, briefly blocking the television screen with her black cloud, just long enough to prick his frayed nerves.

"What?" he barked.

Evangeline stopped and turned to look at him. She looked around the room as if expecting to see somebody other than Patrick. She cocked her head and narrowed her eyebrows, a tiny version of the wrath Emmy would have served if he had yelled at her for no reason.

"Are you talking to me?" she asked.

Patrick regretted shouting at her, but kept with it. That damn cloud had to go. No one else may have seen it, but she *had* started it after all.

"Yes, I'm talking to you."

"I didn't say anything to you. I just walked by."

"I know what you're planning. And I want to know what I did to you to deserve it."

"What are you talking about?"

"You are planning on casting a spell on me. And a dark one by the looks of it. I can see it."

She cocked her head at him again, but this time she raised her eyebrows.

"You can *see* it? Really? That's…so cool. What do you see, exactly? Do you know what I'm going to do?"

"No. I see the spell, like a dark cloud. I can't tell when you're going to strike, or what it's going to be. And I certainly don't know *why*."

She nodded. "Hmm. I wonder if that's because I haven't decided yet."

"You haven't decided why you want to curse me?"

"No. I know why. I just don't know the best way to do it."

"Okay…are you going to tell me why?"

"I saw what you did. In the park, on the Fourth of July."

"I didn't do anything interesting that day…or, any other day for that matter."

"Yes, you did. You stole my spell."

"I what?"

"I cast my repelling spell around the park. You were standing in front of me, also preparing to cast. But when I cast mine, you grabbed my magic out of the air, and made it your own. And you made it better. I've never seen a repelling spell like that. When I lived with my mom, we had repelling spells around us all the time, so I know. You act like you don't know what you're doing, but you stole my spell and made it better."

"Evangeline, I don't have a clue what you're talking about. If I did do that, it wasn't on purpose. And I doubt I did it at all." Patrick thought about the magic he had seen around him that night. The wispy demons. When he cast his spell, they had disappeared, leaving a dense black shell of darkness around them. So, maybe….

"I saw what happened," Evangeline said. "I don't know if anyone else noticed, but I did. Your spell was better. Much better. A repelling spell might confuse people who come around, maybe hurt their vision, but yours…I think we were invisible. No one can cast a repelling spell like that."

"Well, I'm sorry I stole your magic. I didn't do it on purpose. So can you get over it? I thought you were more laid-back than this. Getting pissed about something small and holding a grudge that looks like a swirling vortex of darkness and evil seems more like an Emmy thing."

"That's not what I'm doing," she said. "I'm not mad. Well, I was mad. But that's not why I wanted to cast a spell on you."

"Well, then…" Patrick couldn't finish his question, because the dark cloud swooped in on him. His whole body burned, a cold burn, as if he had fallen in a pool of liquid nitrogen. The chill went deeper than physical pain. The darkness sucked out his light, eating away at him. The darkness that filled his mind felt so complete, so irreversible, it could only be death. But at the moment he thought he might actually die, the sensation faded. He shivered violently. Every single muscle tensed in pain, as if he had gotten frostbite from the inside out.

When he could see again, he had to look up to see Evangeline because he had fallen to the floor.

"Are you okay?" she asked.

His throat felt frozen and clogged. He couldn't talk, but he knew his glare answered her question.

"I'm sorry," she said. "Didn't work, I guess."

She held out her hand to him, and when he didn't take it, she grabbed his arm and pulled on him until he stood up.

"I didn't mean to hurt you," she said.

CHAPTER FIVE

David woke up with a headache. He felt hung over, and wondered if he had gotten drunk the night before and forgotten. But he didn't think so. He remembered watching television on the couch with Amanda, talking about…something. He buried his face in the pillow and tried to go back to sleep. Amanda had left for work and the kids slept in.

After a few minutes of throbbing pain, he gave up. He took three Advil and stumbled to the coffee maker. He stared at the pantry for a full minute before he remembered he was looking for coffee grounds. He wouldn't call himself a morning person, but this was ridiculous. The process of making coffee took three times longer than it should. He rubbed his temples as he watched the coffee drip into the pot.

He had a sudden panic he had forgotten something. Did he have a job? Should he go to work? Should he take the kids to school? There must be something he was supposed to do in the morning.

David felt a presence behind him and jumped.

"Did I scare you?" Xavier asked.

"Yeah, I guess you startled me."

"Did you mean to do that?"

"What?"

"You put juice in your cereal instead of milk."

"Oh…no," David said, looking at the soggy orange mess of juice and granola.

Xavier walked past him to stare into the refrigerator.

"Do you need a ride somewhere?" David asked.

"Where?"

Xavier pulled a carton of eggs out of the fridge.

"I don't know. School?"

"It's summer."

"Right."

Xavier cracked eggs into a bowl. He didn't look up at David to question his behavior.

"And…am *I* supposed to go somewhere?"

"What?" Xavier asked.

"A job or something I'm supposed to do?"

Xavier looked up at him now, and squinted at him with that tiny flicker that showed he noticed something happening outside of himself. That was all the reaction he ever gave.

"No," he said. "Not since last month. You worked for Amanda's brother for a while, but he fired you when he found out you were practicing magic."

"Oh, that's right. Son of a bitch." David had forgotten for a moment, and became angry at his brother-in-law all over again. And the anger distracted him further. He had glared at his reflection in a spoon for some time before he heard Xavier's voice.

"Dad?"

David put the spoon down. "Is there a spell that could give you a bad headache and make you, I don't know…stupid?"

Xavier shrugged. "Sure."

David waited for more explanation, but it didn't come. Xavier lifted the bowl of three raw eggs and drank them in one gulp.

David recoiled. "Ugh. I thought you were about to make scrambled eggs."

"That's a lot of work," Xavier said.

"You can't eat raw eggs. They have salmonella."

"Since when?"

"Always."

Xavier shrugged. "Okay."

David had landed on a coherent thought and now Xavier's *breakfast* had distracted him again.

"You think someone cast a spell on you?" Xavier asked.

Right, that was it. Fortunately, the coherent thought had been related to the only subject Xavier found interesting.

"Maybe. I woke up feeling confused. And my head is killing me. I don't know why."

"Maybe some kind of misdirection spell. It will probably wear off."

Amanda. Nothing she did made him angrier than when she used magic to try and control him. The first time she tried it, she irreversibly removed many of his memories. She thought she did it to help him, but he would never forgive her. He felt so violated when she messed with his head.

"You're sure it will wear off? Some things you can't get back."

"When I reminded you about stuff, you remembered. So the memory isn't gone. So, probably some kind of misdirection, or confusion spell, like I said. Those aren't permanent."

Xavier turned away towards the living room.

"Wait," David said. "Can I talk to you about something?"

"It wasn't me."

"What wasn't?"

"I didn't cast the spell."

"Oh, I know. It's not that…you know, I don't remember what it was."

"Okay," Xavier said. He started to turn away, and then

stopped. "What happened yesterday, after you came back from the mechanic's?"

David shook his head, trying to make sense of a jumble of disjointed memories. After he searched his memory for a moment, he forgot why. Xavier stared at him, with the same no-color grayish brown eyes David had. Xavier rarely looked at him so attentively. Or at anything so attentively.

"Okay," Xavier said. He nodded and pursed his lips together, looking maybe…worried? David had trouble reading Xavier on a good day. "I'm going to go watch TV."

Too confused to do anything useful, David spent most of the day in bed trying to sleep off the spell. He occasionally wandered out to count his children. However, even this confused him. He had lived most of his life with three children, and then lived with five for awhile, and now lived with four. So he found it difficult to remember how many should be there today. How could he love his kids so much and still manage to be such a crappy parent? He couldn't even remember how many he had.

By the time six o' clock rolled around and Amanda came home, David's headache had passed. He still felt confused, but had gained enough coherence to hang on to the fact that someone had cursed him. And he suspected his wife.

In that tiny house, he had nowhere to yell at her without being on display in front of all his kids. He settled for sitting on a kitchen stool and arranging his menacing eyebrows into a glare that would say it all. *I know what you did to me. How dare you?* And several other choice words he would never say aloud, but felt comfortable communicating with his eyebrows.

Amanda put her purse on the counter in front of him and sighed. Maybe winter witches didn't do well in the oppressive heat, but she didn't look well. Her skin seemed too pale and gray, especially for the summer. She put her head on the counter.

His concern distracted him again. He put his hand on her head, smoothing her pale blonde hair.

"Are you okay?" he asked.

She picked her head up, and smiled at him—the transformation too quick. Forced.

"Just tired," she said. "You know, the usual."

"The usual," he repeated.

"How…are you?" she asked.

Something in the tone of her voice and the way she examined him brought David back to his coherent thought.

"What did you make me forget?" He punched each word, so he could give the emphasis of yelling while still keeping his voice down.

"What do you mean?" she asked innocently. *Liar. Liar. Liar.* He had no doubt now. Maybe she could get away with this stuff before he knew he was a wizard. But now, he could see right through her.

His narrowing eyebrows must have said as much, because she sighed. "Calm down. It was a silly little spell. You'll be fine."

She turned away from him and went into the bedroom. David wanted to shoot death rays out of his eyes, and as a dark wizard, he couldn't shoot death rays but he could cause some damage with a look.

She could ignore him if she wanted. He might have forgotten something, but he wouldn't forget she had been the one to take it. Just in case, he had written it down in several places. *Amanda made you forget something.*

"Where's Emmy?" Amanda asked, continuing to ignore his rage. She came back out of the bedroom and had already pulled her hair back and changed into yoga pants.

"What?" David asked.

"Emmy…you know, your daughter. Where is she?"

"She's not here?"

Amanda's pleasantness melted away and she gave him a few curses with her own eyebrows.

"You have got to be kidding me. Your only job is to sit on your ass and watch the kids. And you can't even do that."

"Are you fucking kidding me?" Okay, he gave up. He didn't stop himself from yelling now. "This is *your* fault, Amanda. You did this to me. And then you left the kids with a man who could barely figure out how to feed himself today. You did this. *You!*"

"She's fine," Patrick said, turning around from where he sat on the couch. "She went out with friends."

"What friends? Where did they go?" Amanda demanded, while she dialed Emmy's number. Emmy's phone trilled in her bedroom.

"She leaves her phone at home so you can't track her GPS. We know you do that, you know," Patrick said.

"Dammit, that little…" Amanda trailed off into incoherent hissing. "Who picked her up?"

"Some creepy guy in a van," Patrick said.

"What?"

"Are you guys ever going to get jokes?"

"That's not funny," David said. Adding the only coherent thought he could manage.

"It was a couple girls. In my grade. A Cassie, or Chrissie, or something. Or maybe it's Erica."

CHAPTER SIX

Emmy dragged the vacuum cleaner out of the garage as noisily as possible. For leaving the house without permission, she had been sentenced to vacuuming and shampooing the inside of the truck. Her mom was such a bitch. She had gotten home at 8pm. *8pm*—when nuns and babies came home. She hadn't done anything wrong. Mom claimed she smelled cigarettes and alcohol on her, but she had no proof. But Mom didn't care about proof. She was crazy. And Dad wouldn't stand up to her.

Whatever.

The truck still smelled of Jude—a mix of sweat and body wash. Cleaning the truck was good because she wanted that smell gone. She didn't like thinking about him.

She plugged in her earbuds and listened to angry music— not hard to find in her playlist. She started by vacuuming the air in the cabin as if trying to catch ghosts. She cleaned the dashboard and the windows and mirrors, and found she didn't hate it. She might volunteer to do this every night, for the chance to be alone in the dark and quiet with something to do.

Then she pulled out the floor mats to vacuum and shampoo them on the driveway. Some small pieces of trash had accumulated under the mats and she reached for something silver she mistook for loose change.

The significance of what she held washed over her immediately. The object dripped in magic—an abhorrent magic that felt familiar. Her stomach squeezed into knots. She held Julie Prescott's charm bracelet.

Emmy put the bracelet in her pocket and continued cleaning the truck, with more dedication than she had before. She cleaned everything at least twice, until her hands stung from the chemicals in the carpet shampoo. She stayed out there so long, Mom had to come and call her in to go to bed.

Emmy avoided speaking to anyone when she came in. They probably assumed she was continuing to sulk about her punishment, but her throat felt too tight to speak. She headed straight for the bathroom. When she changed out of her khaki shorts and into her sleeping shorts, she kept the bracelet grasped in her hand.

The bracelet felt hot and pointy, as if she had shoved a cactus covered in fire ants in her fist. She felt about the bracelet as she felt about the girl. She couldn't stand it, without a good reason. Some of the girl's energy stuck to the bracelet, which meant this was Julie's object talisman, a protective symbol wizards kept with them at all times, which accumulated bits of their magic. A talisman Julie had lost. Emmy touched her own object talisman, a glass orb filled with holy water she wore around her neck.

Even though she found the thing innately distasteful, she didn't want to put it down, not even long enough to take a shower. Instead, she turned on the water on so people would think she was showering while she examined the bracelet in the full light of the bathroom. She laid it on the counter, arranging it into a circle. She didn't know what to look for. Some kind of answer. Some kind of information. She tried her usual senses first. She saw some clay mud crusted on some of the charms, but nothing helpful.

If it was Julie's object talisman, she could get some information from it by magic. Maybe get a sense of what spells Julie had performed or where the bracelet had been. She'd never tried to extract information from a talisman and no one had ever taught her how, but it seemed possible.

She held the bracelet between her palms and concentrated. She got an uncomfortable hot feeling behind her heart, but no insights. She tried putting the bracelet on. Other than feeling like the abhorrent bracelet might contract and lop off her hand, nothing seemed different.

Finally, she turned off the water and concealed the bracelet in her balled fist so she could leave the bathroom. If anyone noticed she still had dry hair, they didn't say anything.

Emmy crawled into her bed and Evangeline hovered over her.

"What's wrong?" Evangeline asked.

"Nothing."

"You haven't said anything since you came in. And you usually talk a lot."

"I'm just tired."

"Okay." Evangeline didn't sound convinced, but went to her own bed without saying more.

Emmy kept the bracelet in her fist and slept with the wretched thing right against her heart all night.

CHAPTER SEVEN

The kids had all gone to their rooms. Amanda sat on their bed reading, acting completely innocent. David took his pillow off the bed and grabbed the afghan that was draped over her legs.

"David," she said.

"Don't look at me like that. I'm giving you the whole bed. I'm taking the afghan."

She followed him out into the living room.

"So you're sleeping on the couch," she said—an obvious fact that didn't need stating aloud. "Listen…I'm sorry."

He couldn't remember the last time they fought and she apologized. "You're sorry? What's your angle?"

"My angle is apologetic."

"You messed with my head. I asked you to never do that again."

"Can you please trust me on this one?"

"That's not how it works, Amanda. I don't care if you had the best reason in the world. You don't get to decide what I know and what I don't."

"You don't understand."

"Yes, obviously. That was the point, right?"

"Fine, be mad at me. I guess next time I'll ask you to leave yourself a note."

"What are you talking about?"

"You *asked* me to cast this spell. I thought it was a good idea, so I did. And if I tell you, then you'll just ask me to cast the spell again. And then every day you'll be mad at me when I come home from work. Like some fucked up *Groundhog Day*."

David wanted to yell again, but her words sounded true. Getting that small bit of truth relieved his agitation, as if puzzle pieces in his brain had snapped together.

"Why would I want you to make me forget something? What could have happened yesterday that would be so traumatic?"

"It wasn't like that. You wanted me to counter a spell that had been cast on you. I did the best I could. I'm sorry. I'm not a fantastic witch."

That last line gave David pause. He couldn't remember Amanda ever admitting to not being fantastic at anything. Granted, she had lived most of her life as a non-practicing witch, and had been raised by the same, so she didn't have much training or experience. It probably annoyed her deeply to be a beginner at anything at forty-two. She sat on the couch, and pulled the afghan up to her neck.

"I don't want to fight," she said. "If you really want me to tell you what I distracted you from, I will."

"I…" David's mind had cleared, but he still felt as if he missed important things, like trying to catch smoke. For one, since when did she give in so easy?

"Tell me," David said.

"I don't want to lose you," she said.

David sat next to her. "What do you mean?"

"The good guys always win. *Always*. They talk about dark wizards being dangerous, but that's ridiculous when you think about it. The good wizards win every time. They're the dangerous ones."

"I think you're thinking about Disney movies." He put his

arm around her and pulled her close, even though he didn't understand why he was comforting her. She leaned her full weight into him, as if she might fall asleep at any moment.

"Maybe. I just don't like you involved in summer magic. I don't understand it, and I don't like it."

"Summer magic?"

She leaned over and grabbed the tablet off the end table. After a few swipes and taps, she handed the tablet to David, displaying a news story about Julie Prescott.

David sighed with relief, feeling his brain reorienting itself. He also felt the magic that had propelled him to investigate Julie coming back. Well, not coming back, exactly—it had never left. Now it vibrated in him more strongly than ever, as if the spell had been screaming over loud music, and someone had turned the music off.

However, the feeling of relief subsided, because he also remembered why he had wanted Amanda to make him forget.

David considered asking Amanda to cast the spell on him again, but aside from the grief she would give him, he knew she had been right. Her spell hadn't worked. Amanda's spell and the summer magic would battle it out in his head, which could not be good for him. The spells had fought for less than 24 hours, and he felt as if he had spent that 24 hours binge drinking, or running a marathon, or both.

So, that next morning, he felt sick and sore. But his mind had cleared, and he remembered asking her to cast the spell.

When he told her what he wanted her to do, she said, "Honey..." and patted his arm.

"Nowadays, you only call me 'honey' when you're about to say something patronizing," he had said.

"I think the magic part may be all in your head."

"Yep, there it is."

"I think you're seeing things that aren't there. It makes me worry."

"I'm not crazy."

"I know…I just want you to stay that way." She'd avoided his eyes then, in a way that made her look young. Frightened.

"I'm not making this up, Amanda. Maybe at first I had thought you might be right. Maybe I was just bored. Maybe missing kids get me all worked up. But the magic has been getting stronger. I don't even know if I'll even be able to sleep."

After David had spoken to Patrick and Xavier, the magic had gotten worse. Almost as soon as David showed Patrick the photo and saw him react, the white noise had moved out of the background. The humming vibrated through his brain. The magic screamed. So he dropped the matter and walked out of the room. He could hardly hear his own voice over what felt like a waterfall pummeling his brain. He also left because he didn't want to know any more. And that's why he had asked Amanda to stop the spell.

"It's something Emmy said, too," David said, carefully selecting which part of the truth he wanted to share. "About how any dark wizard would want to attack her on sight. I don't like that…I don't know what that might mean."

Amanda crossed her arms over her chest then. "Oh, I think I see what this is about. Really, David?"

"What?"

"Just because he made one mistake one time doesn't mean he's capable of something like this."

"What? Jude? That's not what I'm saying. I mean, I suppose it's possible but…"

"He's not a psychopath. He made a mistake," she said again.

"Why are you defending what he did?"

"I'm not defending what he did, I'm defending him. He's

my son. And if you're going to accuse him of every crime you see on the news, then hell yes, I'm going to defend him. Because that's not fair."

David's jaw tightened and he had to remind himself to breathe. He hated thinking about what Jude had done. And even more than that, he hated thinking about what *he* hadn't done. He had done so little to protect Samantha from harm and help her recover from it. Instead, he never wanted to look at her or hear her name again. She reminded him of not only of the darkness inside of his son, but the darkness inside of himself.

"I never accused him," David said. "That's not what I was trying to say."

"Because he's a winter wizard and she's a summer witch, he's automatically a suspect? If that's all you're going on, you could just as easily accuse me, or any other winter wizard. It's not exactly an airtight case."

"Yeah…I know."

"Don't even think it. I *know* it wasn't Jude."

"What do you mean you *know?*"

"I know. It wasn't him. He had nothing to do with it."

"When you say you *know*, like that…do mean like 'a mother knows', or you actually *know* something that proves it wasn't him?"

"What's the difference?"

"I think you know what the difference is."

"Don't be paranoid. It wasn't Jude. End of story."

"I don't think it was Jude," David said. "But…I don't want to even wonder. If the spell needs to use me…then I must have some connection to Julie. There must be a reason why it's using me. And it's a summer wizard's magic, so I have to assume the spell wouldn't be kind to me. Just make it stop."

And so she did her best. She specialized in memory magic after all. But the memory of Julie didn't slide out of David's brain. It *fought.* It clawed. It screamed.

David rubbed his forehead and closed his eyes while he spoke into the phone. He had hired a private investigator several times in his life—on multiple occasions, in fact, to try and find Crystal and his kids, and more recently to find Samantha's missing parents. He didn't know why he kept hiring Mundane PIs, because they failed every time. Mundanes just couldn't find missing wizards. He had accepted that, so he wouldn't try to have this man find Julie. Instead, he had asked for a full background check on the Prescott family. He wanted to know about any possible threats or anything unusual. Fortunately, since David had hired this particular PI before, and he had failed to find his children despite guarantees to the contrary, David had been able to negotiate a drastically reduced rate for this search.

When he called to give David the results, the PI started the call with a suspicious tone. "Why are you investigating the Prescotts?"

"That's not really your business, is it?"

"Normally, I wouldn't say anything. But I don't want to get involved in anything nasty. I'm sure you know, their daughter recently went missing? It's all over the news."

"Of course. That's why I'm investigating. The Prescotts are friends of the family, and the police aren't getting anywhere, so I wanted to look into it myself."

The man paused, but David's story must have convinced him enough, because he continued, "Well, I'm not sure what you were looking for. If the Prescotts have any skeletons in their closet, they hide them well. In fact, they seem to be some of the most good and honest people I've ever investigated."

David made an unconscious growling sound that he covered with a fit of coughing.

"John Prescott, is a pediatric oncologist—you know,

helping kids with cancer," the PI continued. "He's on the board of multiple charitable foundations. His wife, Thea Prescott, is a kindergarten teacher. They've been together since high school, and have been married for twenty years, and as far as I can tell, happily so."

"That's ridiculous."

"What is?"

"I don't know. Continue."

"They have five children. All who get good grades, are involved in lots of extracurricular activities, and have no significant recorded behavior problems. Their oldest, Caroline Prescott, is enrolled at the University of Texas. She had phenomenal test scores and went to an accelerated private school for her Junior and Senior year. Nathan Prescott graduated from Sugar Land High School in May and plans to attend Texas A&M in the fall, pre-med. Lucas Prescott will be starting his Sophomore year in the Fall. He takes flight lessons and wants to join the Air Force. Lucas has gotten a couple of speeding tickets and got in a fender bender. His parents took away his car. So, I guess that's a little bit of dirt for you, eh?"

"That's not exactly what I had in mind."

"They're a good family, sure. But I appreciated the challenge. I'm usually investigating cheating spouses who aren't good at hiding their affairs. The Prescotts took work. But I told you I could find dirt on anyone, and I did."

"You mean other than the speeding tickets?"

"Oh, yes. Let me finish."

"I did some extra digging into Nathan and Julie, since Nathan was the last one to see her before she disappeared. I included all of it in the report I e-mailed you. Nothing too interesting. They're both popular, and well-liked, even by the unpopular kids. Julie has a few ex-boyfriends that might be worth checking out, but they all seem like cream puffs, and my gut says they're not involved.

"And I already told you about the parents. Model citizens.

No criminal record, no scandalous rumors, not so much as a parking ticket. However, I did find something that seemed odd to me. Their oldest and youngest daughters...I can't find them."

"What do you mean?"

"Leona never attended middle school. After fifth grade, they withdrew her from public school so they could homeschool her. They cited she had special needs. However, there are no reports of her having any kind of special needs throughout elementary school. Like her brothers and sisters, she excelled and had no behavior problems. So, I don't know why they chose to homeschool her and not their other children. I was curious, so I looked into her as deeply as I could. As far as I can tell, she hasn't been seen in a year. They've given all sorts of reasons for her not being around. Not comfortable in crowds. Sick. At camp. Staying with relatives. No one ever questions them."

"So she never leaves the house?"

"I don't think she's in the house."

"And the oldest daughter, Caroline?"

"Similar story. Like I said, apparently she wasn't challenged enough in public school, because she's the only one of the children who went to private school. I found records of her enrollment at the Sabine Christian Academy outside of Dallas and then later at the University of Texas, but I can't find anything else. She has nothing on her credit report. I haven't found a photo of her more recent than four years ago. And even though the family is in crisis, neither Caroline nor Leona has shown up at the house. Seems odd to me."

"So, you're saying that both of their other daughters are also missing...but they've been keeping it quiet?"

"Could be."

"Why didn't you lead with that?"

"I did all that other research. I wanted credit for it. Besides, you wanted a comprehensive report."

David scoffed. "Alright, that was...useful. Thank you."

CHAPTER EIGHT

The night after Emmy found the bracelet, she woke up before the sunrise. Well, she didn't wake up…really, she gave up on trying to sleep. She had carried the bracelet with her for 24 hours, and the shock had worn off. She wanted answers. And she wanted them now.

She pulled out her phone and read news stories about Julie. She had gone missing on July 22. She searched her memory for what had happened that day, frustrated she couldn't remember the details of such a recent date. But that was summer—every day the same, blending into each other with no meaning.

She looked at her texts and e-mails from that day. Damn. No wonder she didn't remember what anyone had done that day. According to her texts, she had spent all of day at Lexi's house. She remembered now—they had lain out by the pool and made daiquiris with stolen rum while her parents were at work. Emmy had spent the night and didn't come home until the next morning. Just great. She had no idea what anyone else did on that day or who drove the truck.

She knew she should throw the bracelet into the Houston Ship Channel. No cops had come by, so no one suspected them of anything. No good could come from figuring out how the bracelet got in the truck, but not knowing would torture her. She doubted she'd sleep until she found an answer.

So, she cast a mild silencing spell on the house, crept out of bed, and grabbed the truck keys.

Emmy underestimated how long the drive would take. She was so screwed. When she arrived at her destination, the sky had already turned the light purple of pre-dawn. When Mom and Dad woke up and saw she had left…they would be beyond mad. They would also worry. She didn't *like* making them worry, but she didn't have a choice.

She pulled into the Gas N' Go where Julie Prescott had disappeared. Although she knew the police had searched it, they must not have found anything useful, because the gas station was still operating as usual. People went in and out for their morning coffee and cigarettes and such, and cars lined the gas pumps.

People had searched the thick piney woods around the Gas N' Go with a fine-toothed comb. Not only the police, but legions of volunteers. Helicopters. Dogs. And probably other CSI-style gizmos like heat-seeking goggles. Did she think she would find something the others didn't?

Yeah, sure, why not? Most of the people searching had been Mundanes, so what did they know about anything? Certainly some wizards had searched, at least Julie's family. But what did summer wizards know about dark things?

Emmy could feel Julie's noxious presence nagging at her all the way across the length of three gyms at volleyball camp. She knew she could recognize that feeling again. Emmy believed she might see, or at least *sense* something no one else had. At least she hoped so, or she would be grounded forever, and all for nothing.

The gas station itself held no answers. She didn't want to draw suspicion to herself or her family, so she kept a low profile. She pumped gas, and went inside to buy a Diet Coke and gum, and use the restroom. She worried someone would notice that a fourteen year old was driving a car, but no one paid attention to her. She thought she could pass for sixteen. She wanted to do as many things as possible at the gas station to give her time to look around. She even pretended to air up her tires so she could stare into the forest.

As soon as she looked into the forest, she knew she could stop looking in the gas station. The gas station was nothing more than a gas station. But when she peered into the trees, a hard, cold feeling in her chest made it hard to breathe. It felt like fear. She didn't fear the forest, or the dark, or even the monsters lurking in it. The fear was different. It didn't come from her. The fear radiated from the pine needles themselves. The fear breathed in the dark between the trees.

Something magical lurked in the forest, and something very evil. And that meant a lot coming from a dark witch.

She wanted to explore the forest, but a truck left alone at the station might look suspicious. She needed to find a secluded place to park with no security cameras.

She got in the truck and slowed when she saw muddy tire tracks about a quarter a mile away from the gas station. Someone else had also found a hidden parking spot. She turned in the direction of the tire tracks and found herself parked behind another truck—a Ford F-150 exactly like the one she drove now, except dark blue instead of black. The truck even had a football decal in the exact same spot where Jude had put his. Okay, so two guys in Texas drove the same popular model of truck and played the same popular sport. No big deal. But still...creepy.

The football decal was for the Sugar Land Bulldogs. And she saw a small silver decal hanging from the rearview window—the same sun symbol that appeared on the bracelet.

The truck had to belong to one of Julie's brothers.

She got out and scanned the forest. The sun peeked over the horizon, and warm morning light illuminated the road, but the forest stayed dark. However, this darkness didn't feel cool. In the Texas summer, *cool* didn't exist. This darkness felt hot and sticky, like tar.

If a summer wizard lurked nearby, Emmy expected she'd find them easily. She knew which way to walk—toward the jarring, burning sensation. She found him faster than she expected. The hot yucky feeling felt less intense than Julie's, so Emmy thought it came from a distance. But here he was. Not far away at all. As soon as she saw him, she retreated into the thickest thicket she could find, covering her legs with pink scratches. A boy about Jude's age walked in odd patterns around the edge of the forest. He must be Julie's oldest brother, Nathan.

He glanced in her direction when she dove into the thicket, but looked away quickly. Emmy guessed the ambient evil in the forest disguised her own dark energy—like a black cat on a moonless night. Nathan, on the other hand, might as well have worn Christmas lights and jingle bells the way he stuck out.

His magic felt different than his sister's —at least, weaker than his sister's. He had more of a flickering quality, like a candle trying to stay lit on a windy day. The darkness of the forest must be sapping his energy somehow. That would at least explain his bizarre behavior. He skimmed the forest, stepping in and stepping out, walking in erratic circles.

Emmy lurked within the cover of the forest, watching him. She found she could travel through the trees without any problem. And in their shade, he didn't seem to notice her. She could stand there and observe him from ten feet away. He would squint in her direction occasionally, and she thought he might see her. But he seemed to see things everywhere. He darted his gaze in all sorts of directions, looking for invisible monsters.

She watched him for at least half an hour. He looked similar to his sister, but instead of her blonde hair, his was a sun-streaked auburn. He was tall with broad shoulders, on the grown-up side of eighteen. She had never seen anyone so frustrated and determined. He reminded her of a bug crawling out of a puddle even though she kept pushing it back in.

Too late, she realized *she* was the bug—a moth circling a light, getting closer and closer.

Nathan stooped down slowly and picked up a piece of pointed branch. Emmy didn't think much of this, until he suddenly jumped up, and ran directly toward where she hid. Emmy tried to scramble away, but her hiding spot was too good—brush surrounded her and she couldn't move quickly. Twigs snapped conspicuously as she pushed her way through the brush. When she was nearly free, she tripped on a thorny vine, and Nathan found her on the ground clutching her thorn-scraped shin. He yelled out as if he had never seen anything so horrifying. *Rude.*

Emmy jumped to her feet and faced him, preparing to defend herself, even though she didn't know how.

But, his yell stopped abruptly, and he squinted at her as if she was still hard to see. "Wait...you're...*small*," he said.

"I'm not that small. I'm average-sized."

"I mean...you're not what I expected."

"What were you expecting? A big scary monster?"

"Yes, actually."

"What makes you think I'm not a big scary monster?"

"I didn't say you weren't."

Nathan hadn't dropped the stick, even though they stood at least eight feet apart. Emmy didn't know how he saw her, but she thought he looked a little big and scary himself. At least, now that she looked at him directly, her head pounded. But the sensation of unbearable brightness did fade, as if her eyes had adjusted to blinding sunlight after leaving a dark theater.

"You've been following me for a while, haven't you?" Nathan asked.

"Yes."

"Why?"

"It's complicated."

He looked confused at this. Perhaps in his life, nothing was ever complicated.

"You're looking for your sister," Emmy said.

"How did you know that?"

"She's all over the news," Emmy said. "I've been watching you. You know she's here somewhere, but you can't go into the forest. The forest is too dark, and you're too light. You can't see anything very well. And you can't penetrate the darkness much past these trees."

He stared at her. He let the stick go slack in his hand.

"I can go if you want," she said.

"What do you mean?"

"I can go inside the forest. The darkness doesn't bother me."

He squinted at her again, as if she had gone fuzzy. "No. You can't go in there. I don't know who you are or what you want. But it's not safe. You need to go home."

"You may not know what I want, but you do know who I am, or at least *what* I am. You know I can go in."

"Yes, I know what you are. And, I don't know why you'd want to help me."

Emmy shrugged. "I know Julie…sort of. We went to volleyball camp at the same time last year. I can help."

"Maybe you can, but that doesn't mean you should. You might be dark, and you might be a powerful witch, but you're also just a girl. There are plenty of horrible things that can happen to a little girl that have nothing to do with magic."

Emmy shrugged again. "I know."

Nathan jerked around, startled by something Emmy

couldn't see or hear. He looked so afraid. Emmy understood fear. Ever since Jude—her talisman—had betrayed her and left, she felt afraid all the time. But the only thing that made her feel less afraid was pretending she felt brave. If she pretended hard enough, the courage became real.

"Please go home," Nathan said. "I'm not going to let you go in there. It's not safe."

"I get it. You're noble. You want to protect me. It's very boring, you know."

He stopped looking around for invisible demons and smiled. "Boring?"

"Oh, yes. I mean…do people like you have to act all noble all the time? Or can you ever do anything different? It's so predictable."

"Yeah, that's what they say about fire. It's so…predictable."

Emmy gasped. She burned. Her fingers and toes hurt the most, as if she had been frozen and now melted—all her blood rushed in and her nerves flared up. The air in her lungs felt hot, and she coughed, thinking she might breathe fire. She could no longer see Nathan. He'd turned into a bright glowing mass.

The sensation passed and she realized she had fallen. When the brightness passed, she noticed Nathan had gotten much closer.

"Just a warning," he said, standing over her. His brightness had left a—hopefully temporary—mark on her corneas, and an orange smear in the shape of his silhouette hovered by the real Nathan like a shadow.

He reached out a hand to help her up. Emmy didn't say anything, but she chuckled to herself. He couldn't help himself. He was chivalrous even when he threatened her. She hesitated to touch his hand. The burning sensation had passed, but she didn't want to feel it again. They could hardly stand within eight feet of each other, what would happen when they touched? Out of curiosity, she reached up to let him help her.

His hand did feel too hot, but it didn't hurt this time. It felt like beach sand that had soaked up sun all day. She assumed she felt frigid to him, and that bothered her.

"Thank you, for helping me up, I guess. You did knock me down, too."

"I'm sorry. I don't want to hurt you, but I'll do it to protect you if I have to."

"You know what is different about me and you?" Emmy asked.

"I would assume, almost everything."

"I don't have to be good all the time. I can lie. I can tell you I'll leave now and never come back, but you don't know if I'm telling the truth. I could come back tonight. Or tomorrow, or a week from now. You can't know for sure."

"Please, just tell me one thing. What is your date?"

That took Emmy off guard. "My date?"

"Yes, what day of the year does your magic fall on?"

Mom had told her about this. Every wizard's magic falls on a day. The summer wizards had rejected Samantha because she was March 3rd. Too cold. But Mom had said only a wizard with special training could determine your date. Emmy had never been "tested."

"I don't know."

"I hope you're lying, but if you're not, it's even more important you stay away."

Emmy had no idea what he was talking about, and she didn't like that. She wanted to be back in control of this conversation.

"Why do you want to help me, anyway?" he asked.

"Why not?"

"You're going to return to a safe place now," he said.

"You can't tell me what to do."

"Yes, I can."

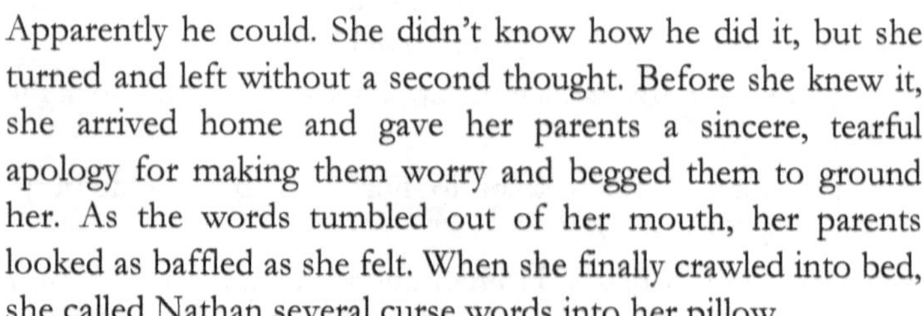

Apparently he could. She didn't know how he did it, but she turned and left without a second thought. Before she knew it, she arrived home and gave her parents a sincere, tearful apology for making them worry and begged them to ground her. As the words tumbled out of her mouth, her parents looked as baffled as she felt. When she finally crawled into bed, she called Nathan several curse words into her pillow.

Of all the nasty spells he could have cast, breaking her free will infuriated her more than almost anything else. She vowed never to let him do it again.

CHAPTER NINE

Emmy held her finger over the call button, feeling nervous. How stupid was that? She used to call Samantha every single day. She had been her best friend. Ever since elementary school, talking to her had felt as natural as breathing. They told each other everything. Well, Emmy told *Samantha* everything. Samantha had kept a big secret from Emmy. The entire time they had been friends, Samantha knew they were both witches, but never mentioned it. When a family decided not to practice, it was uncool to blab to their kids about magic, but still.

When Samantha's parents died, a Mundane social worker sent Samantha to New Orleans to live with her aunt. Emmy had talked to her a few times in the beginning, but then they stopped calling each other. Emmy didn't know if she had stopped calling Samantha, or the other way around. Either way, they hadn't spoken in two months.

Emmy missed her every day, but an image burned into her brain caught fire every time she thought of Samantha—the image of Jude raping her. Emmy knew she shouldn't avoid Samantha for that reason. But Emmy would do anything to take that image away. That image proved that everything she feared about herself, and everything that people believed about dark witches was true—Emmy was evil. She chose not to act. She chose not to save Samantha, and proved her own wickedness.

Emmy told herself that avoiding Samantha because she felt guilty might be cowardly, but it was for the best. Surely, Samantha had discovered other witches and wizards in New Orleans who she liked better. Spring wizards probably. They had fun all the time and nothing bad ever happened to them. Stupid little pixies frolicking in gardens, away from dangerous dark witches like Emmy.

Samantha picked up on the second ring. "Hey!" she said, and the enthusiasm sounded real, which made Emmy smile on reflex.

"Hey," she echoed back. "Sorry I haven't called in a while."

"It's okay."

"How is everything going in NOLA?"

"It's all right, I guess."

"Do you like living with your aunt?"

"She's nice…"

"But?"

"I think she thinks I'm a cat."

Emmy laughed. "What?"

"She treats me like her cats. When she wakes up in the morning and feeds her cats, she also puts out cereal for me. Like I'm a cat with a special diet."

"Does she put it on a table at least? Or does she make you eat on the floor?"

"The table."

"I'm sorry. I shouldn't make fun."

"It's okay. She takes good care of her cats. Never forgets to feed us."

"*Us?* Samantha, you're not a cat."

She giggled. "I know."

"Are there lots of wizards in New Orleans?"

"Yes. My aunt says there is a higher wizard per person ratio in New Orleans than almost any other place."

"So, at least you're not lonely."

"Of course I'm lonely."

"I'm sorry," Emmy said again.

"It's not your fault." A pause passed between them. "So, how is everything with you?"

"It's fine. Boring. Hot."

"I can tell when you're lying you know."

"You don't believe it's boring and hot?"

"You know what I mean."

"Can I ask you a question?"

"Sure."

"Do you still talk to Patrick?"

Samantha paused again. "No. Not recently."

"Oh."

"If you wanted to know, why didn't you just ask him?"

"I don't know. I like talking to you better."

Samantha laughed quietly.

"Well, I wanted to stay with him but it was too weird, you know?"

"Sure…"

"And we're too far apart, and all."

"Yeah."

"How is he doing?" Samantha asked.

"Fine."

"Are you sure? You don't sound sure."

"So, you didn't talk to him at all last week? No texts, nothing?"

"No…why?"

"No reason."

"You can't do that. Now I'm scared," Samantha said. "What aren't you telling me?"

"It's nothing. It's family business."

Samantha scoffed. "Then why did you even call me?"

"I'm sorry. I have to go. I really am…sorry."

David needed to learn more about Leona and Caroline. If the Prescotts had two other missing daughters, but covered it up, then they knew more about Julie's fate than they let on. Perhaps Julie had been too popular. Even if they knew what happened to her, too many other people would notice her absence for them to sweep it under the rug as they had with their other daughters.

He didn't have a good plan. He couldn't walk into their house and look. And he couldn't pretend to be the cable guy or something, because they would recognize him as a dark wizard before they opened the door. But he had to do something.

All four kids watched television in the living room, and he addressed them as casually as he could.

"Hey guys. I'm going to step out for a minute. I'll bring home lunch."

Three of them nodded with expected disinterest, but Emmy stood up. "Where are you going?" she asked.

"The car repair shop. The truck engine is making a funny noise. I want them to look at it again."

"Can I go with you?"

"Uh…you want to go with me to the repair shop…to look at the truck's engine?"

"Yes, I do."

"You're still grounded for sneaking out."

"But I can go somewhere with you right?"

"Um, I guess so. But you wouldn't want to do this. It's not going to be fun."

"I want to get out of the house. I'm going stir-crazy. Give me one good reason why I can't go."

"I…can't think of one." He had tried to think of one, but

blanked out.

"Cool. I'll go get my purse."

David sat behind the wheel with Emmy in the passenger seat. Now he had no choice but to go to the repair shop.

"Where are we going?" Emmy asked.

"Um…I told you."

"No, you didn't. You were lying. We're going to Sugar Land. I saw you getting some directions from Google Maps."

"Oh…"

"It looked like a house in a neighborhood. It's the Prescott's house, isn't it?"

"Emmy…"

"Come on, Dad. It's too late. I found you out. Now, tell me why you're going there." She had an Emmy-ish aggressiveness in her voice, but her eyes told a different story. She looked at him earnestly, almost frightened.

"Why do you care so much?" he asked.

"Why do *you* care so much?" she countered.

"I…" He didn't want to involve Emmy in any of it. He should have told her to get out of the car. But Emmy never cared this much about anything he did, and it felt good to see her care.

"What?" Emmy asked.

"It's nothing to be worried about. I thought I could help find her…Julie. Or, maybe I'm supposed to. I think someone cast a spell to get her home, and I'm part of it for some reason. It's hard to ignore."

Emmy cocked her head to the side thoughtfully. "Oh," she said. "That's it? Really?"

"Yeah, really. What did you think it was?"

"So, if you're part of bringing her home…then you, or

someone you know, must be involved in her kidnapping."

"Not necessarily. And why'd you say 'you.' I hope you don't think I kidnapped her."

"Probably not."

"*Definitely* not. I can promise you I would never, ever kidnap an innocent girl."

"Yeah, I know, Dad."

"Okay."

"So, why are we going to the Prescotts?"

On the drive, he told her about Leona and Caroline, and everything he had found out from the PI. She listened intently, asking questions, but offering fewer opinions of her own than usual. He knew he shouldn't bring his daughter to a home invasion. But in this case, it felt right. They talked to each other as two human beings sharing a common interest, which felt miraculous. Partners in crime, maybe—but at least they were partners in something.

With Emmy along, he knew he would be more cautious. No breaking and entering, just a little look.

"When we get there, do you want me to go peek in the windows? Maybe I could find Leona's bedroom and see if she's there," Emmy suggested.

"No. You're staying in the car."

"Aw, come on Dad. Think about it. If someone sees you lurking around, they'll call the cops. No one is going to take any notice of me."

"Maybe not Mundanes, but a summer wizard would. A dark wizard is a dark wizard."

"Still. They wouldn't hurt a little girl."

"If I were convinced of that, we wouldn't be doing this in the first place."

The Prescotts lived in the type of neighborhood you would expect—an attractive neighborhood near Southwest Freeway, with lots of parks and playscapes and sports fields. The houses were mostly spacious two stories, but nothing ostentatious.

He found himself driving slower and slower as he approached the little destination dot on the GPS.

"This is a bad idea," he said.

"Keep driving," Emmy said.

They could at least drive by the house. He thought he might feel their presence as they turned on their street, he couldn't tell. Summer radiated from all angles at one hundred degree strength.

As he got closer to the house, he saw people standing in the front yard and he slammed on his breaks with a loud screech.

"What are you doing?" Emmy asked. "Drive by and act natural."

"Okay. Get down." He pushed her head down.

"Why? You think they're going to shoot at us?"

"Just do it."

"Fine."

David tried to do what Emmy suggested and drive past them normally. That had to be possible, right? People drove down neighborhood streets all the time for all sorts of normal reasons. Why did that seem so impossible all of the sudden?

He realized quickly that it wouldn't matter how normal he acted. A block away, the three people in the front yard froze and turned their heads in his direction. It reminded him of deer freezing when they hear a hunter's approach. He recognized the three people as John and Thea Prescott, and their oldest son, Nathan. Nathan had either recently arrived or was preparing to leave, and the parents spoke to him while he leaned against his truck.

David had no choice now. They had seen him, so he might as well keep driving. Their stares followed him as he passed, and David gave them a nod and a slight wave. They did not wave back. Just stared, frozen, like big glassy-eyed deer.

As soon as he passed, he pressed on the accelerator to get

out of there as fast as he could without attracting more attention. He hoped they were too stunned to write down his license plate number.

CHAPTER TEN

Emmy managed to wait a whole two days before trying to sneak out again. She knew Nathan had hypnotized her or something. He'd made her go straight home and confess what she had done and ask to her parents to ground her. That was low. Although, his ability to bend her will impressed her. In general, no one could ever get her to do anything she didn't want to do, magically or otherwise.

She needed to go back to that forest. She knew she could go where Nathan couldn't. She could go where, perhaps, few others could. She could walk right into the darkness without blinking an eye. Maybe that's why the catalyst spell needed her and Dad. The magic knew only a dark wizard could save Julie from the darkness. That didn't explain the bracelet, but it did explain why dark wizards had to save her.

Sneaking out of the house wouldn't be easy this time. Her parents had gotten smarter. Mom had started hiding the keys somewhere in her bedroom at night. But Emmy had an extra key she didn't know about. Dad had talked Mom out of putting bars on the windows and locking her bedroom door from the outside because, as he said, that was crazy. If they had a bathroom in their bedroom, he might have lost the fight. But Mom couldn't bring herself to make Emmy and Evangeline pee in a bucket at night in their locked room.

Before she left her room, Emmy sought out the presence of each of her family members, so she could pinpoint their location. She could tell by the nature of the energy whether or not they had fallen asleep yet. She had also mastered the art of quiet. She had honed this skill while she hid from Whitman Colter in the pitch dark desert. She found she could slide through darkness and almost be invisible. Not literally invisible—but if the darkness were water, she could slide through it without a ripple or splash.

When she made it outside, she ran to the truck, her heart racing, cricket song covering the sound of her footsteps. She loved that moment. The moment when she knew she had gotten away with it. She was free. She would probably get caught, and end up more trapped than before. But at least for this moment, she could do anything she wanted. And what she wanted right now was to go lurk through a dark and evil forest.

She enjoyed this time of night. Around 3 a.m., too late for most people to be still up, and too early for most people to start the day. In the Houston Metroplex, people were on the roads all the time, but at this time of night, the roads had more of a hushed quality. And most of the stores were dark inside. Quiet.

Once she made it to the smaller country highway, the darkness became more total. She only passed a few cars. And even then, they were nothing more than anonymous headlights. She was alone. She had her phone off. She was nowhere.

She had to admit, part of her hoped she'd run into Nathan again. She found herself wishing it to the point that she may have cast a spell to make it happen. She didn't know if she could do that. The concept behind casting spells was simple, but she couldn't manage to get anything she wanted anytime she wanted it. Half the time, the spells she cast didn't do anything.

She found the little spot in the trees where Nathan had parked before. She was disappointed to see the spot empty. But as worried as he was about his little sister, she doubted he spent all night, every night looking for her. Last time she had seen him at daybreak. She guessed a summer wizard wouldn't venture out here until the sun came over the horizon.

She sat parked for a while before getting out. Despite her own darkness, the gloom of the forest intimidated her. It seemed as if forest wasn't dark because of the night, but the night was dark because of the forest. Shadows oozed from between the trees like tar, extinguishing all the ambient light from the massive metropolis around it. It reminded Emmy of when the family had called upon the darkness on the Winter Solstice. That darkness hadn't scared her—in fact, she had never been happier. That night they all got to be exactly what they were, but only the best parts of what they were. The twilight on that night had not threatened her, but exhilarated her. Vast and too beautiful for words—a night sky littered with stars, a deep infinity of beauty. Both proof something much greater than her existed in the world, but also proof all the magic and mystery in the world was hers to touch, flowing through her.

Clutching her flashlight, she got out of the car and walked past the tree line. She reminded herself again that darkness wasn't scary. She thought about how the darkness on the solstice had opened up her lungs so she could breathe more deeply and fully than ever before. The solstice darkness felt clean and pure as untouched spring water in a cave. However, this night felt the opposite. It suffocated her. It felt thick. Dirty. Walking through it felt like wading through mud.

She lost track of her path, and turned on the flashlight. The bulb looked dim and orange, as if the batteries had run low, but Emmy suspected the darkness in the forest was draining the illumination. She turned off the sad little light. Flashlights were tools for Mundanes anyway.

The trees seemed unusually thick, and it took forever to cross a short distance. When she finally got a pace going, she found herself back at the truck. She had walked in a damn circle. She slammed her fist on the hood. She turned around and entered the forest at a run, but within a few bounds, she tripped on a root and careened forward in some thick brush.

"Dammit," she said.

If she did make it home without getting caught, she'd have to find a way to explain how she got more red scratches on her arms and face while she slept in bed.

She shook a branch off her leg frantically. She had thought she would have no problem entering the forest. She had thought since she was dark, she had a free pass, and could just walk in. Instead, she felt…rejected.

A repulsion or concealment spell existed in this forest. She knew about these. She and her family had cast these spells before. A concealment spell couldn't actually make you invisible. But it could motivate someone to always look in the other direction. A repulsion would give someone a creepy feeling about a place, like it was haunted. You could also conceal by confusion. Make someone so confused they would forget why they came and left. Wizards had always needed concealment spells, and had gotten good over the centuries.

However, concealment spells, as all spells, worked within the bounds of reality. You couldn't make something invisible. You couldn't set up an actual force field around a place. If Emmy really, really wanted to walk through the concealment spell, she could. She might feel crappy doing it, and all instincts might tell her to run the other way, but she could do it. But if this was a concealment spell, why hadn't Julie's family gritted their teeth and walked in?

Emmy kept working at it, and found she could walk into the forest for a while, but somehow would change direction without noticing and end up at the road. The purplish light of dawn trickled through the trees, so she walked to the truck to check the time. After 6:30am. Mom would wake up soon, but Emmy had a chance of making it home if traffic wasn't too bad and she left right now.

Then Nathan's truck came around the corner, blocking her in. He climbed out of his truck and looked at Emmy. He didn't look the least bit surprised to see her there.

"What?" he asked.

"I didn't say anything."

"Are you okay?"

"I'm fine."

"You called me."

"I don't even have your number."

This started out as one of the weirdest conversations she had ever had, but he squinted at her as if *she* didn't make sense.

"You called me with magic," he said.

"I did? That is so cool."

"You didn't do it on purpose? You don't have any information or need help or anything?"

"Uh…no. I'm sorry."

"If you called me on accident… that means, you just wanted me to be here?"

Emmy felt her cheeks burn and she tried to will the blood out of them so she would stay pale and nonchalant. She had no idea what to say. She hated all of it, just as she hated the forest. She had no control.

"I don't know. I don't know how I did it, or why. It was an accident. That's what an accident means," she said

"You couldn't go in either, could you?"

Emmy scrunched her nose. She didn't want to admit it. "No," she said.

He nodded solemnly.

"What about the Mundanes? The police officers? They've searched every inch of the forest."

"You know how it is. Magic that's obvious to us is subtle to them. They *think* they've searched every inch of the forest.

I'm sure some of them noticed something off about the place. But they wouldn't know what it was."

"That's not a normal concealment spell, right? I didn't know they could be that powerful."

"Do you want to go get breakfast?" he asked.

"What do you mean?"

"Breakfast. It's a meal people eat in the morning," he explained. "Pancakes and bacon and stuff like that."

"I know what breakfast is."

"I came all the way out here. You could at least buy me a cup of coffee."

"You want to eat breakfast with a winter witch? Wouldn't that piss off your parents?"

"Hey, I already wanted to go to breakfast. You don't have to try and convince me."

Emmy turned her phone on and texted her parents. *Yeah, I know. I'm not there. I wanted you to know I am not dead and don't plan on becoming dead anytime soon.*

Then she turned her phone off again. Emmy followed Nathan to a Waffle House only a few miles away. When she followed him in, a waitress greeted him with this sad smile that showed she knew about Nathan and his troubles. No one paid attention to Emmy, but they were Mundanes. They had no idea winter and summer didn't belong in the same booth.

When he asked her to breakfast, she didn't consider saying no, but as she slid into the booth across from him, her stomach did flips and she didn't know if she could keep food down. He wasn't as noxious as Julie, but facing him head on from only feet away, for the time it would take to eat breakfast, horrified her. She couldn't figure out what part of his face to look at, so she scanned the menu for much longer than necessary.

When the waitress took the menus, Emmy had no choice but to look at him. She decided to look at his nose.

"I'm sorry about your sister," she said.

Nathan nodded. She knew it had been a useless thing to say.

"I don't understand why you're here," he said.

"You asked me to breakfast."

"No. The forest. Why are you really here?"

Emmy dropped her spoon. His question had a special quality about it—a command. And the intensity of it startled her. An image of the bracelet popped into her head and she stared at her coffee, trying hard to empty her mind. She didn't know if he could read her mind or not, but it was possible.

She waited a long time before answering. Planning out every single syllable of the words she wanted to say. He squinted at her as she stared at him in silence.

"I don't know," she said finally. She didn't tell the whole story, but didn't flat out lie. She didn't know what spell he tried to cast, but she must have cracked it.

Nathan leaned forward in his booth, as if he expected her to say more. When she didn't he leaned back again.

"I guess you really don't know," he said. "I don't like that."

"What do you mean?"

"Unless you have a habit of driving places in the middle of the night for no reason, it means you're here because of magic. As part of a spell."

"Maybe."

"Are you a *Vandergraff*?" He said "Vandergraff" as if he described a type of mystical beast, not her last name.

"Yes. Emmy Vandergraff."

"I'm sorry, I should have asked you your name. That was rude."

"You're Nathan, right?"

He nodded.

"Or, should I say 'Are you a *Prescott*'?"

He smiled.

"I know your name because your family is in the news," Emmy said. "How do you know mine?"

"I didn't. Not your first name. But we know about the Vandergraffs."

"Oh, do you? What do you think you know about us?"

"Not much."

"That we're winter wizards and there is nothing else you need to know, right?"

"We've left you be," he said, as if ignoring them was a great kindness. "Do you know why your father drove by our house the other day?"

"Yes, I do."

"Okay…why?"

"Oh, basic dark wizard stuff. Stalking the good guys. Being evil for no reason."

He smiled bigger this time. His face had this wilted, tired look, but smiling came naturally to him, he couldn't help himself.

"Is that right?" he asked. His eyes twinkled. Like, for real. As if invisible fireworks reflected in the greens of his eyes.

"Can I ask you something?" she said.

"Sure."

"Have you met a winter wizard before? You know, before me?"

"No. I've seen them. I haven't talked to one."

Emmy sipped her coffee and tried to pretend she didn't hate it. She never drank regular coffee, just sometimes the sugary versions at Starbucks. But she wanted to seem grown-up. Since she'd been driving a car, he probably thought she was older. At least sixteen, and she wanted to perpetuate the illusion as long as possible. "Would you be in trouble if you were caught talking to me?" she asked.

"Yes. Probably."

"Do you think a dark wizard took Julie?" She immediately wished she hadn't asked the question. She didn't want the answer.

His restrained smile faded away again. "I don't know," he said.

She sensed falsehood in his "I don't know." Not a lie, but not the whole truth, by a long shot. She didn't know how to compel him to tell the truth as he could do with her…or as he *thought* he could do with her.

"You know. Not all dark wizards are bad," she said. "I mean, just…mostly."

"You mean, most of them are bad, or they are all mostly bad?"

"Yes."

He laughed, that brightness breaking through again. He had a nice laugh. Even though sadness weighted his eyes, he laughed with abandon, as though he couldn't help himself. He tilted his head back and let the sound rumble though every part of his body.

"Well, summer wizards aren't all good," he said.

"Just, mostly." Emmy said.

"I guess so."

"My dad thinks someone cast a catalyst spell to get Julie back, and we're somehow part of it. Did you, or anyone in your family cast a spell like that?"

"A catalyst spell? Is that like spark magic?"

"I don't know what that is. A catalyst spell is when you cast a spell to get something you want, but you can't decide *how* you get it. Like, you could cast a spell to get a million dollars, and the magic would have your husband get in a car wreck so you get his life insurance settlement."

"Yeah, that sounds the same."

"But when you do it, it wouldn't be bad right? Your magic isn't destructive."

"Since when is fire not destructive?"

"Yeah, but light creates, not destroys. So the spark you lit wouldn't leave a wake of destruction in its path." She could hear the desperation in her voice, and didn't like it. Didn't he see? He was the light. He was the goodness. And if not, then did goodness exist at all?

He gave her a look that combined sympathy and confusion. He could tell what he said upset her, but didn't know why. "Well, it depends. The problem with spark magic is it's unpredictable, like you described. It's like trying to set off an explosion from a mile away. You have to light a long fuse, and the more complicated the magic, the longer the fuse. The fuse takes a long time to wind down, and you hope you set it up right, so the explosion goes off in the right place, or that it goes off at all."

"What do you mean, an explosion?"

"Well, not a literal explosion. At least, not usually. Just whatever you're trying to make happen. Fate doesn't like to be messed with. If you're successful at breaking it, it makes a loud crash. You know what I mean?"

Emmy did not know what he meant, but let it go. She had broken through his shell, and didn't have the patience to wait any longer for answers. "Where are Leona and Caroline?"

His face turned pale. Although it might not have actually turned pale, more as if she could sense his light flickering.

"My sisters?"

"Yes."

"How do you even know about them?"

"Why? Are people not supposed to know about them?"

"No…why are you asking?"

"You're answering all my questions with another question."

"Caroline is overseas doing volunteer work this summer."

"And Leona?"

"It's none of your business. I shouldn't be talking to you

anyway." He stood up to leave.

"Wait." She grabbed his arm without thinking about it. He shuddered at her touch. She pulled her hand away and wanted to shrink under the table.

She thought he would leave, but he didn't. He sat down.

"Are you okay?" he asked. "I didn't hurt you when you touched me, did I?"

"No. I thought I hurt you."

"Oh, no. Maybe surprised me a little."

"What do I feel like to you? Am I really cold?"

He smiled. "No. Not cold…refreshing."

"Yuck. You have to be nice about everything. It's so gross."

"No, I mean it. Do you have any idea what it feels like to be burning all the time? It's 100 degrees outside today. What sounds better to you? Ice water or lava?"

"I guess that makes sense."

"Am I really hot to you?" He blushed a little. "You know what I mean."

"Yeah, you're pretty horrible. I kind of want to gouge my eyes out whenever I'm around you."

"Thank you for sparing my feelings."

"Did you want me to say you were like a cup of hot cocoa with marshmallows?"

"Yes, I did."

"Well…I guess I did exaggerate a little. I don't really want to gouge my eyeballs out when I look at you. At least, not now that I'm used to you."

"Well, that's sweet. I don't want to gouge my eyeballs out when I look at you either."

She felt herself blush again. He hadn't exactly complimented her, but he twinkled far too much when he said it.

"Listen, I don't know what you think about Leona," he said. "But I'm sure you're thinking it's worse than it is. I don't want you thinking bad things about my family, so I'll tell you the truth about her if you want."

"You will, just like that?"

"Well, can you keep a secret?"

"Yes, I can." She shifted in her seat, thinking about the giant secret she had in her pocket.

"She *sparkles*."

Emmy had to stop herself from spitting out pancakes in a suppressed laugh. His tone had been deadly serious, as if he said she had leprosy or snakes for hair.

"What?" Emmy tried to match his serious demeanor, but couldn't suppress a grin. "Like a *Twilight* vampire?"

Nathan looked confused for a moment and then smiled. "No, nothing like that. I'm sorry, I forget we don't use the same words for things. *Sparkling* is a nice way to say it, I guess. We always used that word to not hurt her feelings. I mean, she's a kid. She's fourteen."

Emmy didn't like that, as if he thought fourteen was so ridiculously young that no one could possibly be any younger or naïve.

"What does it really mean?"

"Well, you know how summer wizards can attract people? People are drawn to us without knowing why...present company excluded, of course. Anyway, there is such a thing as too much of a good thing. The term you're probably familiar with is *siren*."

"The beautiful women that sing and make sailors crash their ships?"

"Yeah, that's right."

"So you're saying her curse is being too beautiful?"

"I know you don't think it sounds bad, but it's bad. Especially when you're young like that. It seems to come on around puberty, the hormones or something. When she's older, she might be able to control it better, but not now. She could cause people to lose their minds or be violent, not to mention attract lots of unwanted attention. She can't be around people."

"So, what, she's locked away somewhere?"

"No, not *locked*. She's at a special school, you know where experts can keep an eye on her and stuff."

"Like…a wizard school?"

"Yeah."

"There are wizard schools?"

"Sure."

Emmy stared at him confounded for a moment, before the obvious fact dawned on her. "Oh, you mean, for *some* kinds of wizards?"

Nathan looked at his plate. "Well…"

"No winter wizards allowed, right? Is there some kind of dating process you have to go through? What dates do you have to fall between to be considered worthy?"

"It's not like that," he said. He glanced up and met her eyes, but kept his head lowered.

"Oh, really? How is it like?"

"I'm sure winter wizards have their own things summer wizards can't be a part of."

Emmy glared at him.

"Besides, it's not a place you want to be. More like an institution than a school, I guess."

"Kind of like how you say she 'sparkles,' when you mean she's a dangerous monster? And she's not locked in an institution, she's in *school*."

Nathan bit his lip and poked at his scrambled eggs. He was useless in an argument. As soon as he looked sad, Emmy wanted to back down. No fun at all.

"I'm sorry I said your sister was a monster," she said rolling her eyes. "I'm sure she's just sparkly."

"No, you're right. It's easier not to think of it like that, I guess. It is bad for her. She'll always be alone. She can't ever fall in love or get married."

"Why not? You'd think she'd have her pick of anyone she wanted. They'd have to love her back."

"No, that's not how it works. Anyone she was attracted to would fall under her spell. It's a hormonal reflex she can't control. If she finds someone attractive, it releases pheromones that cause the siren song effect. She'd become like a drug to them. And if they managed not to destroy themselves getting to her, they'd never have a normal relationship. She'd never know if they really loved her or were addicted to her. But the siren effect isn't always sexual. Sometimes it's more like extreme charisma. Some cult leaders have been sirens."

"So, cult leaders, like the ones who lead mass suicides and have a hundred wives. Those have been *summer* wizards?"

"A few have. I told you not all summer wizards are good. Summer wizards are powerful, and power corrupts. It's almost impossible for a siren to avoid being corrupted by their power."

"Are your other sisters sirens too?" Emmy asked.

"No," he said.

Nathan's phone trilled, and he glanced at it. He winced. "My parents are coming out here." He looked her square in the eyes. "You should go home," he said, and he tried to command her.

Emmy did the same thing she had before. She got still and quiet and focused hard on what she would say next. The reaction, the easy thing, would be to obey. But she could resist him if she concentrated.

"No," she said finally.

He raised his eyebrows. "No?"

"No."

He sat up straight and looked confused. He looked at his phone, and then out the window, and then back at her. He looked so lost.

"Oh, calm down," Emmy said. "I don't want to get you in trouble. I'll go. I just wanted you to know that it was up to me."

He nodded slowly, as if now he was the one in the trace. "Okay. Thank you."

He insisted on paying for her breakfast and she didn't know if that meant it had been a date, or if it was a side effect of his unstoppable niceness.

He also walked her to her truck, keeping his eye on the road the whole time.

"Can I see your phone?" he asked.

"Why?"

"I know you don't need my phone number to call me. But it is a lot easier."

"Oh," she said. She turned on her phone and handed to him.

When Emmy got home, Mom and Dad waited for her. But they didn't yell, they just glared at her. Their seething silence intimidated her more than yelling.

"So, where were you?" Dad asked.

"I was at a strip club smoking crack. And then I robbed a convenience store."

Mom and Dad glared harder.

"You know what, Emmy?" Mom asked. "I don't even care. It doesn't matter what I do. Nothing I do or say matters. You're so selfish and childish, you're beyond hope."

Mom handed her an envelope and Emmy stared at it.

"If you're working as a stripper, dealing crack, and robbing convenience stores," Mom said. "Then I'm going to ask you to use your ill-gotten gains to pay this credit card bill."

"I was obviously joking."

"Then, go get a real job."

"I'm fourteen."

"Are you? Really? I thought you were a grown-up. You know, since you can do whatever you want all the time and don't have to listen to your parents."

"I—"

"Do whatever you want, Emmy. I don't care. I give up." Mom went into her bedroom and slammed the door.

Dad continued glaring at her.

"So, am I grounded, or what? Are you going to take my phone away? Why don't we skip to the punishment part?"

"What's the point of that? You're going to find a way around it," Dad said. "We're trying to keep you safe. Why do you to have to make that so hard for us?"

"I'm not putting myself in danger. I can take care of myself."

"You have no respect for us. And you have no respect for yourself."

"Would you please punish me already?"

"Are you sneaking out to see *him*?"

"Who?"

"Your brother."

"What, you can't even say his name now? Are we going to call him he-who-must-not-be-named?"

"That's not funny."

"No, I'm not seeing *Jude*. We haven't spoken." Her voice hurt when she said it. She felt her throat tightening.

"I obviously don't think you should see him. But if you have, you can tell me. I know it's difficult to be away from your talisman."

Just hearing him say it out loud made her chest hurt. It also made her eyes hurt, and the bottoms of her feet hurt.

"Why don't you just punish me?" She had to push the words out of her constricted throat.

"I will. When I think of an appropriate punishment. One that might actually work."

"So, you're going to hang the axe over my head and not

even tell me?"

"Just go to your room, Emmy. Get some sleep."

She started walking away and then turned around. "Dad, I wanted you to know. I don't think Leona and Caroline are missing like Julie. Caroline is in some third world country building wells or whatever…that's why she hasn't come home right away. And Leona is at some kind of institution for messed up wizards."

Dad's curiosity must have gotten the best of him, because his glare melted. "How do you know?"

"I'm trying to help find Julie. Just like you. And that's what I was doing. If you must know."

"You can't go around investigating summer wizards on your own. They're dangerous."

"You told me to go to my room and go to sleep. That's what I'm going to do."

CHAPTER ELEVEN

Patrick couldn't sleep. He would lie down and breathe deeply to relax and his heart continued to race. So, he tossed and turned and got up to play a video game, and then check Facebook, and then he'd try to go to bed again. Xavier slept like the dead. In fact, to pass the time, he would lean over Xavier and check to make sure he hadn't stopped breathing.

At around four in the morning, he went out into the kitchen to get some food. As he stared into the pantry, he felt a dark presence behind him. His already racing heart managed to race faster. But he forced himself to take a breath. He lived with five monsters, and sometimes they lurked in the dark. And he didn't need to fear them…not really.

He turned around, and sure enough, he saw Evangeline standing in the middle of the living room. The only light on was above the stove, so he knew she could see him, but he couldn't see her well. He could make out her pale skin standing out against the darkness, and her dark hair laying flat across her shoulders, but the darkness obscured her features. She looked like a little girl ghost from a horror movie. He reminded himself she was no ghost. She was his little sister. A normal, living person.

"Eve, could you turn on that lamp next to you, please?"

"Why?" she whispered.

"Just do it."

She flicked on the little lamp, and the orange light bathed her in a comforting glow, making her look human again. She walked towards him, but left a good amount of space between them.

"You look scared," she said. "Are you scared of me?"

Patrick didn't know how to answer. The truth was, *yes…..so, so, so much.* But he couldn't admit his wispy, quiet little sister scared the crap out of him. When she had cursed him several weeks ago, he considered telling Mom and Dad, but he couldn't bring himself to tattle on her for bullying him.

"I told you, I'm sorry I cast the spell on you. I wasn't trying to hurt you."

"What other reason could you have?"

"I wanted to see what would happen."

"That's not better."

"It must have been pretty bad, for you to still be this freaked out," she said. "Was it bad?" she asked with a scientific curiosity.

"Yes. It was bad."

"It was my magic. I was trying to give it to you."

"It's fine. I'm not mad. I'm going to go back to bed now, okay?" he said in a pacifying way, as a hostage negotiator might.

"I don't think you're hurt though. Not really. Getting hit with magic like that could really hurt most people. Make them crazy. Or really depressed. Emmy got a taste of Jude's magic and threw herself down the stairs. What I gave you was much more than that. But you're okay. That's pretty special."

"I don't know if I'm okay."

"Well, if you're not okay, it's not because of me. It's for other reasons."

"Why are you standing out here in the dark, anyway?"

"I was waiting for you."

Patrick felt panic coming on. He looked around the kitchen to find the best way to get around Evangeline. She looked like a stiff wind could blow her over, but her magical presence took up the whole room. His hands shook. All right, he could admit it. She terrified him. He knew how she could make him feel, and he never wanted to feel that way again.

"What do you want from me?" he asked.

"Please don't be scared of me," she said.

"All right. Whatever you want. I'm not scared."

"I wanted to talk to you when no one else was around."

Patrick heard a crunch and realized he had dropped his box of crackers and then trampled on them backing away from her.

"About what?" he asked.

"Xavier told me about how you freaked out when dad showed you the picture of that missing girl. I thought it was weird no one asked you about it. Not Xavier. Not Dad. But then I realized. They were scared of what your answer would be. So, they didn't ask the question. But I think that's silly. Because, your answer couldn't be scary. You're not a scary person. But…you are hiding *something*."

She pulled out a folded piece of paper and gently unfolded it. The creases looked worn. She lay the same flyer with a footprint on it that Dad had shown him on the counter. He averted his eyes and stared at a crack in the linoleum on the floor.

"Why don't you want to look at her picture?" Evangeline asked.

"What do you all think? You think I had something to do with her disappearance? Is that what Dad thinks? And Xavier? That's insane. How could they think that?"

"I agree. So, then tell me what you're hiding. Do you know her?"

"I haven't lied about anything. Before Dad showed me her

picture, I had never seen her before."

"Tell me the truth. I know you're not a bad person. The truth can't be that bad."

"I told you, I'm not lying. I've never seen her before. But I think…I *will* see her."

After a moment, comprehension flashed on Evangeline's face. "Oh. You mean when Dad showed you the photo, you had a vision of the future."

"I think so."

"That's incredible."

"It wasn't really."

"What did you see?"

"I don't like talking about my visions."

"Maybe it could be useful. Maybe it could help find her. You should tell Dad."

"It's not useful. It's horrible. What I saw, was…bad. Either she has, or she will be…tortured. It's the worst thing I've ever seen. I'm sure her family is already imagining the worst. So, I don't think it would be helpful for them to know they're right."

"I see." Evangeline picked the flyer back up and stared at Julie's face. "You should tell Dad. And Xavier."

"Fine."

"Have you seen anything else?"

"What do you mean?" he asked, even though he knew exactly what she meant.

"About the future."

"No."

"You're lying."

"Just leave it alone. Please." His "please" sounded so pathetic, so supplicant, he must sound pathetic enough to leave alone.

She shrugged.

"You know, maybe you should see a doctor. I think you have pre-traumatic stress disorder."

"That's not a thing."

She shrugged again. "Good night, Patrick…sweet dreams."

Her "sweet dreams" sounded so ominous, and he didn't know if she meant to be a threat, or jab. But that's just what people say.

CHAPTER TWELVE

Amanda pushed David's laptop screen down so he had to look at her. She had a cup of coffee in her hand. It must have been morning. He had meant to go to sleep before Amanda woke up for work and discovered he'd stayed up all night, but he must have lost track of time. Her eyes looked more shadowed and creased than usual, as if she had been the one who hardly slept last night, not him.

"Oh good, you're still with us," she said.

"What?"

"I was talking to you, and you were ignoring me."

"Sorry, I didn't hear you."

She must have noticed him looking her over, because she glanced away from him and tucked her hair behind her ear self-consciously.

"Are you all right? You look tired."

"Of course I'm tired. It's six-o-clock in the morning. And the man I share a bed with can't lie still for more than two minutes."

"I'm sorry. I couldn't sleep."

Amanda opened his laptop again and turned it to face her. "I should have guessed," she said, and sat down next to him at the kitchen table.

David had been scouring the Internet looking for traces of Leona and Caroline Prescott since four in the morning.

"How strange is it for teenage girls to not have any social media accounts?" David asked.

"Stop trolling Facebook for teenage girls."

"Leona is still fairly young, and if she went to a special school like Emmy said, maybe they aren't allowed on the computer. But why not Caroline? She's a twenty-year-old college student."

"She's also a witch. Wizards like to shun technology. Like how Evangeline and Xavier use their cell phones as paperweights."

"Xavier uses his cell phone…just not to talk to people. And Evangeline drew that really cool owl on hers."

Amanda laughed. "That's not what I meant by 'using' the phone."

"All the other Prescotts have Facebook accounts. John, Thea, Nathan, Lucas, Julie—and between the five of them I think they have 10,000 friends. I also found relatives of theirs on Facebook, cousins and such. They are probably wizards, and they use Facebook. Emmy won't tell me how she found out about Caroline being overseas doing volunteer work, but I don't think it's true. None of the other Prescotts have posted anything about it. Isn't that something a parent would want to share? And she would have graduated from high school two years ago, and the Prescotts were on Facebook then. No photos of graduation, prom, senior pictures, nothing. No Caroline."

"Wow, you've been reading two years of Facebook posts? That is some expert level stalking."

"Investigating. If they didn't want me to know this stuff, they should haven't shared it on Facebook."

"True."

"Are we out of half and half?" David asked. "I couldn't find it."

"I think we're out. We should have enough money in the bank account for you to go to the grocery store today."

"I can do that."

"Wait until Emmy wakes up and then take her with you, otherwise she might bolt."

"I was wondering…is there a wizard way to keep her from sneaking out?"

Amanda gnawed on her lip. "I've thought about that. I don't know, maybe if we weren't dark wizards. I can't think of an appropriate curse that wouldn't be borderline abusive. Even if I could think of something humane, we could make a mistake."

"You're right. Nevermind."

Amanda pressed the laptop closed again. "At least you're sparing some thought worrying about Emmy. You're spending way too much time and energy worrying about other people's kids."

"Are you implying that I'm not worried about my own?"

Amanda chewed her lip again. "Have you been paying attention to Xavier?"

"Yes."

"You don't think there is anything strange about him?"

David chuckled dryly. "I don't know how to answer that question, Amanda. He drank raw eggs for breakfast the other morning. He wore the same shirt for three days and didn't even notice until I said something. He's almost sixteen and doesn't care about learning to drive. Yes, he's strange. But considering what he's been through, I'm impressed that he's as normal as he is."

"I'm just…I'm worried that he might be dead."

"What?" David might have laughed if it hadn't been so sick. "That's a ghoulish thing to say about my son."

"I'm serious."

"Oh, you're serious," he said sarcastically. "Well, since hopefully we can both agree that he's walking around and talking like a living person, what type of undead creature do you think he is? Is this more of a zombie or a vampire situation?"

"I mean that his soul could be dead, not his body."

"Oh, that's better."

"Honey, I'm only saying this because I'm worried about him. I care about him. I don't want it to get worse. Souls can die. We know this. That's one of the most important dangers of dark magic. Especially magic that kills."

"He has never killed anyone. What happened to his mother was an accident."

"Still, causing death is dangerous for the soul. But that may not be the cause. He's good at hiding from pain. He may have gotten lost behind the veil. Or perhaps his stepfather destroyed him, with dark magic, or otherwise."

"I'm done with this conversation."

"You know I'm right. If you didn't, you wouldn't be so defensive. I'm just trying to help your son. *My* stepson. Ignoring it won't make it go away."

"I don't understand what you want me to do," he said. "Who do I call about this? The pediatrician? Or is missing soul more of a problem for the psychiatrist?"

"I don't know."

"Well, then leave it alone."

"I'm not saying I think it's too late for him. But I'm worried. The psychiatrist calls it dissociation. But he's a wizard, so it could be more than that. If he wanted to stop existing, maybe he could—if he wanted it badly enough. If anything else were to happen to him—"

"Why would he get worse? I may not have given him the perfect life, but I think everyone would agree that things are looking up."

"Of course, babe. But that's not how trauma works. It doesn't go away just because the abuse has stopped."

"What do you know about it?"

"I know how abuse affected you," she said quietly.

"That makes one of us."

Amanda sighed and stared at her coffee cup with glazed eyes.

"You want to know the truth?" David asked. "I'm more worried about Evangeline."

"Why?"

"When a child has suffered that level of abuse, you expect them to have issues like Xavier does. Evangeline is so…well-adjusted. I find it unsettling. Something's not right."

"That's a strange concern. If it makes you feel better, I think Evangeline is very unusual. And I'm happy that she's doing well. Perhaps she's just a strong person. Resilient."

"Did you eat breakfast?" David asked.

"I'm not hungry."

"You've lost weight," he said gravely.

"Thank you."

He hadn't meant it as an insult, but not a compliment either. She didn't need to lose weight. He could see her collarbones more sharply than usual.

"You would tell me if something was wrong, right?"

"Nothing is wrong." She smiled and squeezed his hand. "In fact, I feel better than I have in a while. Hopeful."

As promised, David brought Emmy to the grocery store after Amanda left for work. Emmy seemed quieter, and more vigilant, constantly waiting for her punishment. David let her wander around the store while he shopped for groceries. Amanda would have kept a closer eye on her. But he knew she had a serious case of cabin fever. He doubted wandering the aisles of the HEB would help much, but he would at least give her that moment of freedom.

"David Vandergraff. As I live and breathe." David's hand froze over a loaf of bread. He turned around to see a woman he recognized from church. He couldn't remember her name…Janet…Janice…something with a "J". She was in her sixties, and had a pleasant face.

"Hello," he said.

"We haven't seen y'all at church recently. I hope everything is okay."

"Yeah, everything is fine. We moved," he said, as if somehow that explained everything. He wouldn't mind if they went to church. He thought it would make Amanda happier, in any case. No one in the congregation of Mundanes would have any idea what they were, but he figured she still felt as if she didn't belong anymore.

"I see. Well, we'd love to see you back," Janice or Janet said with a bright smile.

"Yeah, definitely."

"Oh, I saw your boy up at the outlet malls last weekend. He's looking good."

"What boy?"

"Jude, of course. Saw him shopping at The Gap with his girlfriend. They are an adorable couple. I don't know if I've ever seen him so happy. And I can see why. She is a cutie, looks like a real sweetheart. You know, we have a Sunday School class for young couples, to help them strengthen their relationship and prepare for marriage. Oh, but listen to me, sticking my nose in. They're young. Probably not thinking about that kind of thing."

"What?"

"I'm so happy to see him doing well. I know Amanda was worried about him and praying for him. Looks like the good Lord has answered her prayers."

"What?"

"So, where is he going to school in the fall?"

David stared at her. He had wandered in to an alternate

timeline. A timeline where Jude had never turned to darkness and had continued to live the life David had expected him to. A place where Jude was happy and successful. An impossible place.

She gave him a concerned look as he continued to stare, so he played along.

"UT," he said finally, happy to pretend for a moment. "He's going to the University of Texas."

As they got closer to home, the truck's engine made a knocking noise, making Dad's lie from before, true. *That's what he gets for lying.* Emmy would have laughed, but the car breaking down had gotten old.

Emmy went in first, while Dad stayed outside glaring at the engine. She thought if he kept giving the engine that evil glare, he would end up breaking it more.

Emmy found Xavier and Evangeline staring at something on the kitchen counter as if it was an alien head they dug up in the backyard.

"What are you weirdos doing?"

"Look at this," Evangeline said. "It's like flowers, but it's made of fruit. Isn't that amazing?" She pointed towards an Edible Arrangement on the counter.

"Yeah…weird things impress you," Emmy said.

"Look at this little daisy made out of a pineapple," Evangeline said.

"Yeah, it's a bouquet made of fruit," Emmy said. "A normal thing. Where did it come from?"

"Someone brought it to the door," Evangeline said. "It's for Amanda."

"What for?"

"I don't know."

Emmy snatched the note. It's like they grew up on Mars.

"Can we eat it?" Xavier poked at a chocolate covered strawberry.

"No. It's for Amanda," Evangeline said.

Emmy read the card aloud. "Get well soon. Your friends at Vector Petrochemicals."

"Is she sick?" Xavier asked.

"No, she's fine," Emmy said, although the card implied otherwise. She scanned the signed card full of co-worker's platitude. *We miss you…I hope your surgery goes well…Relax and enjoy your leave.*

"Okay, that's weird," Emmy said.

"Why do they think she's sick?" Evangeline asked.

"I don't know," Emmy said. "But she's either lying to us…or to her co-workers."

Emmy thought about Dad glaring outside and thought Mom had probably lied to him too. Of course, Mom owed Dad a good lie.

"Maybe we *should* eat it," Emmy suggested.

However, they would have to do it *really* quickly for that to work. Dad burst through the front door, a smudge of grease on his face. "I can't believe it actually started making a noise. God hates me. And He thinks He is *real* funny, too." Dad looked around the living area. "Where is Patrick?"

"Sleeping," Evangeline said.

Dad looked at his watch and then huffed. Emmy clutched the card, and the three of them stood there waiting for him to notice. They didn't have a chance to hide it.

"We can't afford to get any more repairs done. Period. We'll have to walk everywhere. But it's not like the tollway has a sidewalk. Why are you guys looking at me like that?"

Emmy handed Dad the card, and he saw the arrangement. "Who would send us a gift?" he asked, and then looked at the card. His eyebrows narrowed further.

"I don't understand," he said, waving the card in her

direction, as if this was her fault too, just like everything else.

"We don't know any more than you, Dad," Emmy said. He must have believed her because he didn't say anything else. He took the card into his bedroom and slammed the door.

CHAPTER THIRTEEN

Amanda heard her son's voice. And that was all there was in the universe. Everything else was darkness. She didn't remember how she had gotten to this dark place, but she instinctively moved towards her son.

"Mom. Mom!"

Amanda opened her eyes. Her son was not lost in the distant darkness, but right here, inches away from her face, shaking her. Jude looked at her with clear blue eyes—eyes full of concern, full of love, brimming with everything that made him good. And that made it all worth it. She smiled at him, but he didn't smile back.

"Dammit, Mom, you lied to me. I shouldn't have trusted you. I should have gone with my gut."

She wanted to come up with some an excuse, some argument, but she couldn't remember how to work her mouth, let alone her brain.

"I'm taking you to the hospital," he said.

This jarred her back to reality enough for her to find her voice.

"No. I'm fine." Her voice sounded raspy and unfamiliar. "Besides, the Mundane doctors wouldn't be able to help anyway."

"Fine then, I'll call Dad. Or, Uncle Carson. Or, Grandma."

"You're going to call my mom? Now, you're just being mean," she said, trying to lighten the mood.

"It's not funny," he said.

"Please don't call them," Amanda said, her voice too meek, too pleading. None of them could know for one simple reason. *They would try to stop her.* "They wouldn't know what to do either. It would just worry them. Please, honey, just let me rest for a minute. I'll be fine."

Before he could respond, she closed her eyes and lost consciousness again, or at least she must have, because she woke up somewhere else. She heard beeping. A hospital. She wandered into consciousness just enough to verify this. Yes. An IV poked into her hand, and it smelled of anesthetic. She felt Jude's presence, but no one else. If he had called anyone, they hadn't arrived. He probably hadn't called. He would avoid calling David at all costs.

She could work with this. As soon as she came to a little more, she could call home and say she needed to work late. Then she'd try to get discharged as soon as possible. That shouldn't be a problem. The Mundane doctors would run some tests, see nothing wrong with her…at least nothing *they* could diagnose. They'd send her home with a prescription to get more rest and drink more water.

Or she'd walk out if she had to. She didn't think she could get up and walk now, but she'd feel better soon. She always did. Each time she had cast the expungement spell on Jude she had felt the darkness permeate her. But she could handle it. It had gotten worse each time, but she always felt better after some rest. She just had to sleep it off. The expungement spell was complicated, but similar to the spell she had cast on David to expunge his memories. This time though, she didn't aim for memories. She wished to remove something much deeper, and more complex.

Her spell had worked. She could lift the darkness away

from her son. It appeared that the darkness had not become engrained in his sense of self, nor had it destroyed the good man inside. The darkness had come into him recently enough that it lifted right out—a stubborn stain in the hands of an accomplished homemaker.

"Mom? Are you awake?"

Jude grabbed her hand and she turned towards him and smiled.

"I told you not to take me to the hospital."

"What were you thinking? This was so short-sighted." He let go of her hand and wrung his own. He tapped his foot up and down. "What do you think would happen if something happened to you? I'm barely hanging on as it is. I couldn't handle it if something happened to you. Especially if it was my fault. And what about the rest of the family? What about Dad? He couldn't make it without you. If you died, there would be no point to any of this. It would all get worse."

"Died? Honey, no. I'm not going to die."

"I need to call Dad."

"No, you don't. I'll give him a call and tell him I'm running late."

"Mom…you're not leaving today."

"What do you mean?"

"They said your white blood cell count is high. And some other stuff I didn't understand. It's just…it's not good."

"I…what?"

"They won't know anything for sure until they run a few more tests. They're ordering a CT scan."

"No, I'm fine. I just need to go home and get some rest."

Jude shook his head, his eyes on his hands.

CHAPTER FOURTEEN

"Evie?" Emmy asked.

Evangeline looked up from her book, then immediately put her book down and stood up. She must have seen the urgency in Emmy's face.

Mom should have come home from work an hour ago and wasn't answering her phone. For some reason, that had been the final straw. The bracelet had burned in her pocket for too long. Her secret about Nathan had burned in her for too long. She didn't want to be alone anymore.

"What's wrong?" Evangeline asked.

"It's not a big deal. Well, it sort of is. It might be. Can I tell you something?"

"Yeah, sure."

Evangeline shut the door, and then followed her to sit on Emmy's bed. Evangeline blinked at her with the same green eyes Emmy's grandmother once had.

"You have something in your pocket, don't you?" Evangeline asked.

Emmy's throat tightened. She stared at Evangeline open-mouthed.

"Don't be upset. You've been carrying it around with you. Something magical. But…something that doesn't belong. The energy coming off it doesn't match yours."

"Do you already know what it is?"

"No. I was curious, but you were trying so hard to keep it secret. I figured you would tell me if you wanted me to know."

Emmy doubted anyone could be *that* noble. Emmy could never let something go that easily. She would have pried the secret object out of Evangeline's clenched fists.

"Are you lying? You didn't sneak a peek while I was sleeping or anything?"

"No, I'm not lying. Besides, you slept with it under your pillow. Do you really think I'm going to sneak up and try to take it while you're sleeping? That's a good way to get cursed."

Emmy had to smile. "Okay, then."

She pulled the bracelet out of her shorts pocket and handed it to Evangeline. Evangeline reached out to take it, but pulled her hand away suddenly, so Emmy laid it on the bed instead. Evangeline reached for it again, more slowly this time. She picked up the bracelet by the clasp with two fingers and held it a good foot away from her face while she examined it. Emmy watched her expression. She could tell Evangeline had never seen the bracelet before. Evangeline had more of a detached curiosity, like an archeologist examining a rare find.

The bracelet must not serve as an explanation in itself because Evangeline lifted an eyebrow and waited for Emmy to explain. Emmy told her everything. *Everything.* It all spilled out, bursting at the seams. About how she had found Julie's bracelet in the truck and not told anyone. About how she had snuck out to the forest and met Nathan. About how she drove to the Prescott's house with Dad and all the things he told her about them. About how they both believed someone cast a spell on Julie's behalf and the magic needed them to save her. And most importantly, that she believed Julie was trapped somewhere in that forest, hidden by a powerful concealment spell.

Evangeline had put the bracelet back on the bed. She

listened to Emmy's story as she usually listened. Intently. Quietly. Patiently. She listened well—Emmy's exact opposite in that way. So calm, too. She didn't add to Emmy's fears by injecting any of her own. However, Emmy had mixed feelings about this. The same calm indifference that had comforted Emmy when she first handed Evangeline the bracelet now gave her chills. She had a look of unbothered interest, as if she were listening to an interesting story about strangers or characters in a novel, not her own family.

"Do you understand what I'm saying?" Emmy asked.

"Since you found the bracelet in the truck, you think someone in our family was involved in her disappearance. And now you want to try and find her and help her."

"Yeah, that's pretty much it."

"Hmm."

"Is that your only reaction? Doesn't any of this bother you at all?"

"Of course it does."

"Do you know anything you're not telling me?"

"No."

"As soon as I get the chance, I'm going back to the forest and trying again. I have this strong sense I'm *meant* to. I'm the only one who can help her. Do you get that?"

"Sure. But if there is magic in play, you don't know whose magic it is, or what they want. It may not be what you expect. Could be dangerous."

"Yeah, that was the first and only lesson in Mom's dark magic for beginners course. I get that."

Evangeline chuckled.

"Rule 1. Magic is bad," Emmy continued. "Rule 2. Never do magic. Rule 3. No, seriously magic is always bad. I really mean it this time. And so on, and so forth."

"Okay, I get it. I'm sorry. I don't know how I ended up sounding like *your* mom. Maybe she cast a spell on me."

"She totally would. She would cast a anti-magic spell on

you and not understand why that made her a huge hypocrite."

"Okay, so what is the plan? When do we go?"

"*We?*"

"Of course. I want to go with you. I can help."

"That wasn't what I meant when I told you."

"I have the same reasons to care that you do, and you need me. I'm a much better witch."

"How *dare* you?"

"Oh, you don't believe me? Why don't you attack me with magic to prove me wrong?" She waited. "Go ahead. Anytime. Oh, wait. You have no idea how to do that."

"Just because no one has ever taught me. Whenever I do learn, I will attack you. Just for being such a bitch right now."

"Okay then. In the meantime, you could use my help."

"I'm not letting you come with me."

"Why not?"

"Because you're my little sister."

Evangeline paused before responding. Emmy realized she had never called her 'sister' aloud.

"I'm not much younger than you," Evangeline said.

"Yeah, but you're…"

"What?"

Damaged? Traumatized? Broken? She couldn't think of a good way to say it, so she should shut up before she got cursed into oblivion.

"You've already been through a lot."

"So what's the point in trying to protect me now?"

"Okay."

"Okay?"

"Yeah. We'll do it together. But you better not slow me down."

"You either."

"They've made it pretty impossible for me to get out of the house. But I'm sure we can still manage it. Let me talk to Dad, see if I can find out when he'll be out of the house next.

Now that we have both cars back, it will be way easier."

Emmy and Evangeline left the room. Emmy tried to look casual. Evangeline didn't have to try. Effortless indifference came naturally. Dad continued to stare at the pineapples and melons cut into hearts and flowers in the kitchen.

"Hey, Dad," Emmy said.

Dad's phone rang in his pocket. He ignored Emmy in favor of his phone. Usually, that would be rude, but he'd been waiting to hear back from Mom. He stared at the display on his phone for a long time without answering. He let the phone ring in his hand while he stared, oblivious to Emmy standing in front of him. It must have rung six times. She wanted to grab it out of his hands and answer it herself. Finally, he answered the phone.

"Hello?"

He stayed silent while he listened to whoever spoke on the other line, his face a pale, frozen mask. He looked into Emmy's eyes before he spoke. Emmy felt frozen too. She could feel the weight of the words without having to hear it.

"Okay," Dad said, in a whispery croak. "I'm…I'm on my way."

Dad put his phone back in his pocket.

"Is everything okay?" Emmy asked. "Is Mom okay?"

"Yeah…yeah," Dad said. "That was her…the Expedition broke down again. I have to go pick her up."

"Really? You sound like you're lying."

"I have to go now. It may…be a while…are you guys going to be okay?"

"Yeah, of course," Emmy said.

Dad headed for the door. As he searched for the keys on the table by the door, he knocked some mail and other stuff off the table. As soon as he found the keys to the truck, he rushed out without another word.

Emmy looked at her feet. When he'd scattered the mail, Patrick's keys had slid across the floor, right to her.

"Whoa," Emmy said. "What just happened?"

"I'm going to say…magic. And it wasn't subtle."

"Did you do that?"

"I don't think so."

"I guess it could be a coincidence," Emmy said.

"It's never a coincidence." Evangeline motioned toward their bedroom. "What about the guys?"

"It will take them a while to notice we're gone," Emmy said. "Probably like several weeks."

Emmy didn't talk much on the drive, and as expected, Evangeline didn't either. Emmy figured magic was in play, but she had never seen it so aggressive or to the point. The magic liked Emmy and Evangeline going to the forest right now, and bent fate so that could happen. Emmy kept going back and forth in her head. *This is a bad idea. Imagine what Mom and Dad would say if they knew I blindly followed magic…but Dad was doing the same thing. No, I'm sure it's fine. It could be a coincidence anyway. Mom brainwashed me against magic. I'm trying to save Julie, and that can't be evil, right? But if it's summer magic, then it's against me.* She could talk too much even in silence.

Emmy didn't want to voice any of her thoughts aloud, because she didn't want to accidentally talk Evangeline out of coming. Maybe Evangeline wouldn't realize how stupid it was until Emmy said something. However, Emmy doubted Evangeline had any of these same fears. On all accounts, Evangeline appeared to be the contemplative and reasonable one, and Emmy, the erratic, irrational one. Emmy could understand why people thought this, but she didn't think it was true. Emmy knew she was the reasonable one…a terrifying thought. Unlike Emmy, Evangeline didn't battle with magic. She wasn't stuck between two worlds, and didn't feel conflicted about who she was or whether she made the right choices. Evangeline didn't read the Bible in secret, trying to find some explanation she had missed. She didn't pray. At least not to any Christian God.

Evangeline was not stuck between two worlds at all. She lived 100% in the magical one—a place where following the whims of magic, regardless of consequences, was the reasonable thing to do. Emmy doubted if Evangeline understood any other option. Or, maybe Emmy was the one naïve enough to believe other options existed. In any case, despite all the quiet reading of paper books and good listening skills, Emmy suspected Evangeline didn't have a rational bone in her body.

When they arrived at the fated gas station, they had plenty of light left in the day. Dark witches or not, Emmy thought the daylight would make the forest easier to handle. And having Evangeline by her side would make it much easier too. She had a good feeling about this. Everything had aligned in her favor now. This would work.

Emmy parked at the side of the gas station where Nathan had parked when Julie disappeared.

"This is where it happened," Emmy explained. "She disappeared from this parking lot in the middle of the day. No one saw anything. And they've searched the forest up and down and haven't found anything."

"Well, the *Mundanes* and *summer* wizards haven't found anything," Evangeline said.

"Exactly."

"But Nathan thinks she's still here, close by?"

"Yes, he thinks he can feel her presence. He just can't get to her."

"That makes sense. You said her presence is strong, and Nathan would know it well. He'd be able to sense her. You've felt her presence before, too. Do you sense her nearby?"

"No. Although, I'm not sure I would be able to.

Besides…do you feel that? That feeling coming from the forest? It feels like darkness, but not the good kind, you know what I mean?"

"Yes."

"I guess we can look around a little bit. Maybe you'll see…or feel…something I didn't."

"Okay."

Evangeline wandered into the parking lot, examining the asphalt with peaceful contemplation, as if searching for shells at the beach. Emmy should have asked her to look more normal so they wouldn't call attention to themselves, but such a request would confuse her, as no word for "normal" existed in her language.

Since they were acting strange anyway, Emmy went around the back of the gas station this time, a section she had avoided earlier since she couldn't think of a normal reason to examine the area. She walked up and down the back wall, which appeared gray and dirty, and ordinary. While she looked at the wall, she felt the weight of the forest on her back, breathing on her. Emmy reminded herself she wasn't afraid. Not of trees.

Emmy forced herself to turn and face the forest; she saw something glinting between the trees. The sun hit a piece of metal in a way she would have missed when the sun was lower in the sky. The bizarre sunlight glinting in between the trees filled her with a dread she could not explain. *That is not scary. That is not scary.* What could be scary about sunlight reflecting off of metal?

She walked toward the metal to investigate, a nearly impossible task. The fear threatened to paralyze her. Her throat became tight and she struggled to breathe. Her heart pummeled in her chest. She felt lightheaded at first, and then her head throbbed. But she kept walking toward the metal object. She had never felt anything so evil.

Her chest hurt now and her face dripped with both tears and sweat. She wiped away the moisture, half expecting blood.

By the time she stood in front of the object, she felt as if she was at the bottom of the ocean. She couldn't breathe and the pressure threatened to crush her bones. But it wasn't cold and dark like the sea. It was hot and bright. Burning. She could barely open her eyes.

She covered her mouth to try and keep herself from vomiting, and forced her eyes to focus on whatever metal object lay before her. She kept blinking at it. She saw a mangled car bumper. By the level of rust, someone had tossed the bumper here years ago, from some long-past collision on the highway.

This object should not terrify her. It had been here too long to have anything to do with Julie's disappearance. Nothing made any sense. This realization terrified her more. She hated things that didn't make sense. And she hated feeling afraid. If she was afraid, there better be a damn good reason. She couldn't take the fear anymore.

She turned and ran out of the forest at full speed. So fast, she tripped on a branch and scratched up her palms and knees yet again, but she hardly noticed the burning scrapes. She jumped up and kept running. The evil car bumper seemed to loom closer, following at her heels. She made it to the edge of the forest and had never been so happy to stand under the oppressive August sun. The forest still seemed to breathe it's hot breath on her neck, so she pressed her back against the gas station so the forest couldn't sneak up on her, and focused on breathing.

After a few minutes, she realized something was off. She had stood there drenched in sweat and hyperventilating loudly for at least two or three minutes, but no one came to check on her.

"Evangeline?"

The side of the parking lot was empty except for Patrick's car. A different fear crept in now. A very real fear. One she could define. *Don't panic. Don't panic. She probably just went inside.*

Reminding herself not to panic didn't help much. Most people didn't have to jump to the most terrible conclusion. They could think the more obvious thing could be true. But for dark wizards, the most terrible conclusion was almost always the right one.

Emmy practically flew around the pumps and into the store looking for her sister. She threw open the door to the station bathroom and darted up and down the aisles, ignoring the alarmed looks of the station attendants and patrons. Then she ran around the perimeter of the station calling for Evangeline. The reality creeping in…growing stronger and stronger…filling her with more and more dread.

With no sign of Evangeline anywhere around the station, she ran back into the forest. For some reason, the fear of losing her sister made the fear living in the forest less powerful, much less real.

"Evie!" She screeched the name with an intensity she didn't know she was capable of. Her screech vibrated the air. She thought she could breathe fire if she wanted to, but didn't know what good that would do anyone.

She kept running, deeper into the forest, with no idea which direction she ran. Whatever kept her out before, didn't stop her now. Nothing could stop her now. Eventually, her lungs and legs failed her and she had to stop running. So she walked. And walked. And walked. She saw a clearing ahead and started running again, just to find herself running right back into the gas station parking lot. The forest had once again swallowed her and spit her right back out.

Furious, she ran back in, thrashing through the thick branches as if she hoped she could hurt them, but only getting her arms and legs covered in more scratches.

"Fuck you," she yelled at nothing. "I'm right fucking here. Come on, take me too! Why won't you take me too!?"

She threw a rock at a tree as hard as she could.

"Or are you too scared?" She held her hands out in

welcome. "Come on, motherfucker! I'm right here!"

She sunk to her knees. Her sister was gone. And it was all her fault.

Emmy kept walking until the sun sunk low in the sky. She knew if she hadn't found Evangeline yet, she wouldn't. But she thought maybe she would fall into the same rabbit hole. Why not? Why Julie and Evangeline, and not her? If she could get the evil to take her too, she could follow Evangeline in. She could find her. She could bring her home.

But part of her knew that wouldn't happen. She had walked through the forest several times, sometimes alone, at night, and nothing snatched her. Julie and Evangeline got within arms reach of the forest during the day, with someone else, and they vanished into thin air. If the darkness wanted her, it would have taken her.

Now, she just delayed the inevitable. As soon as she got in the car and left, it would be real. Official. She'd have to tell Dad. And Xavier. She'd have to tell them what she had done.

CHAPTER FIFTEEN

David must have fallen asleep in the chair, because he found himself standing in front of Crystal—Xavier and Evangeline's mother who had died last year. She glowed with happiness and health. Her black hair shone, and her skin looked tan and rosy. She had white teeth and bright red, sparkling lips. She didn't look anything like he remembered her, perhaps a sign she was nothing more than an illusion, a Crystal that never existed anywhere but in his own head.

The real Crystal would not have appreciated what David had done with her in his subconscious mind. She might have tolerated the cheerleader smile and the ample amount of naked skin. But she wouldn't have liked the gold sequined bikini and gold high heels, or the bizarre gold crest perched atop her head, like a Vegas showgirl. She twirled two chains around her, both with a fireball at each end. She danced and swung the fire in the air, making elaborate patterns, and just missing her bare flesh. The image, however ridiculous, mesmerized him.

She stopped her dance, and looked right at David, still twirling her lit chains. She shook her head and snickered at him.

"David, why are you looking at me?"

"How could I not?"

"You silly man. You shouldn't look at me."

"Why?"

"Because that's what he wants."

"Who?"

She looked into the darkness behind David. "The magician."

David spun around. He saw a dark theater with only one occupied seat. The lone figure appeared as nothing but a mass of darkness. No face. No features. No body. Just darkness. The more David squinted toward the figure, the more the darkness swelled. The dim lights faded, until he could no longer make out the seats or the aisle. He turned back to Crystal, but she had disappeared too. The darkness became absolute, but he was not alone. Somewhere, in the darkness, lurked the magician.

Perhaps the fear woke David, because he jolted awake with his heart racing. He felt out of sorts, as if he hadn't slept for three days but had drunk copious amounts of espresso. Exhausted and panicky at the same time. Despite a bad night's sleep, he couldn't believe he had drifted off. He couldn't imagine ever sleeping again until he knew Amanda would be okay.

He and Jude waited outside the radiology department for the doctors to run more tests on Amanda—an experience so surreal, he hung on to the hope this was all an elaborate nightmare.

As Janet or Janice had said, Jude looked good. Too good, if that was possible. As Crystal had looked in his dream. Seeing Crystal so healthy and happy reminded him she wasn't real, and that's how he felt now, looking at Jude. Of course, he was real. He had driven Amanda here. He had called David. He had talked to doctors and nurses. But something about him didn't feel real. Altered.

"Did I really fall asleep?" David asked.

"Yeah."

"I can't believe I did that. I didn't miss anything, did I?"

He shook his head. "I can't believe how long this is taking."

"Why are you here?" David asked.

"I'm waiting to hear what the doctor says."

"No, I mean, why are you *here*? Why were you with her when she passed out?"

"Oh. That."

"Yeah. That."

"Maybe I should let Mom tell you."

David turned and glared at his son. "I have no patience for bullshit right now. Tell me what's going on."

"I'm sorry, Dad."

"Tell me *now*."

"I wouldn't have let her do it if I knew it would hurt her. She kept telling me she was fine. She hid it well."

"Dammit Jude, start at the beginning of the story, not the end."

"She was trying a spell. She thought she could remove the darkness…or whatever…from me with magic. Like she did with your memories."

David didn't say anything for a while. He had no doubt his son told the truth. It sounded like something Amanda would do.

"So, I guess that's why you're all…*clean*." He said the word "clean" with distaste. He meant it as a euphemism for something terrible, although he didn't know what.

"Her spell worked. Mom is incredible."

"Of course, it fucking worked. All the crap that was in you went right into her. Energy can transform, but it can't die. So, congratulations. You moved it to your mother. How could you be so selfish?" *How could she be so selfish? How could she take herself from him?*

"I told you, I didn't know." He averted his eyes. "I'm

sorry."

David's throat felt dry. He wanted to fall asleep again.

"So what then, you're fine now? Just a normal guy?" He asked it sardonically. He couldn't believe that.

"Well, it's more than that. I have something else."

"What?"

"I met somebody."

David didn't respond.

"She's amazing. She's *beyond* amazing. I'd like for you and Mom to meet her."

David shot his words at him. "You think I care about that right now? You killed your mother and you want to introduce me to your girlfriend? I—do—not—care."

"I just…"

"Maybe your mother thought your life was worth more than hers, but I don't. I'm sure that's why she didn't tell me. I would have stopped her. I would have never let her sacrifice herself for you. Your soul is not worth hers. Not by a long shot."

"I didn't…"

"Why are you still here? I'm going to have to tell your brothers and sisters about this, and then they'll come up here. And you can't be here. Get out."

"You can't do that. What if she gets worse? What if she… I want to be with her."

"Get—out."

Jude stood up and grabbed his keys and his phone like a ghost fumbling through long-forgotten tasks. David saw an elderly woman watching them from several seats over.

"*Damn*," she muttered under her breath, giving David a sour look.

David felt as if he watched a giant wave swelling in front of him. He swam away as fast as he could, but he couldn't swim forever. The wave would crash right on top of him. But for now, he swam away. He couldn't accept that anything was wrong with Amanda. He couldn't handle it. He didn't have the strength or the courage. And as bad as it would be for a Mundane, the loss could devastate a dark wizard. She was his talisman. He needed her.

While David waited, he tried to pray, but it didn't work. He ended up yelling at God in his mind. He tried to ask God to protect her, but ended up making demands. *No. This is unacceptable. You can't do this. I won't accept it. Don't even think about it. Who do you think you're kidding? Un-freaking-acceptable. No. No. No. Not happening. Amen.*

A nurse finally came out and said they'd moved Amanda back to her room and she was waiting for him.

When he came to her bedside, she'd never looked so happy to see him. Her whole body melted in a sigh. She reached for him eagerly. This shook David more than anything else. He had never seen her look so frightened. *She* was the strong one.

"David," she whispered his name like a poem. "I'm so glad you're here."

He did the best he could to gather her in his arms with her hooked up to several tubes and contraptions. She pressed her face into his shoulder and wrapped her arms around his back so hard, it hurt.

"It's going to be okay," David said, aware that the platitude meant nothing.

"Where is Jude?"

David swallowed a growl. She had reached for David so desperately, but mere seconds later she asked for Jude, the one who had done this to her.

"I asked him to leave."

"David" she chided.

"I don't want to talk about him. I only want to talk about you."

"I suppose he told you."

"Yes."

"I know you're angry. That's why I didn't tell you. I'm sorry this happened, but I won't say I'm sorry I did it. He's our son."

David couldn't say anything without sounding selfish. What he had said to Jude about him not being worth saving had been cruel and untrue, but he still wouldn't have traded Amanda for him. A horrible thing to think about his own son, but true. Jude had done something terrible, something he could never take back. Amanda sat at the center of his universe. Without her, everything hurtled out into space.

"Did you tell the kids?"

"Not yet." David glanced at his phone as he said it, and wondered why none of them had called. Not that they longed for parental supervision, but dinnertime had come and gone, and they had yet to call to demand food. Or to ask why he and Amanda hadn't come home yet. Or…anything. "I don't know what to tell them."

A doctor came in and introduced himself as an oncologist. David wondered if somewhere in his degree-laden mind, he realized he spilled his guts as soon as he introduced himself.

David's stomach coiled into a hard ball as he listened to the man talk. He tried to listen. Like Xavier, he sensed he could slip out of this conversation if he wanted to, and had to work hard to resist the temptation. He realized that was how he "fell asleep" in the lobby. He could turn himself off. He didn't know if he could control it.

Amanda had advanced breast cancer that had already spread to her liver and lungs. Amanda argued she had gotten a mammogram four months ago that came up clean. She also said breast cancer didn't run in her family. Of course Amanda would want to argue with cancer. As if she believed that if she came up with a rational argument against cancer, it would disappear.

But David knew none of those arguments mattered. He knew the darkness she had taken from Jude had invaded her body – and it had already taken root.

CHAPTER SIXTEEN

It had taken several hours, instead of several weeks, but Patrick had called Emmy twice and texted her, "YOU STOLE MY CAR." Then, "Eve with you?" And later, "Are you okay? Where are you? TEXT ME BACK."

Dad must still be occupied with his mysterious, urgent task because he hadn't called. Neither had Mom. 99.9% of the time, Emmy would have relished their sudden lack of stifling attention, but now it infuriated and frightened her. Not because she was mad at them for turning a blind eye, but because the magic had tricked her. Their inattention and the timing of Dad's sudden departure were way too convenient to be a coincidence. And as Evangeline said, there were no coincidences. Somehow magic called them away, but she didn't know if something dark had called them away so Evangeline would be free for the taking, or if she herself had managed to will them away for her own ends.

Even if Emmy *would* find Evangeline, she knew she couldn't go on for any longer. She felt dizzy, and had even venturing into the forest a few feet confused her. She sat on the side of the road, the dry pine needles and twigs digging into her thighs. Her head throbbed as if her brain might start oozing out of her ears.

She had already stalled way too long. She had to get it over with and call someone. Do something. Stop being selfish. Evangeline needed help and she couldn't provide it on her own. After staring at her favorites list for a while, in a state of paralyzing indecision, she took a far right turn and pulled up Nathan's number. She had never called it, but had liked knowing she could. And as soon as she thought of it, she didn't have to sit in a pool of worry and indecision. She pressed call.

"Hello?"

"Nathan?"

"Hang on. Let me go somewhere else."

"Wait, just…"

"Hang on."

Emmy heard chatter in the background. Nathan must be with people, and didn't want to get caught talking to a winter witch. She had to sit there and wait while he made some excuse and walked to the ends of the earth to find a place to talk to her.

"Nathan…Nathan…Nathan!"

"Okay, now I can talk."

"Nathan, something happened."

"What's wrong?" His tone shifted in a heartbeat.

Emmy could feel heat in her eyes but tears didn't come. She willed herself to form words.

"Emmy? Talk to me."

She took a deep breath. "It happened to me, too."

"What? What did?"

"My sister…she disappeared. In the same spot. At the same gas station. I looked everywhere." Her voice cracked on "everywhere" and she had to stop talking.

Nathan didn't reply. She heard a stilted whispery sound as if he tried to say something, or several somethings, and it didn't come out right.

"What?" he finally said. His strangled tone made it clear

he'd heard exactly what she had said, so Emmy didn't repeat it. "When?"

"Just now. Well, a few hours ago. I've been looking and looking…I didn't want to stop looking."

"Have you called the police?"

"No."

"Jesus, Emmy. Why are you calling me? Call 9-1-1."

It must have been the witch in her, because she hadn't considered that. But anything seemed better than calling home.

"Okay. You're right. I will."

"Where are you?"

"At the gas station. Sitting in the car."

"Stay there."

Nathan hung up the phone. Emmy had the feeling he planned to "rescue" her, which she didn't usually appreciate. She was not, never had been, and never would be the damsel in distress. But she had hardly ever felt less like the brave knight. She was a stupid little girl. A stupid little girl dark witch, and brought nothing to the world but destruction and pain. She felt so resolved to stay put, she wondered if Nathan had made it so. But she didn't care either way. She picked her phone back up and called 9-1-1.

The police arrived first. One car, with a man and a woman, who both looked pretty young. An ambulance came behind them and the paramedics started poking at her even though she said she was fine. The police asked a lot of questions, and asked for her parents' names and phone number. She guessed that meant the police would call her parents, and she liked that. She couldn't do it herself. She didn't have the courage. She couldn't hear the pain in Dad's voice, when he found out Evangeline had gone missing yet again. In danger, again. She couldn't do that to him.

The paramedics claimed she suffered from heat exhaustion, and tried to take her away. Emmy flat-out refused. She said she wouldn't go without her brother, who should arrive soon—a weird lie, and kind of gross, because she didn't think of Nathan as a brother, but the lie tumbled out. She thought it would work better than saying she needed to wait for some random guy she hardly knew who may or may not have cast a spell on her making it impossible for her to leave anyway.

When Nathan arrived, the paramedics didn't question him when he crawled into the back of the ambulance with Emmy. Nathan's yellow green eyes became glassy and frozen when he saw Emmy on the stretcher.

"Before you freak out, I'm completely, absolutely fine," Emmy said. "These people are crazy."

"Your sister is fine," the paramedic explained. "Just dehydrated from being in the heat. We want to monitor her for a while."

Emmy cringed. If the stretcher and the IV didn't freak him out, her claim to be his sister might, especially considering the fact his actual sister was not fine.

Nathan paused before speaking, but rolled with it. "Okay, thanks," he said. "Can I ride with her?"

"Sure."

Fortunately, the paramedics and policemen were Mundanes. They would have no idea Emmy and Nathan being brother and sister was as ridiculous as claiming a mouse and an elephant were brother and sister.

When the paramedics left Nathan and Emmy alone in the back, Nathan took her hand. She was glad she had called him. It felt good to have someone comfort her without being simultaneously devastated and furious with her. Dad would be too distracted about Evangeline to worry about her, which she guessed was fair. She resolved not to drop Nathan's hand, even though his touch seemed to make the heat exhaustion worse. Her eyes felt so dry and hot, they might have turned to glass. She blinked at his blurry face.

"I'm so sorry," he said.

"It's not your fault. It's mine. I shouldn't have brought her here."

"I didn't even know you had a sister. I never thought to ask about your family. I saw you weren't at risk, and didn't worry about anybody else. Stupid of me."

Emmy didn't get that, but her head hurt so much and she felt foggy, so she didn't question him.

"What is her date?"

"What?"

"Your sister's date. On the solar calendar. How dark is she?"

"I don't understand. Why are you asking me that right now? You want to know if she's worth caring about? Worth using up any energy to find?"

"No, no, of course not," he said. "I'm sorry. I know this isn't the right time…if you don't know your own date, I'm sure you don't know hers. I shouldn't have asked."

She wanted him to stop talking. No more confusing questions. No more reminders that he knew more than he let on. She squeezed his hand tighter, hoping to give him a clue as to what she wanted from him. Just to be there.

He got the hint because he didn't say anything else, and stroked her palm with his thumb. He looked so sad. The word that came to her mind was *eclipse*. As a summer wizard, Emmy figured he was good at faking happiness. He could smile and laugh and joke around, but if he stayed still long enough, the clouds would roll back in.

For the first time, she noticed a shiny pattern of burn marks on the inside of his forearm and twisted under his sleeve, like a angry, red, distorted snake. She could tell he caught her looking, and Emmy pulled her eyes away, cheeks burning. He didn't say anything though, and Emmy didn't either.

"Where are your parents?" he asked. "I didn't notice anyone else around."

"I never called them. I couldn't do it. But I think the police did. Evangeline has a different mother anyway. And she's dead. We have the same Dad."

Emmy didn't know why she explained all of this, but Nathan nodded.

"Do you think your parents will come?"

"Of course. They're my parents." Emmy didn't like the implication. He must think that because her parents were winter wizards, they must be assholes who didn't care about their kids. Sure, they were assholes, but not *that* kind of assholes. "They're good people," she continued. "They love me. And they love Evangeline. Even my Mom."

"I should leave before they come for you. I don't want to leave…But I don't think me being here will help anything."

Emmy agreed, but didn't like it.

"But I'm not going to *leave* leave," he continued. "I'll be around. I'm going to make this right. You don't have to worry. It's going to be okay."

"Do you really believe that, or are you just saying it because that's what people say?"

Nathan paused as if considering it. "No, I believe it," he said finally. "I have to. You've gotta have hope, you know? That it's all going to work out in the end. That's what gives you the strength to make it there."

But could it work out for both of them? Or, did he mean it would work out for the good guys? It all works out in the end for the hero. Not for the villain.

"That's a nice idea," she said.

When David finally decided to call Patrick and tell him to bring his brother and sisters to the hospital he saw he had a voicemail from the unknown caller he had ignored earlier. He planned on deleting it without listening, then the same number called again as he held his phone.

"Hello?"

"May I speak with David Vandergraff?"

"This is he."

"This is Officer Yolanda Trevino with the Sugar Land Police Department. You're the father of Evangeline and Emmy Vandergraff, correct?"

The panic ran through him like an electric current. This reminded him so much of the call he received last fall when his children were found, but this time, the news could only be bad.

"Yes, I am," he said, his voice a whispery croak.

Nathan kept his promise and stayed by her side until about three minutes before her family arrived in the ER. One nice thing about being a wizard was some awkward encounters could be avoided because Nathan could sense a Vandergraff coming from about a mile away.

Patrick came around the white curtain, which surprised Emmy. Even though Evangeline's disappearance would devastate Dad, she still expected him to come for her—to gather her in his arms as he did when he found her in West Texas. Perhaps it was too late for that. She had pushed it too far this time and he wouldn't forgive her. He had already been so angry at her for sneaking out, and now…she had destroyed everything.

Xavier followed behind Patrick, which surprised Emmy even more. The sight of her *other* brother made her stomach lurch. If she hurt anyone more than Dad, it was Xavier. Dad had plenty of people to love. For Xavier, the world began and ended with Evangeline.

She sat on the edge of the hard bed, discharge papers all ready, and shrunk at the sight of them. She thought they might yell at her, but they didn't.

"Are you okay?" Patrick asked.

Emmy nodded.

"Was there a summer wizard here?" Xavier asked. Hearing Xavier talk always alarmed Emmy, and this time, the words crawled up her back like snakes. He spoke the words calmly, but they came so unexpectedly and so soaked in hate.

"No," she said too quickly. "I don't think so."

Xavier stared her down, and she shrunk more. *Had he always been so frightening?* Her mouth felt dry and she appreciated Patrick's presence. Xavier's eyes looked different. They had always looked so empty, but not anymore. Instead of Evangeline's disappearance causing him to shrink back more into his shell, it had brought him to life. His no-longer-empty eyes—so much like Dad's—focused on her. She didn't think he'd ever held eye contact with her so long.

"They said you can go?" Patrick asked, ignoring Xavier's unexplained hunt for summer wizards.

Emmy nodded again.

"You're sunburned," Patrick said.

Emmy shrugged, feeling defensive, as if she needed to argue this fact.

"Come on," Patrick said. He took her hand to pull her up. Emmy must have imagined any accusation. Patrick pulled her into a quick hug. She couldn't remember that *ever* happening before.

She buried her face in his shoulder and didn't want to let go. She felt herself shaking and hoped he couldn't feel it too.

"Where's Dad?" Emmy asked.

"Uh…let's get out of here. And I'll tell you."

Emmy scrunched her nose at this evasion. She didn't like

the sound of it, but feared the answers too much to ask any questions. She grabbed her phone and discharge paperwork and followed her brothers out of the ER.

Chapter Seventeen

Someone slapped David in the face. The slap must not have satisfied the assailant, because then he was punched. When the pain exploded in his jaw, blood rushed back to his brain as well. He looked up and saw the face of his brother-in-law, Carson, right before he punched him again.

"Stop it, honey. That's not helping anything." That sensible woman's voice had to be Jess, Carson's wife.

For a split second, seeing his former best friend again made him smile, even though he had just punched him. But then he remembered the whole Oppenheimer family—Carson, Jess, and Amanda's own parents—had turned their back on their family when they learned they were practicing magic. At least they finally reappeared when things got bad enough, but David should be the one doing the punching.

David must have slipped out of reality again, and he wanted to go back. Back to the nothing. But seeing Carson's mean blue eyes, made him think of Amanda's mean blue eyes. And that made him think of his children. All the people who needed him here in reality. For about the hundredth time, he wished he was a stronger man. A better man. But until then, he would have to fake it for the people he loved.

"David?" Jess asked. "Are you with us?"

"Yes."

"See, punching helped," Carson said.

"Where am I? Where are the kids? Amanda?"

"Oh, so now you care," Carson said.

"Stop it," Jess said. "He's not himself."

"I'm not so sure," Carson said.

"What's wrong with me?" David asked.

"I don't know," Jess said.

"I know," Carson said. "He's lost his mind. Just given up and gone like so many of his kind. Too weak to stay and fight like a man—bails when things get tough."

"Perhaps, but can you imagine what it must be like? How would you feel if you were in his shoes? How would you feel if you lost me and one of your girls in the same day?"

This argument did quell Carson. "Don't even say things like that."

"Exactly. A reality too horrible to consider. But that's his, so you are the one who needs to man up, and show a little compassion."

It took David a moment to understand they were talking about him. As soon as the reality needled back in, he could swat it away like a buzzing fly.

"Lost?" David asked. "Amanda didn't…?"

"No, no, I'm sorry," Jess said. "I didn't mean that. No one is *lost*. I…" Jess must have run out of things to say, mid-sentence. "It's going to be okay," she concluded, finally.

"Oh my God," David said. Reality floated back in now in stronger waves and he tried to hang on, no matter how much it hurt. "Evangeline. I…what is wrong with me? Why do I keep forgetting? I need to go find her."

The horror floated in now at full strength. Evangeline's disappearance was made more frightening by the fact that he couldn't keep hold of his mind long enough to do anything about it. He felt as if he had forgotten something important, but a hundred times worse. He had wanted to float out of reality the way Xavier did, and he had managed it. Now, he had to find his way back.

He grabbed Jess's arm and must have done it too aggressively because Carson looked ready to punch him again. He backed away from her.

"Jess, please. You have to help me. What is this magic? Is it some kind of misdirection spell meant to confuse me? Or am I losing my mind?"

"I'm sorry. I don't know. It could be either. It could be both."

"How do I make it stop?"

Jess shook her head. Her deep brown eyes implored Carson. "You know more about this kind of magic."

"Yes. A little too much," Carson said. "There's nothing that can be done."

"I don't believe you," Jess said. "Think about your sister. Think about your Patrick and Emmy. There has to be something."

"I don't know any spell or anything, if that's what you mean." Carson looked David in the eye now. "Our parents taught us we have choices. Wizards always think they're subject to forces outside of themselves they cannot control. And that's true. But it's not the only thing that's true. Free will is a real thing. And sometimes the simplest magic is the strongest. If you want something bad enough, it can be so. But you have to be strong person to have a will strong enough to counteract other magic."

David could tell Carson didn't think he was up to the task, and he agreed with him. "So I can make it go away?"

"That's what I've been trying to tell you. *Be a man*. The darkness can't take you if you don't let it. They need you. Be a husband. Be a father. Just do it."

David's head swam. He could feel the darkness polluting his brain, its own kind of cancer. He saw how easily it could make its way in. He only had to lose hope for a second, and he began to drown in it. He had never lost hope so thoroughly as he had today. And now he knew. One more second of lost hope and he would lose himself, and lose everything he loved along with it. If he almost slid into oblivion now, he knew he wouldn't survive losing his talisman.

"Okay," David said.

"Okay?" Carson asked.

"You're right. I can do it. I have to do it. Just point me in the right direction, please."

"Go home," Jess said.

Home. Right. But home wasn't a place. Home was his family, and that wasn't one single place he could go. He had to go back to the hospital to be with Amanda. He had to go to the forest to look for Evangeline. And he had to go back to his other children, and be there for them.

Jess seemed to read his mind. "The police are looking for Evangeline. The doctors are taking care of Amanda. For now, go home."

David knew the Mundane police wouldn't find Evangeline any more than they had found Julie. And the Mundane doctors couldn't do whatever needed to be done. He was alone.

Chapter Eighteen

Patrick thought he ought to stop believing in God. He didn't know why his parents still did. God hated them. Maybe since Patrick was a fall wizard, and not inherently evil, God would spare him. But he didn't care. He loved his family. And if God didn't love them, he had no use for God. And God seemed to want to destroy them.

"Patrick, tell me what you know. I *need* to know there is hope. It's important," Dad said. He sat in the living room with Dad, Xavier, and Emmy. A way-too-small version of their family.

Patrick sighed. "I told you. I can't tell you the future. I told you about my vision of Julie. That's all I have, I'm sorry."

"There has to be more. Please."

Patrick stared at Julie's bracelet on the table. Emmy had shown it to all of them, and none of them had any idea how it got in the truck. The only person left to ask was Mom.

Dad, Emmy, and Xavier all continued to stare at Patrick as he stared at the bracelet. Pleading in their eyes. Waiting to lap up whatever he had to say like water in the desert. All three of them wanting him to do something so badly at the same time gave off a tangible energy that made his stomach burn. He had a feeling of power over them, and he didn't like the way that felt. He wanted them to turn away. Leave him alone. But the time for inaction had come and gone. He knew if he could do anything to help Evangeline and make them feel better, he should.

"I don't know much. It's not very helpful."

"I don't care," Dad said. "Just tell us."

"We'll find Evangeline. I don't know how or when, but I know she's not going to die now. Because I've seen a vision of her in the future. So, I know I'm going to see her again."

"What is the vision of her?" Dad pressed.

"A vision of her alive in the future. That's all you need to know right now. Somehow or another, she makes it out of this."

"And your mother?" Dad asked.

He could lie and say she'd survive too, but he feared he wouldn't get away with it. What he said about Evangeline was true, and he didn't want them to doubt that by lying now.

"I have no information about Mom."

"You don't have any visions of her in the future?" Emmy asked, breathless.

"Yeah, but it doesn't mean anything. I can't see the future like I'm looking through a window. It's just certain things. It could be a good thing I don't have a vision. If Mom gets better and lives a normal, happy life, I wouldn't see visions of that. I just see the things that…I don't know, leave a mark. On time, or fate, or whatever. So, I think that means Mom is not going to die, at least if she does, it's not soon. I'm not close enough to see it yet."

"Okay, thank you," Dad said.

Patrick could hear a difference in his voice. Patrick's vague pronouncements actually did change something in him. At least they gave him a reason to keep going.

"And Julie," Dad continued. "If there is anything else you've seen about her you're holding back, now is the time. Everything is different now. Whatever has happened to her has probably happened to Evangeline. It's personal now."

Patrick tasted bile in the back of his throat. He had only shared the details of the vision with Evangeline. He had told the others he had seen a vision of her and that's why he reacted. But he didn't tell them about the torture. Now, he was so grateful he had left that part out.

"Well, in my vision, she's alive too. But that's about all I know. It does mean there is still hope. I'll pay attention. Keep looking for new visions," Patrick said. "But right now, there's nothing new. Like I said, everything around her is darkness. I didn't see anything useful about where she is or who might have taken her. That's the truth."

Dad nodded solemnly. He had been right, of course. What once happened to strangers now happened to them. No longer a curious mystery to fill their summer boredom, this was their story now. But it had been personal to Patrick for a while now. Patrick's powers had limits. He couldn't foresee a deadly earthquake in China or the results of a Presidential election, no matter how much of a "mark" those things might have on the fate of the world. When he said he saw things that left a mark on fate, he meant things that left a mark on his fate. Due to selfishness or the limitations of his magic, Patrick had never foreseen anything that wouldn't occur right in front of his face.

Chapter Nineteen

David didn't know how he would have made it through the next few days without Carson's advice. "Just be a man." Whenever David felt he might fade away, he repeated those words to himself. *Be a man.* And when David said this to himself, he didn't mean it in the gender specific way. He really meant, *be a person. Be a human being. Do what people do. Breathe in. Breathe out. Feed your children. Feed yourself. Do the dishes. Sleep at night. Wake up in the morning. Shower. If your wife is sick, you take care of her. If your children are scared, you tell them everything will be okay, even if you don't know if it will. You pray to a God you're not sure is there. Do what people do.*

This basic sentiment kept him together. As Carson said, sometimes the simplest magic was the most powerful. And as a dark wizard on the brink of losing his mind, the chance to actually be a person—be a husband, be a father, was the most beautiful and unattainable magic he could imagine.

However, although this kept him sane from moment to moment, he knew he would need more in order to save his wife and daughter. He needed to be a wizard. The root of his problems was magical, and would need a magical solution.

When Mom came home from the hospital, she looked really sick. Emmy had never thought of Mom as a happy, upbeat person, but she must have smiled and laughed more than Emmy had realized. Because now she didn't and Emmy noticed the absence. Mom stayed in bed most of the time. And next week she had to start chemotherapy, which would probably make her sicker. As soon as she got the chance, Emmy showed Mom the bracelet, too. And told her where she had found it. Mom's normally bright blue eyes had turned grayer. Cloudier. She stared at the bracelet a long time before answering, not even sitting up in bed.

"In the truck?" she asked.

"Yes. Do you know how it got there?" Emmy asked again, trying her best to be patient.

Mom used the tip of her fingernail to touch one of the charms—an ancient symbol for the sun—a circle with a dot inside.

"I don't understand," Mom said.

"Yeah, no one understands."

"This is why you cared so much. Why you kept sneaking out. You thought Julie had some link to our family, and that scared you. If it hadn't been for the bracelet, would you have gone to that forest? Would you have taken Evangeline there?"

Emmy considered it for a moment. "No, probably not."

Mom nodded. Her skin looked gray too. "I wish I had a good answer for you, Emmy. But I think the bracelet found its way there as part of a spell. Probably the same spell that affected your father. Maybe it wanted Evangeline all along, and that's how the spell bent fate to make it happen."

"That's not how magic works. A bracelet cannot materialize in the truck."

"I know. I'm sure it didn't," Mom said. "Perhaps I tracked it into the truck on my shoe or in the folds of my clothes."

"Okay…so where were you where you might have just happened to get the bracelet stuck to you?"

Mom stared at the ceiling. They both must have had the same thought, because Mom said, "Not your brother's apartment."

"How do you know?"

"I've been skipping out on work, visiting him almost every day to work on my spell. It's complicated. Takes time. I was with him when Julie disappeared."

Emmy thought Mom would lie to be Jude's alibi, but she had this weakness in her voice. She sounded too tired, too unfocused, to come up with a proper lie. As if she talked in her sleep.

Emmy collected the bracelet in her hands. She had grown used to it now. The jarring energy of the bracelet had grown comforting. As her own talisman provided a source of protection and strength she could touch and hold, Julie's talisman served as all of Emmy's fear and weakness bundled up in an object she could touch and hold, that she controlled, that she could break if she wanted. But she had no interest in breaking it. She put the fear right back in her pocket.

Evangeline had gone missing three days ago, which in missing person time, meant bringing out the corpse-hunting dogs. Of course, Julie had gone missing weeks ago. Long enough that the news had grown stale, at least until Evangeline's disappearance. Now the news believed a serial kidnapper was preying on the local teens, and everyone needed to feel afraid all the time.

Emmy's family could use magic to keep annoying people away. The press. Curious neighbors. Even detectives had trouble finding them. They would ring the doorbell and then immediately turn around and go back to their car, as if they had waited there for ten minutes instead of three seconds.

Emmy didn't like this. The Vandergraffs got what they wanted. They had become invisible to the world, but that meant Evangeline had become invisible too. The news people rarely mentioned her name and called her "the second victim." As much as she doubted the abilities of the Mundane police, she didn't want them to forget about Evangeline altogether and stop looking for her. Everyone would cry for Julie, but this "second victim" would fade out of their memories.

She wondered if the spell worked on their own family too. Uncle Carson and Aunt Jess didn't come back after they had visited Mom at the hospital. Uncle James didn't notice or care his niece had gone missing. And Me-Maw and Pa-Pa, Mom's own parents, hadn't come to see their daughter at all. If the spell wasn't working on them, this proved dark wizards who didn't practice magic were exponentially more evil than those who did. How could they think practicing magic was more evil than abandoning their family?

Dad drove out to the forest alone every single day, and spent most of the day there. Emmy assured him she would look after Mom while he looked for Evangeline. Patrick helped too, but he also picked up a few more guard shifts at the pool to help with money…or just to escape. Emmy thought they should pay him more than ten dollars an hour, since he could prevent accidents before they even occurred.

This left Emmy alone in the house with Mom and Xavier a lot. She didn't know which of them depressed her more. At least she understood Mom's problem. Xavier scared her. He had stopped going through the motions of watching television or playing video games and did nothing. *Nothing.* A combination of sleeping and staring into space.

Emmy had to take care of Xavier too, because if she didn't make him sandwiches and bring him water, he would die. She had tested this by refusing to bring him breakfast and lunch. Finally, at 3pm, she gave in. She barged into his room without knocking. He sat at his desk tapping his fingers. When he didn't acknowledge her, she dropped the peanut butter and jelly and plate in front of him with a loud clatter. He looked at it, but his reaction was still miniscule, so she kicked him in the shin as hard as she could.

He gasped and finally looked at her, clutching his shin. Still not satisfied with his response, she pushed him hard enough that he had to catch himself from falling out of his chair. That time, he pulled back like he prepared to strike back.

"Good," Emmy said. "Hit me. Curse me. *Do something.*"

"Why do want me to hit you?"

"I don't." Emmy felt her eyes burning with tears yet again. "I just want you to stay. I'm not asking you to be happy, or normal, or not a psycho. I just want you to stay."

Xavier continued rubbing his shin, but the anger in his eyes faded again. Emmy had to stop herself from attacking him again. "I'm sorry," he said. "I'll try."

"I need to go somewhere," she said, still wiping away tears and hating herself for it. "Can you keep an eye on my mom?"

"What do I do?"

"Nothing. Just pay attention enough so if she needs help or something, you actually notice."

Emmy found it unbelievable and aggravating that, despite their identical predicaments, the Vandergraffs and Prescotts continued to ignore each other. Emmy believed this was stupid and arrogant on both sides. Julie and Evangeline didn't fall down the same rabbit hole by coincidence. They had some link to each other. There *had* to be a reason why someone wanted them and not Emmy. Or Nathan, for that matter. Julie and Evangeline had to have something in common. However, she had no idea what. She couldn't imagine any two witches so different. And she could not imagine any plausible circumstance where they would have come into contact with each other, or anything else that tied them together.

However, she knew whom to ask. She may have just wanted to see him again, but she didn't care. When Emmy asked Nathan to pick her up from the grocery store, he agreed right away. He checked several times that she didn't have any of her family members with her. And she said, several times, yes, she had ridden her bike there to pick up some prescriptions, milk, and coffee.

When she saw his truck pull into the parking lot, she felt so nervous her tongue swelled. She had asked him to come pick her up, but hadn't given any specific reason, which made it feel like a date.

When she climbed in, she still felt nervous at first. And felt very aware of the bulky bag of groceries she had with her. Their time together had an expiration date, because she had brought unrefrigerated milk with her. Not brilliant. But she felt better quickly. He had a reassuring presence about him. He kept his brow and lips in a firm serious line, but radiated a warm glow despite himself. She felt her cheeks grow warm too.

"Is everything okay?" he asked.

"I guess it's not any less okay than it was before."

"Fair enough."

"Are you okay?"

"Same. Not any less okay. I worried that since you called me, something might be wrong."

"No. Nothing specific. Is it still okay I called you?"

"Yeah. You want to go somewhere?"

"Sure."

"Anywhere in particular?"

"I don't care."

He started driving and Emmy felt relieved. She didn't care where he took her. She wanted to get away. And away with him was even better. And she liked his truck. It didn't smell like Jude. It smelled of sunscreen and cinnamon gum.

"I wanted to talk to you, anyway," he said. "I wanted to finish the conversation we started in the ambulance about your sister. There are things you should know. Things I should have told you in the first place. I didn't realize you needed to know. And you know, wizards don't spill their guts to everyone they meet. Especially not a dark witch…no offense."

Emmy felt like she was about to be given a present. Or had scratched off a winning lotto card. She was right. He did have the key. He would tell her everything.

"Tell me."

"Well, I don't know anything for sure. But my family has a theory about why Julie was taken. And Evangeline may be able to help us confirm that theory."

"Okay."

"Julie isn't an ordinary witch. She's special. You know how every wizard falls somewhere on the solar calendar?"

"Every wizard has their moment."

"Yes. Some wizards claim to be able to narrow it down to the minute, or even the second, although they might be full of it. In any case, we know we can narrow it down to the day. And some days are more important than others. Julie's date is June 21st. She's a summer solstice witch. And that's rare and special."

"So, what does that mean?"

"She's more powerful than most, pretty much all, other wizards. At least when it comes to summer magic. There may be some powerful spells that only she can cast. And some believe she has even more importance and power. In any case, we tried to keep it quiet. We always knew that her being a solstice witch would lead to unwanted attention at best, and at worst, something like this."

"But she's the one with the power. What use would she be to another wizard? Do they think they can get her to cast spells for them?"

"Well, you know, there are ways to take someone's power.

I don't know much about it, of course. I don't know if that's what happening or not. I hope not." His voice got softer and softer as he spoke, and "I hope not" was barely audible.

He had said "you know" as if he assumed she did know about that kind magic, probably because it was some kind of dark magic.

Emmy waited for him to continue, but he didn't. He pulled into the parking lot of a small park.

"It's too hot for any kids to play here. All the slides are burning up and the fountain is off and grills closed because of the drought. So no one will be around."

Emmy smiled to herself. Her family had visited a different park on the Fourth of July, but had the same reason. They went at night so no one would be around. Nathan had the exact same idea, but he chose the middle of the day in the summer.

Emmy followed behind Nathan, the air so hot she thought her skin might cook. The drought caused Nathan to track dust and pieces of dead grass into the air as he walked. The dust burned her eyes. She wanted to point out that everyone else in the world had the right idea by avoiding the park today, but she wanted to be with him. And she wanted to know what he had to say.

They found a well-shaded picnic table, so the heat and humidity still made it hard to breathe, but at least the sun wouldn't cook them alive. The walk from his truck to the picnic table took about thirty seconds, but sweat and dirt coated her skin as if she'd wandered the desert for hours.

"Does the heat not bother you?" Emmy asked.

"I don't mind it too much. But it's not like I can't feel it. We can go somewhere else if you want. I just thought Mundanes wouldn't be around."

"No, this is fine," she said, as she wiped a droplet of sweat from her temple. "So, you were talking about spells that can take someone else's magic."

"Yeah," he said.

"For that kind of magic, would Julie and Evangeline have to die?" Emmy asked. She knew many bad things could happen before death. But she assumed that any other trauma could eventually heal. Some hope existed. Only death was irreversible.

"I don't know if that's part of the plan. It could be. Sometimes. There are dark spells that require human sacrifice. As I said, I don't know much about prax portentia. But I know it's not always about death. I know Julie isn't dead. I can feel her presence. As a solstice witch, she has a strong presence. And if that light went out, I'd know it."

"So, there's still hope. Like you said."

"Yes. I think so."

"Prax portentia. What does that mean?"

He looked up at her. Previously, he had kept his eyes on the ants crawling across the surface of the table. "You've never heard that term?"

"No."

He raised his eyebrows. Perhaps he didn't understand how he could know about a dark spell and she didn't. But he didn't know she barely knew anything about magic. She definitely didn't know any fancy names for spells.

"Well, that's good, I guess," he said. "I'm glad you don't know."

"So, what is it?"

Nathan picked at his cuticles and made a face, as if the explanation tasted bad in his mouth.

"It's hard to explain," he said.

She could tell he meant, *I don't want to explain.* And she didn't ask him again. For most people, she wouldn't give up until they told her what she wanted to know. But she felt different about him. She didn't want to make him say things he didn't want to say. She didn't like seeing him struggling.

"And you want to know if Evangeline is a winter solstice

witch?" Emmy asked, changing the subject.

"That's right. We always just thought it was about Julie and her power. But having the power of both the poles, that's unthinkable. Maybe they were waiting for both. Used magic to call for both. Evangeline just came second."

"If they were waiting for both poles, then…"

"Then, now that they have Evangeline, they might do…whatever it is they plan to do. Time might be running out. Unless…"

"Unless, what?" Emmy asked.

"Unless they want all four."

"You mean, spring and fall too?"

"Exactly. Equinox wizards. If having the power of summer and winter was unthinkable, having all four…I mean, they could do anything. The solstices have the power, but the equinoxes have the precision. Together, they're sometimes called 'the four events.'"

"So, if they're greedy, they'll wait until they have the full collection."

"Maybe. But that would not be easy to get. Finding one of the poles is rare. Finding two is astronomical. Finding all four…I don't know. I would have thought it was impossible, but now I'm not so sure. Whoever did this, used magic to bring Julie and Evangeline to the forest, which meant manipulating a complicated string of events. It's possible the spell has been working for years, gradually aligning the fates. Who says they couldn't use that same magic to call spring and fall too?"

"So that's why we can't find them. The magic only 'calls' the ones it wants."

"Yeah, we think so. It's a magical snare. But it only traps the wizards that meet its qualifications."

"So, then Evangeline *must* be a solstice witch."

"I take it you don't know for sure."

"No. None of us know our dates."

"Is your sister powerful? And darker than you?"

"Yes, she's powerful. And pretty dark, but not evil. But she's a good person. She's not the darkest moment of the darkest night."

"As you might have already figured out, I'm not like a lot of other summer wizards. I don't believe all dark wizards are bad. We all have our kind of magic, but we're still just people. Not angels or demons. People. Julie is a good person. She's a great person, probably the best person I know. But if you were to listen to legend, you'd think the summer solstice witch would be more superhuman, like an angel. And as good as Julie is, I wouldn't say she's *that* good. She has flaws like anyone else. I assume it's the same with Evangeline."

"Yeah, well you said that even though Julie isn't perfect, you said she's the best person you know. Evangeline is not the worst person I know. Not even close. Hell, she might be the best person *I* know." Her voice wobbled.

"I didn't mean that." He put his hand on her back, and then must have thought better of it, because he pulled away.

"I'm not crying," Emmy said, even though salty tears and sweat stung her eyes. "It's okay. I know what you're trying to say. This just sucks."

"Yes, it does."

"So, you're saying there is no chance the Mundane police will find them."

"Probably not."

"So, it's up to us."

"Yes."

"Alright then. We should do some kind of spell together. Like you said, combining magic from the two poles can be very powerful. Maybe if we worked together—"

"I don't think magic is the answer," Nathan said.

"Why? Because it's dangerous? Because it has unintended consequences? I've heard it all before. But I'm not talking about using magic to open a pickle jar. This is to save our sisters. It's worth the risk."

"No, you don't understand. I'm saying our magic wouldn't be powerful enough. Whoever is pulling the strings here is incredibly powerful. They enacted a complicated spell with many variables that was able to bring two powerful magical families to their knees. They could snuff out anything we tried to do. We'd end up hurting ourselves."

That made Emmy feel small. Being a witch meant she didn't have the same limits the Mundanes did. She was special. Powerful. And she couldn't imagine anything worse than not saving Evangeline because she wasn't special *enough* or powerful *enough*.

"So you're saying we can't use magic to find them. And we're not going to be able to find them by looking like humans would. So what, there's nothing we can do?"

"I told you. We have to keep the hope. We have to assume there is something we can do. I just don't know what it is yet."

"Can you tell me my date? Do you know how to do that?"

"Yeah, I can," Nathan said. "You want me to?"

"Yes." She wanted to know her date, but that's not what got her heart racing. She'd seen this done before, so she knew it meant he would have to get close to her. He'd have to touch her. Maybe for several minutes.

"Okay. I'm not an expert. I might be off by a day or two. But I have studied this practice. Go ahead and stand up and face me."

He stepped close to her and placed his fingers behind her head, interweaving through her hair as he did—the exact position someone might take before they pulled you into a kiss.

"You know, you don't have to stop breathing...or you know, blinking," he said.

"Oh...right."

"Does that hurt?" he asked.

"No."

"I've never tried this on a winter. It's different. But I think

I can find it."

He closed his eyes and furrowed his brow in concentration. Her head felt warm and tingly at the spot where he touched her, and she felt lightheaded. But no, it didn't hurt. It felt wonderful. His touch drew out all her happy memories. They rolled through her mind as if he called them.

She thought of the day in the winter before everything got weird, when the roads iced over and the power went out. No one could go to work or school, and the whole family stayed inside, played board games. and drank hot chocolate. She thought of the day Samantha and Emmy skipped school and jumped the fence at a neighbor's house to spend the day at their pool, and sipped wine they hated, just to feel grown up. And she thought of little things, like jumping off the high dive. Watermelon snow cones. Sprinting toward the castle at Magic Kingdom as a little girl, with Dad running after her, trying not to lose her in the crowd.

"I think January 22nd."

"What?" She had almost forgotten why they did this.

"January 22nd, maybe 23rd."

"Oh."

He unraveled his hands from her hair. "You look disappointed. Did you expect something else?"

"You mean about my date?"

"Yeah."

"I guess not. A friend of mine told me I was a January. What does it mean?"

"It means you're a winter witch, but more than 30 days after the winter solstice, so you're not that dark. Since you're on the spring side of the solstice, we say you're a winter witch, tending towards spring. Which means you may have some spring characteristics too."

Emmy scrunched up her nose.

Nathan laughed. "It's not a bad thing And I'm sure it's no surprise to you It means you're a little…stormy. Impetuous.

Passionate. You follow your heart. And you're not afraid to live life with abandon. I don't have to know you well to know that's true."

"Maybe."

"I'm June 5th, so I tend towards spring too."

She couldn't stop herself from smiling. She liked that they had at least one small thing in common.

"What does that mean about you?" she asked.

"Well, according to my parents anyway, it means I can get lost on my way from the driveway to the front door."

She laughed. "Is that true?"

"I don't get lost. I might decide to go somewhere unexpected at the last minute. Or, I might get distracted by something shiny."

"I know what you mean about…shiny things." By *shiny things*, she had meant him, but she wished it hadn't been as obvious. He blushed, which made her blush five times worse. He smiled as if he couldn't help himself, which made him shine even more.

"Since we both have that crazy spring in us, I think we should made a pact," Nathan said. "We have to avoid wandering into oncoming traffic or off cliffs for at least a couple more years."

"Why do you say that?"

"Because I want to kiss you. But you're too young."

"You're saying you're going to wait a couple more *years* before you kiss me? I don't think so."

"All right. You convinced me."

Emmy's heart leapt into her throat. She couldn't believe it was really happening. Right in that moment. He put his hand in her hair again, as he had done before, but this time he did pull her close to him. He kissed her as if he wanted to make it count. Slowly, and with great attention, as if he wanted to memorize every cell of her lips. Emmy didn't know what she was doing, but kissing Nathan turned out to be easy. Natural, as if she'd done it a million times before. She thought their opposing energies might fight against each other, but they didn't. They complemented each other like hot apple pie and ice cream. A perfect fit.

Nathan had to pry Emmy off him, because she had no plans to end the kiss.

"I shouldn't have done that," he said.

"No, you definitely should have done that."

"Why do you have to be so young?"

"Why do you always have to do the right thing?"

"I know I was joking when I said we shouldn't walk into oncoming traffic, but I'm serious, too. You put yourself in too much danger. And you're too strong-willed for me to put any long-term spell on you that would make you be safe. Can you please take care of yourself, so someday I can do that again?"

Emmy didn't respond. She didn't like the terms of the agreement.

But he didn't make her agree. He pulled her into a hug, a hug that somehow made him feel big and her small, but in a good way, as if he had her wrapped in a warm cocoon.

She knew the hug meant goodbye, and she tried to think of ways to make it not be. Maybe she could use magic to make him stay. She didn't want to go back to her winter world.

Apparently, she could not force him to do things, because way too soon, he dropped her off again at the grocery store.

It didn't take long for the warm feeling to disappear and the sense of dread to return. The cold seeped back in, from her core, out to her extremities, burning and prickling as it went.

CHAPTER TWENTY

David combed his fingers through Amanda's hair, gently removing the tangles. Since she had gotten sick, they had more moments like this. The cancer slowed her down. She had become a quieter version of herself. Normally, she wouldn't stay this still for long, her head resting on his chest while they lay in bed in silence.

He felt the warmth of her body, the rise and fall of her breathing, the heaviness of her head, very aware of the heart inside her—a heart, far too flimsy. That small beating thing kept all the energy and life and beauty that was Amanda. How could something so precious be snuffed out so easily? These moments felt bittersweet now. He couldn't enjoy them. Every time he was reminded of how much he loved her, he couldn't help but think about how it would feel to lose her.

I don't want to think about it. Please, God, just stop me from thinking about it.

"I wish we were ordinary," David said. In a way, continuing his prayer, talking to God and Amanda at once. "I want us to complain about things like traffic and the heat. And fight about money, and the kids. I want normal."

"If it makes you feel better, we do all those things," Amanda said.

"You know what I mean. I don't understand why I can't have that. I don't want much. I don't need wealth or power or anything I didn't earn. I just want my wife and my kids, and for all of us to live to be old. Why can't God give that to me? Is that really too much to ask?"

"So, this is the, 'why does God let bad things happen' question?"

"I suppose."

"It's a stupid question."

"How is it a stupid question?"

She intertwined her hand with his and fiddled with his wedding ring. "I don't pretend to understand God's plan. But clearly, the world is meant to be horrible, and cruel, and unfair. It always has been. Always will be. Life is supposed to be that way. That's what God intended. The world is horrible…but it's also beautiful."

The ceiling above him faded away. At first, he panicked, thinking he must have gone mad. But it didn't take him long to realize what Amanda had done. She had done the same thing when she first told him he was a wizard. She immersed them in one of the "sticky" memories she had kept. She wanted to show him "beautiful."

The ceiling blew away to reveal a thick blanket of stars. He had never felt so close to the sky. He knew this moment right away. Their honeymoon. They had lain together in the warm, white sand, in almost the same position they lay in now. Music from the nearby cabana drifted through the sound of the waves. He dug his toes into the warmth of the sand and inhaled. He could smell the salty ocean, and he could smell Amanda, with a hint of coconut on her skin and rum on her lips. He pulled her face toward him to kiss her, but the image faded.

"No," he said. "Please, no. I want to stay."

"It's just a memory, David. We're here, not there."

"I know." The room and Amanda went back into focus.

She peered up at him with her pale blue eyes, and it hit him hard. She was twenty years older, and they lay under a bland white ceiling instead of stars and on a lumpy mattress instead of sand, but he loved her as much as he had in that moment. The contrast made that clear. Life had been filled with more hope then, but the love felt the same. In fact, now it felt exponentially stronger.

So he leaned in to kiss her anyway.

When he pulled away, she was crying. He hated to see her cry.

"I don't want to die," she said. "I want to stay here with you."

Her blue eyes pleaded with him, as if he could grant her request. He didn't think he could say anything back without crying himself, so he squeezed her tighter.

"Please don't stop praying for me," she said. "I don't want you to stop praying."

"If there is only the slightest chance there is a God listening to my prayers, I'll pray for you. I won't stop unless someone proves to me there is no God, and probably not even then. I'm stubborn like that."

Patrick woke up coughing. His lungs burned. His eyes burned. *What the Hell? What was wrong with him?* The dark bedroom seemed normal. No smoke. No fire. In contrast, the room seemed oddly still, perhaps magically so. He couldn't hear Xavier breathing, or the gentle tick of his alarm clock, or crickets outside. But he did smell…

His stomach lurched. Gasoline. He smelled gasoline.

This was no nightmare. This was a vision. And not the distant, blurry kind. The right here. Right now. The *you have seconds to spare* kind. He hoped he hadn't spent his entire advance warning coughing.

Despite his coughing, Xavier didn't stir. Patrick flew out of bed and shook Xavier as violently as he could. He opened his eyes, but didn't react, so Patrick dragged him out of bed and kicked him in the stomach.

"What…the…fuck?" Xavier spluttered.

"We don't have much time. Go wake up Emmy and get out of the house. I'll get Mom and Dad." He had to push against a hard wall of silence to get the words out. Something muffled all the sounds in the house. A silencing spell, maybe. He hoped Xavier could actually hear him.

The room filled with orange light. And Patrick could see Xavier's eyes bathed in the firelight, coming into full focus as he realized what had happened. *Shit.* Time had run out. Patrick tensed up, waiting for an explosion, but none came. The fire stayed outside the window, or *on* the window.

Being kicked in the stomach and having his room set on fire jolted Xavier awake. Without a word, he ran out of the room, and Patrick hoped he followed his instructions.

Patrick followed him out and headed to his parents' bedroom. Smoke had already filled the house, but the smoke alarm hadn't gone off yet. He thought it wouldn't, or at least, they wouldn't hear it. The silencing spell would take care of that.

Flickering yellow light bathed his parents' bedroom too. From what he could tell, fire encircled the house, as if someone drenched the outside in gasoline and lit a match. Dad was a much lighter sleeper than Xavier, and Patrick's presence in the room was enough to wake him. Patrick pointed to the window. Dad muttered and Patrick couldn't tell if the spell made it so he couldn't understand him, or if Dad babbled incoherently due to fear. But Patrick had already used all the spare freak-out time for himself.

"Help me with Mom," Patrick commanded.

Mom could walk, but she couldn't walk fast. Dad didn't

take the time to wake her. He pulled her out of bed and into a standing position. Mom woke with a gasp as Dad pressed her into Patrick's arms.

"Help her out," Dad said. His voiced sounded odd, as if they had a bad cell phone connection. Dad made a dash to leave and Patrick grabbed his arm.

"They're already outside. We're last." Patrick hoped it was true, and that Dad could understand him.

Patrick thought he could make out a confused squint on Dad's face, perhaps noticing how strange Patrick might have sounded.

When they left the bedroom, Patrick saw that the fire had made it into the kitchen. The drapes around the kitchen window had lit up, and threatened to serve as kindling for the rest of the room. The same drapes hung right over Emmy's bed, and he hoped again Xavier had come through.

Patrick was grateful—for the first time—their house was small. The walk to the front door felt endless, but it must have taken seconds. Mom pointed toward Emmy's room, but Patrick and Dad pulled her out of the house anyway, not taking the time to explain.

The fresh air outside felt hot and suffocating, but still a relief. And to his greater relief, Patrick felt Emmy careening into them like a cannonball before he could blink away the burning smoke. Xavier stood on the sidewalk.

As Patrick coughed and tried to catch his breath, he looked out at the street. Whoever had done this had already made their getaway. He thought he might see some brake lights disappear several blocks down. Even if he wanted to follow, the keys sat inside the burning house.

Patrick looked at the street while everyone else looked at the house. As Patrick had guessed, gasoline-fueled flames licked up the sides of the building at every angle. The flames were crawling inside through the windows like eager intruders. Their dry, dead lawn had caught too, and Patrick thought he saw the remnants of something more well-planned than spare embers catching the straw-like grass. A large triangle, like the one on Julie's bracelet, had been drawn in the lawn with gasoline.

Magic had nothing to do with the silence that followed. Patrick could imagine everyone felt what he felt. Shock, gradually melting into a hot, black rage. Rage too deep and pure to require shouting or cursing or crying. Someone had tried to burn them alive.

CHAPTER TWENTY-ONE

David knew Amanda must be really sick, because she fell asleep at the police station. David thought he would never sleep again, nor would his kids. They popped around him, from chair to chair, to the vending machine, to the bathroom, to the water fountain, pop, pop, pop. They radiated rage and frustration, and had nowhere to direct it. David could guess that, because he felt that way too.

A wizard reporting a crime to a Mundane detective was frustrating. David had already learned this when Evangeline went missing. The detectives assigned to Evangeline's case came to talk with him about the arson, presuming there had to some relation.

A forty-something woman with red hair and a pretty, but tired, face was the lead detective on Evangeline's case and she sat with David alone in an interrogation room.

"Can you think of anyone who wishes you harm?" she asked.

"John Prescott," David said. He realized immediately that he shouldn't have voiced his suspicions aloud. He was just too damn tired to talk in circles with this woman. Besides, magic or no magic, Mundanes could understand arson. Maybe she could find some real, non-magical evidence against him.

"Why?"

"He doesn't like my family."

"Why? According to you both, and all the evidence we have seen, the two of you have never met, nor do you have any connection to each other whatsoever. Are you telling me now that you have met John Prescott?"

"No. Not that I recall."

"Then why do you believe he wishes you harm?"

David didn't answer. He glared at her, again wishing he had kept his mouth shut. The Mundane police had never managed to help him an ounce, and he didn't know why he thought things might be different now. He felt dark magic radiating from him and the detective glared back at him. She must feel something. If anything, his magic must cause her to either fear or hate him, even if she didn't know why. If she "followed her gut" as they did on the T.V. shows, she'd investigate him next. He wanted to rein in the ambient evil that surrounded him, but he felt too angry, tired, and sad. The detective was trying her best, and he didn't wish to curse her consciously or subconsciously.

"Mr. Vandergraff," she continued. "I've been doing this for long enough to know things aren't always the way they seem. But I've also been doing this long enough to know in most cases, things are exactly as they seem."

"And how do things seem to you?"

She didn't answer. He could read her well. Something about all of this seemed wrong to her, but she didn't know what and she hated that. This case kept her up at night, nagging at her. David could also sense she was smart. Not the reactionary type. Even if David radiated evil and John Prescott radiated good, she knew she was missing something. She wanted facts. Something tangible. David wished he could give it to her. But she wouldn't believe the truth if he told her every last detail.

"You want to know how things seem to me?" she asked.

"I think you're telling me only part of the story. I'll ask you again, why do you suspect John Prescott of setting your house on fire?"

"I guess I have no reason. It doesn't matter. Investigate him. Don't investigate him. You won't find anything."

"I'm trying to help you, Mr. Vandergraff."

"I know you are."

"I can't do that if you're not honest with me."

"Is this an interrogation? I thought I was the victim."

"If you're the victim, then stop obstructing my investigation. All, you're doing is making it harder for me to find your daughter and catch the people who tried to hurt you and your family. I can't imagine why you would want to do that."

"I told you. John Prescott. Or someone he is associated with. I told you exactly who did it. I don't know how I can be more helpful than that. Now, I'm done talking. I need to take my wife somewhere she can rest. And then I need to figure out what the fuck I'm supposed to do now."

"Do you have any family you can stay with, or should I have Victim's Services set you up with temporary housing?"

David paused. "The temporary housing will be fine. Thank you."

"When you decide you want to help me find your daughter, give me a call."

"Where do they live?" Xavier asked. "What was it, Candy Land?"

Patrick figured that nearly getting burned alive had been enough to shake Xavier back to life. He had the look of someone who had woken from a coma to find the hospital burning around him.

While they waited for Dad to finish talking to the police, everything was opposite. Xavier paced and talked in the waiting area, planning a counter attack, while Emmy sat quietly in a plastic chair, watching Xavier's feet.

"Sugar Land," Patrick said. "It's called Sugar Land."

"Why do you think it's the Prescotts?" Emmy asked quietly. Patrick almost believed someone had cast a spell on them and they'd switched bodies.

Xavier laughed, and Patrick shuddered. He rarely laughed, and it sounded wrong, especially now.

"Who else?" Xavier asked. "A week after Evie disappears, this happens? It's because they know about us now."

Emmy had her arms crossed in front of her and cradled one with the other.

"What are you hiding? Did you hurt yourself?" Patrick asked.

She looked at him as if he had accused her of something. She looked small.

"I'm fine," she said.

"Show me."

With her eyes averted, she held out the arm she had cradled. She had covered a blistery pink burn mark on her forearm.

"Ouch," Patrick said. "Why didn't you say anything?"

"It's no big deal. I got hit with an ember."

Emmy pulled her arm to herself again. Patrick thought her behavior was strange. Why did she hide an injury from the fire they all knew about? He had the strangest sensation—a vision, but more delicate. He could sense a secret, like a rabbit's cottontail he glimpsed for a moment before it ran back into the brush. He could go after it if he wanted to. He could hunt it down. He didn't know how, but he had the urge to grab her burned arm, as if when he touched her, he would know her secret.

But he resisted. He might want to know what she hid, but

he wouldn't draw it out in front of Xavier. Xavier animated and Emmy meek was not just weird, it terrified him. He had no idea what either of them might do.

"Why would the Prescotts want to kill us?" Emmy asked, looking to Patrick for the answer.

Patrick had no good answer. Why would *anybody* want to kill them? Not kill them. *Burn them alive.* All of them. His sick mom. His little sister. Every time he thought about those brake lights, his whole body went cold. He felt raw. Naked. He could see how anger and fear were related. He felt both so strongly that they were almost the same emotion.

"I don't know," Patrick said.

"They don't want to hurt us," Emmy said. She sounded less confident than usual. Patrick could sense the little secret hopping around again and he wanted to grab it by the ears. "They may not like winter wizards, but they don't think we took Julie. I mean, why would we take Evangeline too? That's not what they think happened." She sounded more confident as she went along. "Xavier, I don't know what you think you're going to do, but I'm not going to let you."

"What?" Xavier spat.

Emmy stood up. "The Prescotts did not set that fire. And I'm not going to let you, or anybody, go and burn down their house. That's going to make everything even worse…if that's possible."

Xavier stared her down, but didn't reply. Perhaps there was only enough energy in the world for one of them, and they had to take turns.

"You sound pretty sure, Emmy," Patrick said. "What do you know?"

"Fine," Emmy said. "I know one of them. Nathan. We've been talking. They think Julie and Evangeline were taken because they're both solstice witches. And they don't have any more idea who did it than we do. They're not the enemy. Someone or something else out there is the enemy. And as long as we're fighting against the same enemy, the Prescotts and us are on the same side. We need to be working together."

"Oh, my God," Xavier said. His voice sounded as if it came from far away. But The quietness of his tone didn't fool Patrick. He could feel Xavier's anger building, simmering closer to the boiling point. Xavier looked up at Emmy as if he had found the target for all that rage.

Patrick moved between them without thinking about it, and Emmy hovered close behind him.

"You did this. It's your fault," Xavier said.

"I…" Emmy started, but she trailed off.

"You're so fucking stupid."

"Hey, that's not cool," Patrick said. "Calm down, man."

"Fuck you!" Emmy shouted from behind him.

"You don't even know what you did," Xavier said.

"I didn't do anything," Emmy said. "I don't know what your problem is."

"You trusted a summer wizard," Xavier said, and let the statement drop hard as if he didn't need further explanation.

"Oh, my God! You're really upset about me being friends with a summer wizard?" Emmy stepped back out to face Xavier, but stayed close to Patrick. "That's insane. You're insane. He's a nice guy."

"Oh, I'm sure he's *really* nice," Xavier said. "The nicer they are, the more dangerous they are. You seriously don't know how dangerous summer wizards are, do you?"

"I…" Emmy stopped. Patrick could tell she wanted to argue. "You're insane," she said, again.

"Yeah, no, you don't know. None of you know. You pretend you're wizards, but you don't know anything about anything."

"You're right. We don't," Patrick said. "That's what we need you for. Maybe if you talked once in a while, we'd learn something. You're talking now. So, why don't you go ahead and say what you want to say, and lay off Emmy? She didn't do anything wrong."

Xavier looked slightly quelled, and Patrick let out a sigh of relief.

"You're right. I should have said something. As soon as David mentioned that summer witch. I should have known we were marked."

"Marked?" Patrick asked.

"Summer wizards live for killing winter wizards. It's their mission. Their whole lives are centered around defeating us. And they usually get what they want. They're extremely powerful, but also tricky. That's why they're so dangerous. They don't come right at you. They cast intricate spells to draw you in. And it all seems so warm and safe…until you're dead. It's a siren song."

"Siren?" Emmy asked.

"And they always get away with it," Xavier continued. "They'll kill us, and then everyone will go on loving them, and hating us. The best thing you can do is avoid them. That's what my mother told me. Don't fight with a summer wizard, because they always, *always* win. Keep your head down, and stay away. I'm sorry Emmy, but this guy does not like you. All he wants to do is light you on fire, and watch you burn."

"That's a lot of words you said," Emmy said. She looked small again. That moment of confidence had faded away.

"I'm sorry I yelled at you," Xavier said.

"It's okay."

"I want to get her back. I *have* to get her back." Xavier's voice shook. Patrick didn't know what terrified him more, Xavier yelling or Xavier crying. He didn't want to see either.

"Do you think Julie is even missing?" Emmy asked. "Or was it all a trick? She's probably hiding out somewhere. She's probably fine."

"She's not fine," Patrick said. Xavier's argument about summer wizards sounded solid. They may have started the fire. But that didn't explain Julie. The image of her in his mind was so strong. Deep burn marks on her back. He could hear her screams. Smell her burning flesh. No one could tell him that wasn't real.

"I told you," Xavier said. "They can trick you. They can get into your head if they wanted to." He must have known what Patrick had thought.

"And into the truck," Emmy said. "They must have planted the bracelet. That's what made me care so much about Julie. That's why I looked for her. That's why I brought Evangeline out there with me. Because of the damn bracelet. I can't believe I was so stupid."

"I don't know," Patrick said.

"What do we do?" Emmy asked, looking at Xavier. "I'll do anything to help get her back. Just tell me what to do."

Patrick felt a chill as he witnessed the alliances in the room shift. Emmy had joined forces with Xavier, and Patrick knew their combined energy would be both powerful and devoid of reason, even worse than the Emmy-Jude alliance. And when Emmy said she would do anything, Patrick knew she meant that literally. She would do anything. And Xavier would too. Absolutely-fucking-anything. And now that the summer wizards had violated them so much, even Patrick felt as if he didn't have much to lose. And he was the sensible one.

Xavier looked at Emmy warmly now. She must have given him a tiny flicker of hope. However, he didn't spout out any instructions for her. He looked paralyzed under the weight of her allegiance. That would at least delay Emmy and Xavier from doing their *anything*. The willingness to do anything didn't mean they had any idea *what* to do.

"I know where they live," Emmy said.

Xavier ran his fingers through his hair as if he wanted to wake up his brain. Patrick knew he was not used to being a leader in the Vandergraff family. He wasn't even a follower. He was barely a participant.

"No," Xavier said. "You were right the first time. We have

to assume the fire was all a part of their strategy. They would expect us to go running after them. So, we can't do that."

Patrick nodded, wishing to encourage this rational line of thinking. "Remember, Evangeline's safety is the most important thing. All of this feels like a distraction to me. We can't go running off seeking revenge. We can't do anything that takes away focus from finding Evangeline. Agreed?"

They both nodded.

"So, unless you think Evangeline is at their house, there is no point going there. Maybe we should go to the forest."

Emmy groaned. "Are you serious? I have been there a million times. Dad has been there a million times. There is nothing to see."

"Well, I haven't been there yet," Patrick said.

"So?" Emmy said. "What do you think you can do that no one else can?" She said it with a hint of an eye roll, and Patrick scowled. But he didn't have a good answer for her question…at least not one he wanted to share.

"Besides," Emmy said. "Did you already forget? The last time I brought someone with me to the forest, they disappeared. We thought, 'Oh, yeah, let's check it out. What's the harm?' There is no way you're going there. I am not going to make the same mistake twice."

"It's either that, or do nothing," Patrick said.

Patrick knew his sister well enough to know that the argument would work. Nothing was not an option.

"Yeah, but what if I lose you too?" she asked.

"That's not going to happen."

Emmy didn't see through his lies. Patrick had his own secret. He knew at some point or another, he would see Julie. Tortured right in front of his face. He didn't know what to believe, but he had to trust his visions had some meaning. His vision had saved him and his family from the fire. Regardless, he knew he had to go to that forest. None of this could end until he did.

When they made it to the motel, Dad took the guys out to get some food and Emmy stayed with Mom. As soon as the guys left, she couldn't keep it in anymore. She cried. And like a little girl, she crawled into bed with Mom and cried into her shoulder. Mom stroked her hair and Emmy listened to her heartbeat. And it made her cry more. What if her mother would never hold her again?

Mom liked to fix things, but this time she didn't try. Maybe she was too sick. Or, maybe she knew things were beyond repair. But she didn't make Emmy talk about it. She didn't offer any suggestions. She didn't tell her it would all be okay. And Emmy appreciated that. She didn't want to hear any lies. Mom held her and let her cry. She felt the warmth of her body and the rise and fall of her breathing, and that provided comfort enough.

Emmy cried for everything. She cried for Mom. She cried for Evangeline. She cried for the dumb old dolls that had burned in the fire. She cried because all of Evangeline's weird, mismatched clothes and books had burned away too, as if she had never existed at all. And like a stupid girl, she cried because Nathan had broken her heart.

CHAPTER TWENTY-TWO

Thea Prescott pulled over to the side of the road at the exact intersection in Houston where most of the city's murders took place. She should have felt frightened. She knew if she stayed here long enough, someone would carjack her at gunpoint. But she knew the oracle would come when she called him. If he ever didn't show up, that probably would mean he had died.

Sure enough, a tattooed young man appeared from around the corner. He carried a gun in plain sight and circled her car once, looking around before he climbed into the passenger seat.

"You crazy bitch," he said. "You can't park here. You're going to get yourself killed."

"Yes, but if I park here, I know you'll come faster because you want to protect me from danger. You're a good man, Carlos. But don't worry, I won't tell anyone."

"Drive."

She pulled back onto the street. Carlos kept looking around, holding his gun. His other hand hovered in Thea's direction, as if he prepared to grab her and push her out of the way of gunfire.

"Man, your car smells like peach pie. It's disgusting," he

said.

"I'm surprised you can smell it at all, because you smell terrible."

"It's hot out there, woman. What, your men don't sweat in the heat?" He lowered his gun and adjusted the air conditioner vents to hit him in the face. "You haven't found your little girl yet?" he asked tenderly.

"No."

"I can give you a potion to dull the pain. And I've got the Mundane shit too, if you prefer to go classic."

She spared one glance away from the road to glare at him.

"I know, I know," he said. "You have a different weakness, right?"

"If you consider love for my family weakness, then yes, watch me crumble at your feet."

Carlos made a gagging noise.

"You know I can pay."

"Drive us at least past Lark Street."

She did as he asked, and pulled in the parking lot of an abandoned building covered in graffiti.

"I'll take your money if you want," Carlos said. "But I take my work seriously. I'm not going to fill your ears with all kinds of shit just for something to say. And I'm not just going to tell you what you want to hear."

"I know. That's why I come to you."

"What do you want to know?"

"I want to know if anything has changed. Your prophecy about the Vandergralls. Has it changed?"

He took her hand and closed his eyes. She looked at the tattoos on his arms while he searched the future. From far away, his tattoos made him look frightening, but they were lovely up close. He had branches that spread up his neck and down his arms. She assumed they sprouted from a tree on his back. On his muscled forearm, he had the names "Isabella," and "Elena". On his other forearm it said, "It is not for you to know times or seasons that the Father has fixed by his own authority." Acts 1:7.

He released her hand. "No. If anything, the prophecy has grown stronger. And more complex. I'm sorry."

She nodded. "When you said a Vandergraff would murder a Prescott. Did you envision it would be through magic? Or in a more traditional sense?"

"I see blood. Much blood will be spilled."

"And you still do not know which Vandergraff will kill which Prescott?"

"When I have my visions, they come to me in symbols. It's hard to explain, but I do not see earthly things like names, faces, locations, or dates. I only see the symbols."

"What symbols do you see exactly?"

"The demon slaying the deity. Spilling blood. With great anger. Perhaps in vengeance."

She nodded. He hadn't mentioned vengeance before. And that might mean she had found a way to turn the fates.

"And from that you know it's a Vandergraff killing a Prescott?"

"I'm sorry Miss Thea, it's hard to describe in words. I make it sound simpler than it is. Something happened recently that has made it messier, more confusing, than the first time I gave you the prophecy. What has happened?"

"Many things. Our families are more intertwined than when we spoke before."

"That fits."

"I no longer believe I can cancel out the prophecy. It's too late for that. I just hope to alter it."

"You may shine brighter than the rest, but you are not one of God's angels. And fate is not yours to bend."

"I never said I was one of God's angels. But if God wants my babies to suffer and die, I don't accept that. If that's God's plan, you better believe I'll defy Him. I'd burn in Hell for eternity for the chance to save any one of them."

"I hope you find your little girl," he said. "Both of them. They are together."

Thea expelled a long pained breath, as he answered the question she hadn't asked. The question she hadn't dared ask.

"No charge today, Miss Thea." Carlos stole the half-drunk bottle of water in the cup holder and jumped out of the car, leaving Thea staring at her steering wheel, feeling frozen.

CHAPTER TWENTY-THREE

Sneaking out of the hotel was easier than sneaking out of the house. So easy, Emmy could do it during the day. The two tiny rooms drove all of them crazy, and everyone but Mom kept leaving on random errands…vending machine, ice, coffee, fitness room, pool, parking lot, it didn't matter. They didn't announce where they went or why anymore, they just wandered. So, Emmy took the truck keys off the T.V. stand and walked out. She drove to what remained of their home.

The fire department had come fast enough that the whole house didn't go up in flame. But the summer wizards had done their best. Gasoline drenched the outside walls and brush, with special attention paid to the wooden doors and window frames.

This house had never felt like home, but seeing it destroyed made Emmy's stomach hurt. It reminded her of looking at the version of her mom with cancer. Something so familiar had gone so wrong. The house was a blackened shell, surrounded by charred and barren brush and trees. It looked odd set among all the normal, non-burned houses. One cancerous cell in a healthy host. Now the whole house didn't belong in the normal, Mundane neighborhood, as the family inside hadn't.

She could smell the wet ash from the sidewalk. She feared everything had burned, but Dad had assured them they hadn't lost everything. The outside looked bad, but the fire never took the house. "Only skin-deep," he had explained. However, smoke and water from the firemen had damaged everything that hadn't burned.

She looked around carefully as she walked down the driveway. The police had put yellow tape over the door and warning signs against entering. However, she had already prepared some good sob stories in case she got caught. She wanted her teddy bear. She wanted a picture of her mom from before she got cancer. She wanted her kidnapped sister's pillow to see if it still had any of her smell. Yeah, she doubted anyone would put her in handcuffs. Especially, because she *did* want all those things, so she wouldn't have to lie. However, she had come for something else.

To avoid disturbing the crime scene seal, Emmy entered at a spot where the wall had burned away…in her room. When Xavier had first grabbed her in her bed, she had to admit, she freaked. But only for a second. He just had to look at her and she knew what to do. She remembered seeing her bedside lamp reflected in his gray eyes, and thinking the lamp looked like fire, and just knew. They ran out—not one word spoken between them until they got outside.

Emmy had realized they were alone outside and went to run back in. Xavier held her back, and said, "They're coming." Emmy knew right away something was wrong about the fire. It leapt up the walls with unnatural vigor, and spread out in lines in the yard that formed a triangle, the ancient symbol for fire, and one of the charms on Julie's bracelet. It was magic.

Later, the police asked them asked several times if they had seen anyone outside. Emmy hadn't looked. She hated herself for this now. They must have set the fire minutes before. But Emmy didn't remember turning around at all. She just looked at the house. And Xavier had been distracted keeping her from running back inside. The arsonist could have stood right behind them.

The fire had blackened Emmy's bed. The sight of her bed made her throat fill with bile. She pictured her own blackened skeleton there. The fire didn't get Evangeline's bed as bad. Her story about wanting to find something with Evangeline's smell now seemed stupid. Ash and water stains covered Evangeline's bed. And the smell of fire overwhelmed everything. Nothing here smelled like Evangeline anymore, and maybe nothing ever would again. The thought made her throat tighten with constricted sobs.

The living room looked better. Emmy's flip-flops were still where she left them by the TV, but the room looked odd. The electricity was off, and the room was dark, with bright patches of sunlight poking through holes where the fire made it through the wall. The sunlight caught ash and dust floating in the air. It didn't look anything like home anymore.

In Mom and Dad's room, the carpet had caught fire and the room had a sickening burned plastic smell. She went straight to the closet. The fire hadn't made it inside.

Mom sold a few of her guns when they had to move, but still had some in a locked chest in the closet. This was a fireproof chest, and way more high-tech than the lockbox she had kept a handgun in at their house before. That one had a key Emmy could find. This one had a combination. Emmy had no idea how to break into this lock, or any lock, so she would have to use a mixture of magic and guessing.

She put her hand on the wheel of the lock and cleared her mind. She waited for numbers to pop into her mind. For some reason, she could only think of Jude. She had this super random memory of playing this vicious—but crazy fun—game of air hockey with Jude at Party Station Pizza. But when the puck flew off the table and nailed Patrick in the face and made him bleed, Mom made them stop. Emmy had been angry that

Mom made her sit in a corner behind the crane game for five minutes. And Jude got to go back to his friends because it was…

"Oh," she said aloud.

She entered the numbers 4596, Jude's birthday—April 5, 1996. The lock clicked open. She took a moment to scrunch up her nose and feel angry Mom had chosen Jude's birthday of all the birthdays she could have picked.

Emmy let it go, and she looked through her choices. Two hunting rifles and two handguns. She took a handgun and a box of bullets, checked the safety, and put it in her purse.

Emmy took several deep breaths before she called Nathan. She had to admit she feared him, and that made her feel weak. She was the wicked witch—he should fear *her*. But he was the kind of monster she didn't understand. She didn't know how to outwit him. But she wouldn't let the fear dampen her resolve. She let the fear soak through and turn to anger, because she knew anger would make this easier.

She listened to his phone ring on the other end, the electronic ring trilling through her brain.

"Hey," he said.

Emmy didn't answer right away. She listened to that "hey" with as much magic as she could muster. She hoped she could hear his thoughts through his voice. A thought like, "You should be dead." Or maybe she could hear the surprise in this voice. Or a forced attempt to sound natural, since he knew what had happened to her family and had to pretend he didn't. But no special insights came to her. She just heard, "Hey."

"Emmy? Are you there?" He said her name quietly, as if he didn't want anyone to overhear.

"Yes, I'm here."

"You okay?"

"Yes."

"You don't sound okay." Could he hear her thoughts through her single word? What did her "yes" tell him?

"I guess, no. I'm not okay," she said. "Can I see you?"

"Sure. Where are you?"

Emmy had him pick her up at the Starbucks down the street from her ruined house. She had to wait twenty minutes, and it felt like an eternity. Her jaw tightened with fear and rage, and she didn't know if she could open her mouth to talk when he arrived. Out of nerves, and for something to do, she went to the bathroom in the Starbucks three times while she waited. Every time, she found more ash on her. Even though she had removed most of it, she surely smelled of fire. The smell in the house must have seeped through her clothes and hair. And she had a bandage on her arm.

Emmy thought back about the burn marks on Nathan's own arm. She saw them in a whole new light now. Who had he set on fire, when he accidentally burned himself? Did the whole family do it together? Did they set winter wizards on fire as a wholesome family activity, like mini-golf or bowling?

When Nathan's truck pulled into the parking lot, she went out to meet him. The hot air on the black asphalt choked her, as if she were running through the fire again. The burn on her arm simmered in the painful August air.

She crawled into the passenger seat of his car, and although the air conditioning enveloped her, she felt hot enough that she might spontaneously combust.

Nathan reached for her bandaged arm. "What—,"

"Don't touch me," Emmy said.

He pulled away. Concern sparkled in his green eyes. Lies. *All lies.* "What's going on? Are you okay?"

"Drive, please." Emmy said.

Nathan did as she asked.

Now, in his presence, Emmy found it easier to read

between his words, as few as he had spared. His blazing energy felt more uncomfortable, as if it had become dirty with radiation. But the mere fact that he didn't talk told Emmy what she needed to know. If he had no idea what was wrong with her, he would have pressed her until she gave in. He wouldn't have this glaring sense of guilt, or nerves, or fear, or something, all intertwined in his usual heat.

"Can you pull over behind this building?" Emmy asked.

"Why?"

"Please? I want to show you something."

"Okay."

Nathan pulled around the back of a half-vacant shopping center. She had picked out this spot earlier. Unless someone specifically went back there for some reason, no one would see them. And she needed the fence.

When he stopped the truck, Emmy jumped out and walked to the fence on the edge of the woods. Nathan followed her. All too easy—because he trusted her. Or, because he was so arrogant he didn't see her as a threat.

When they got to the fence, Emmy faced him. The look on his face was inscrutable. Well, a Mundane might consider his face easy to read. Worried. Confused. But they didn't know how well he could wear a mask.

She held out her non-burned hand to him, and without hesitating, he took it. She had to admit this didn't feel right. It felt like *she* was the siren. She told him what to do and he did it. He should run. He should at least resist. He may not know what she had in mind, but he had to know the jig was up. He didn't need to wear the mask anymore.

In a swift, practiced motion, she pulled a pair of handcuffs she had swiped from the police station out of her back pocket and wrapped one half around his wrist, and the other around the steel pole of the fence.

"What the fuck?" he asked. She had not heard him curse until then, but his voice didn't sound harsh or angry. His tone stayed kind, and pleasant. Which made her hate him all the more.

Emmy pulled the gun out of her purse and pointed it at his head.

"Oh, my god," he said. "Emmy, what are you doing?" To Emmy's satisfaction, at least he now sounded afraid. His green eyes went wide and he didn't blink.

She could feel her pulse in her temples, and behind her eyes. It made her head feel hot, and the nearly one hundred and ten degree temperature didn't help, either. The gun might ignite on its own, or melt. She felt sweat pouring from her neckline into her bra, but as an extra offense, Nathan didn't look sweaty at all.

"Emmy," he said evenly. "Put the gun down."

Her head felt fuzzy. It could have been nerves, or the heat, but Emmy knew better. She had made an important mistake. She had planned a way to restrain the man, but hadn't thought about restraining the wizard. What if he used his powers to get her to put the gun in her own mouth and pull the trigger?

She shook her head from side to side, to free herself from the sensation. She knew the action made her look more insane. But that was good. Anything to scare him. Her blonde hair fell in stringy strands around her face.

"No," she managed to say. "I'm not putting the gun down." She punched each word. She could barely say it. She had to tap into her strong reservoir of stubbornness, but she could fight his command.

"Emmy, please. Why are you doing this?"

"You know why."

"I don't."

Emmy thought she heard it that time. The lie. Something about the "I don't" wavered.

"Tell me what happened," he said, a sense of command returning. "Tell me why you're angry at me."

Emmy found it harder to resist this time, because she

wanted to spill her guts. She wanted to yell at him until she got heatstroke again.

"I know what you are," Emmy said.

"Yeah, a summer wizard. You didn't realize that until now?"

"I don't hate people because of what they are, I hate people because of what they do. You're a siren. No, that sounds too nice. You're a killer. And a coward. And a liar."

"Why are you saying these things? What do you think I did?" His composure faltered, and he matched her tone, shouting back at her, tugging at his handcuffs.

"I want you to say it. I want you to say one thing that's not a lie."

"I'm *not* lying."

"Fine. I guess you haven't given up the game. As long as you know you're the only one playing it."

"Why are you doing this to me?" He had stopped shouting, and looked scared. She didn't like him looking at her that way—like a monster, a villain. But she shook the feeling away. She knew his sad puppy dog eyes were all part of the magic trick. The siren song.

"I'm doing this to you because you tried to execute my entire family. You tried to burn us alive. However, unfortunately for you, you underestimated my brother's powers. He saw what was going to happen and got us out. Aside from a few minor burns, we're absolutely fucking fine. The house is gone, but we don't care about that. You didn't do anything to hurt us. All you did was make us mad. And that's not going to end well for you or your family."

Nathan didn't say anything at all. Despite the oppressive heat, he looked frozen. Pale, cold, and unmoving. She didn't wait for him to spout out any more lies, she just kept going.

"You know, I underestimated you, too. You put together one impressive magic trick. You know which part floored me? When you gave my mom cancer just to distract my Dad so you could kidnap Evangeline. I mean, that's really, really cold. And that's coming from someone who's supposed to be nothing but ice all the way down. Yeah, you're a powerful wizard, but you know what? I think, in the end, it doesn't matter. I think your brains and blood will splatter all over the dirt, just like they would if you were a Mundane. What do you think?"

"I…I'm sorry your Mom has cancer. I didn't know that. And I didn't know about the fire either. I'm sorry about that, too."

"Are you fucking kidding me? That's all you have to say?"

"You're wrong about me. I didn't do any of those things you're accusing me of. And part of you knows that, so *you're not going to shoot me.*"

"You know, you're not as good at that mind-control thing as you think you are. I can break it."

"I know. I'm not commanding you not to shoot me, I *trust* you won't shoot me."

"Why not? Isn't that what winter wizards do? We're hopelessly evil, remember? We need to be cleansed from the earth."

"I don't believe that," he said.

Emmy laughed as coldly as she could.

"Hold a gun to my head all you want. I'm never going to confess to something I didn't do. You're wrong about me…but you're not wrong."

"What do you mean?"

"You're just not wrong. You should stay away from me. Your family should leave town."

"Are you threatening me?"

"No. I mean, yes. Whatever you want me to say. Whatever gets you away from me." His voice had fallen flat now.

The apathy made her want to shoot him more. As natural enemies, he should at least fight her. After everything he had done, he should at least be honest. If he was the enemy, at least things would make sense.

She approached him and put the gun against his temple. He tensed up and closed his eyes. She thought at least in that moment, he feared for his life. But she had never intended to kill him. She refused to be the villain he wanted her to be. She reached into his pocket and took his phone and his keys and then turned away from him.

She got into the driver's seat of his truck, drove back to the Starbucks, parked it, and drove back to the hotel in her own.

The air conditioner in the motel room blasted defiantly and enveloped Emmy in frigid air as she entered. Despite the wintery coolness, the room smelled of fire. No matter how many showers they had taken, or how much laundry they had done, the smell of the fire haunted them.

"Are you all right?" Mom lay alone in bed, watching the weather channel, a depressing spread of record breaking highs—each day marked with a cheerful looking sun, that was anything but. No rain. No break. No change.

The question surprised Emmy. She had left several hours ago. And she had grown accustomed to a greeting of, "Where have you been?" or some variation thereof.

"I told you, I went to Starbucks to meet a friend," Emmy said, answering the unasked question out of habit.

"And how did it go?"

"Fine."

"Are you sure? That's not the face of 'fine'. Tell me, did he admit to anything, or did he keep on lying? I'm guessing the latter."

"What?"

"Sweetheart, you're not as sneaky as you think you are."

"So, you…"

"I know you've been sneaking around with that summer wizard."

"How?"

"You're not going to like the answer. But you didn't leave me much choice."

"*How?*"

"You wouldn't tell the truth, so I took it for myself. I looked at some of your memories while you were sleeping."

Emmy knew what her face might look like. Her eyebrows in a "V," her mouth in an "O." For once, she had no words. Most girls just had to worry about their Mom reading their diary. This was so, so, so much worse.

"I understand you're upset," Mom said, sitting up slowly. "But I only did it because you wouldn't tell me anything about where you were sneaking off to. And I was worried about you. If it makes you feel better, it's not something I do often. It's difficult, and I find I'm better at removing darkness than finding light. I may not have seen him at all, if you hadn't been thinking about him a lot."

That last part made her madder. So, Mom knew how stupid she had been. How much she had liked him. How much hope and happiness she had wrapped up into a guy she barely knew, and a summer wizard at that.

"Why didn't you say anything? Why didn't you stop me?" For some reason, her words came out more sad than angry.

"Because if I told you not to see him, you would have married him just to spite me. Instead, you figured it out on your own. Besides, I don't mean to bruise your teen ego, but I have bigger things to worry about than you having a secret boyfriend. Honestly, I was relieved to find out that was all it was."

"He was never my boyfriend. And you should have said something. You let me do this. This is all my fault."

"Oh honey, it is not."

Mom seemed oddly complacent. Peaceful, but in a bad

way, as if she had already given up. Emmy hated it.

"Does Dad know?"

"No. I guess I should have said you're not sneaky enough to fool *me*."

Emmy felt tears burning in her eyes and she fought to keep them back. She had no use for crying, but she'd tried to keep from crying ever since she left Nathan handcuffed to the fence. And she had reached her limit.

Emmy sat on the edge of the bed and Mom put her arm around her. "I'm sorry, honey."

Emmy didn't like any of it. She wanted so badly to hate Mom. She *was* furious with her. But what if they would never speak again? And she hated Mom's new calm, the way she spoke to Emmy like a stupid little girl who had had her stupid little heart broken for the first time. The fact that it was true made Emmy hate it all the more.

When Mom released her, she had the gun. She must have grabbed it from Emmy's purse, when Emmy looked away. She examined it peacefully.

"It hasn't been fired," she said.

"I wasn't really going to shoot him. I'm not a murderer."

"I know. What did you do?"

"I um…handcuffed him to a fence and held the gun to his head."

Mom laughed. "Wow, that *is* a bad break-up. Although, for a summer wizard and a winter witch, it sounds about right. Could have been worse."

"I just wanted him to tell me the truth. I wanted him to feel bad about what he did. Or, at least feel scared. He *was* scared." Emmy didn't think she'd ever forget that moment when she put the gun to his temple, the way his whole body tensed, and he didn't breathe. In that moment, he thought he might die. And she had made him feel that fear.

"And do you feel better now?" Mom asked.

"No," Emmy said without having to think about it.

"That's good. Remember that. When you hurt someone, you always damage your own soul, and it doesn't feel good. A good person can feel it happening. A bad person doesn't notice until it's too late."

More "death-bed" style wisdom Emmy didn't like. No life lessons. No words to remember her by.

"So, you think I'm a good person?" Emmy asked.

"Emmy, you're more than a good person. You're a great person. You know you drive me crazy, and I don't agree with a lot of things you do. You're reckless and sometimes downright foolish, but you're also brave. You put yourself in danger to help others, even others you have every right to hate. That's what heroes do. I'm proud you're my daughter."

"Mom…" Emmy swelled with pride, but also swelled with fear. She hated this. All these nice things Mom wanted to say now…in case she never got the chance later. It made Emmy's stomach burn.

"I wanted him to tell me the truth," Emmy said.

"What truth were you looking for?"

"The *truth*. That he never liked me at all. That it was all a trick. That he wants to light me on fire and watch me burn." She quoted Xavier's words. They had rattled around in her brain ever since he had said them.

"And if that's not the truth?"

"Summer wizards lit that fire. They tried to kill us. And Xavier told me what summer wizards are really like. How they trick you. And the nicer they are, the more dangerous they really are. It all fits. Right?"

"Oh, I do think summer wizards lit that fire and tried to kill us. But that doesn't mean it was your friend. I know how you feel. You want it to be simple. You want him to be wrong and you to be right. Him to be the bad guy, and you to be the good guy. But that's not how it works. And no one should know that better than a winter witch. You wouldn't want him to judge you by where you sit on the solar calendar, or by what people like you have done, so don't do that to him."

"So, what? You don't think he did anything wrong?"

"Baby, I have no idea. He could be the mastermind behind it all, but it's just as likely that he's a nice kid mixed up in something bad."

"Mom, this is not helpful at all. Why are you doing this to me? I already felt like shit. Either he's completely innocent in all of this, and I'm a psycho bitch that left him handcuffed on a fence. Or, he's the dangerous psycho that played me. Both of those things really, really suck."

"But you showed him you're not to be messed with. Whether or not he set that fire or is involved in Evangeline's disappearance, he's a summer wizard. Sooner or later, he would hurt you. I was afraid to give you this speech earlier, because I knew you would rebel and do the opposite. But maybe now you will listen. Whenever a summer and winter wizard cross paths, it never ends well for the winter wizard."

"Don't worry. I'm never going to see him again."

Mom squeezed her hand. "I hope that's true. I love you, baby."

Emmy scowled. She knew her mother loved her, but did she have to sling it around all the time?

"I love you, too," Emmy said.

CHAPTER TWENTY-FOUR

David's younger brother James leaned against his car in the parking lot of the motel.

"When you called and said you needed help, this is not what I expected," he said. "I thought you needed help with money, or with the kids, or with Amanda, or with getting a new place. I mean, you do need help with those things, you know."

"It wasn't easy for me to call you and ask you for help."

"I don't know what you think I can do. I'm not a practicing wizard."

"But you were. And *you* remember it. I'm going to go after Prescott with or without your help. And he is a practicing wizard, and probably a good one. I don't know shit about magic. You don't have to do any actual magic if you don't want to, just tell me what to do. Tell me how to beat him."

"I didn't come by the decision not to practice lightly. You can't change my mind."

"Oh, bullshit. If you're like all the other supposedly non-practicing wizards I have known, you won't be as hard to convince as you'd like to think. You, Amanda, Carson, you're all dying to do magic. And you can find any excuse to break your beliefs."

"Yeah, no kidding. You're offering a drink to man who's been sober for five years. You're a real hero."

"Five years? Are you saying you stopped practicing magic five years ago?"

"Yes."

"Five? As in, 2009."

"Yes, that's what I said."

"I...I assumed you had been younger, like I had been. I gave it up in college. Or, as Amanda tells me I did. 2009?" David wished James would take off his sunglasses so he could see his eyes, maybe then he could read him better.

2009...the year their parents had died. Their father of an aneurysm, and then their mother committed suicide four months later. David wanted to know if any of that had anything to do with why James gave it up...if maybe he had something to do with their father's death... But he also didn't want to know. "You started dating Justin that year," David said.

"Yeah."

"So you went from being a full-fledged practicing wizard, to giving up magic completely and moving in with a Mundane?"

"How many times are you going to ask me the same question?"

"I'm sorry. It bothers me when I learn something that big. Something I should have known."

"It's one of the main reasons we haven't been close as adults. I was practicing, and you weren't. You disapproved. At least, I had thought that was why. What's your excuse now? Is it the gay thing?"

"No, it's not the *gay* thing. Hell, I don't know why we haven't been close. I'm sorry. But now it's the other way around. So, you should have more sympathy for me. You *were* me."

"Look at what has happened to your life since you found

out you were a wizard. Look at what's happened to your family. In less than a year. Your life is barely recognizable."

"It's not like I haven't fucking noticed. You don't need to tell me. Don't act as if everything that has happened has been my choice. None of this had anything to do with me practicing magic. I *barely* can. I don't know shit about it. If I could have done *anything* to prevent my family from being hurt, I would have done it. And don't think I haven't already tried to do everything a normal man can…to try to find Evangeline…to save my wife. It's not going to be enough. I agree with you, magic is shit. Magic caused all of this. A wizard took my daughter. A wizard burned down my house. Magic made my wife sick." His voice cracked and he had to stop talking. "I need magic to make it better," he added after a pause.

"Magic might not make it better," James said. "It could make it worse."

David laughed a watery laugh. "I know it's bad luck to say this, but really? How much worse could it get? I've lost almost everything I have."

"Okay, David."

"Okay?"

"I'll help you. With magic."

James stepped away to call Justin.

"What did you tell him?" David asked when James walked back to the car. He wanted to get out of the heat and move on with this. His skin had already grown an extra ten years older, wading through the sun and heat every day looking for Evangeline in that godforsaken forest. He could feel the sunburn on the back of his neck burning hotter.

"I didn't lie. I said my brother was a total fuck-up and I had to save his ass."

"I see."

"I pick which part of the truth I want to share."

"I don't understand how wizards don't get found out. You'd think eventually a Mundane would see something they shouldn't."

"I'm sure some Mundanes know," James said. "But as powerful as magic is, the Mundane is powerful, too."

"What do you mean?"

"Like, you know, how Mom used to describe it."

"No, I don't know," he said through gritted teeth.

"Right. Well, she said that even though magic is all around, it's hard for the Mundanes to see it. Magic seeps into Mundane culture all the time, but it doesn't often make enough of a mark to be taken seriously. It's so hard to break out of that Mundane world. The drudgery of day after normal day, deep in the mire of ordinary and bland. It sucks you in—blinds you, suffocates you. Even those who want to see the magic have to fight through a thick fog of humanity to even catch a glimpse before falling back into the mire."

"Yikes," David said.

"What?"

"You really paint a picture. You sure you're okay with not practicing magic?"

"Just get in the car."

"Let me drive."

"It's my car."

"Please. I can't just sit there the whole way. I have to be doing something."

On their drive to Sugar Land, David spotted a dark-haired woman walking on the side of the highway. She drew his eye for two reasons. For one, he could tell she was a witch from a distance. And two, she looked like Evangeline. Something about the way she walked and the way her long dark hair fell down her back. As he got closer, he could tell she wasn't Evangeline, but still…so familiar.

He slowed as he passed her. She turned and looked at him. David's entire body froze. He had never felt so cold. He slammed on the brakes, which caused the car to skid and veer off the highway into the median.

"Son of a bitch," yelled James as the car skidded to a dusty stop.

David looked back and saw no one. He searched the dry dusty roadside and didn't see her lying on the ground either, so he didn't hit her. She had never been there at all. Those sad brown eyes hadn't looked right at him.

"Ghost," David said, barely able to catch his breath.

"What?" James said.

"Did you see her?"

"Who?"

"The woman on the side of the road."

James turned around in his seat and scanned the highway. "Uh…no."

"Wizards are real. Are ghosts real?"

"I don't…think so." He didn't sound sure.

David pressed his hands to his eyes. He didn't know if he wanted to scrub her image from his mind or memorize every detail.

"You're really not okay, are you?" James asked.

"No, James. I am not okay. I don't think I've ever been less okay."

"Let me drive. You're too distracted."

David paused. Something James said shimmered in his brain.

"What?"

"Give me the keys," James said. "You're going to wreck my car. You probably already messed it up randomly driving off the highway."

"No, what else did you say?"

"Uh, I said you seem distracted."

"Oh, God."

"What?"

"Oh, no."

"David, what?"

"I'm *distracted*. I don't know if it was a ghost or what, but it was a reminder. A clue I'm on the wrong track. She wanted me to remember what she said before. About misdirection. I'm misdirected, James. It's what the magician wants."

"What?"

"Where is my phone?"

"What you saying? That the good doctor didn't start that fire? This is some kind of trick?"

"I don't know if he did or not, but I know it doesn't matter. Not right now, anyway."

"What do you think you're being distracted from?"

"I don't know. Something bad happening to someone I love. Because I'm not watching over them. Because I'm a fool. Where is my goddamn phone?"

"It's here," James handed him the phone.

As the most likely to find trouble, he called Emmy first. As the phone rang, he pulled back onto the highway heading toward the motel, too close to an oncoming car that blasted its horn.

"David!" James looked as if he prepared to grab the wheel.

Emmy picked up on the second ring.

"Where are you?" David asked before she could say hello.

"At the motel, with mom. Where are you?"

"So, you're both fine?"

"Yes. Why?"

"I know you never listen to anything I say, but I'm begging you…stay there. Please, please stay there."

"What's going on?"

"Where are your brothers?"

"I'm…not sure. Patrick's car is gone. They probably went to get food or something."

"Dammit. Okay. Stay there, Emmy. I love you."

"Wha—"

He hung up the phone and called Patrick. Xavier rarely had his cell phone on or with him. But Patrick *always* had his with him. He'd seen him sleeping with it in his hand on more than one occasion.

He heard Patrick's recorded voice on the voicemail. "I'm not in. Leave a message."

"Patrick, this is your father. Some kind of magic is happening. You have to call me back, immediately."

He tried Xavier and heard, "The person you have called has a voicemail box that has not been set up yet. Goodbye."

"Damn this thing." David opened his window and chucked the phone into oncoming traffic.

"Oh my God," James said. "That was stupid. For so many reasons."

"No. I rely too much on my phone. I'm not thinking like a wizard."

"Yeah, but still. There is a reason why wizards still carry cell phones. Steve Jobs bested us on that one."

"Stop talking. I need to think."

CHAPTER TWENTY-FIVE

athan didn't know if he wanted to see a car come around the building. If he did, then someone could help him. But then someone would also have to see him handcuffed to a pole. He could cast a summoning spell so the closet person would decide to come behind the building. But he couldn't cast a spell to get the handcuffs off. He tried. He thought maybe he could burn them off. But he only managed to make the metal hot, which left scalded rings around his wrists, adding a fair amount of pain to everything else. Eventually, he'd have to give up and summon someone. His eyelids hurt when he blinked, which meant the sun had burned him to a crisp. And without water soon, he might have a serious problem.

Half the time, being a wizard was useless…God's joke on them. They had the power to get almost anything they wanted, but handcuffs thwarted them. God said, "Hey, you down there. You think you're so great? Try this." And then, God laughed while Nathan burned his own damn self trying to get out. As Emmy had said, he may be a master of the flame, but his flesh burned like anybody else's.

When a car did come, Nathan could sense it before he could see it. He should have cast a summoning spell. Then, someone random would come around the corner. Some Mundane. They might laugh at him, but that would be all. He'd waited too long and someone who could do much worse had found him.

His father's car came around the side of the building and stopped in front of him. He could tell by the jerky way he drove that he was mad. But when he got out of the car, he just shook his head. His look said something between, "you're disgusting," and "you're an embarrassment."

"How did you find me?" Nathan asked.

"You're not as sneaky as you think you are."

"You knew?"

"Of course. *Nothing* gets past me. I would offer up some kind of punishment, but that seems hardly necessary. I couldn't think of a better way for you to learn your lesson about winter wizards. Maybe I should leave you here for a while. And you can soak it all in."

"Fine. Leave me here."

"This is just like you. You didn't like that we were paying attention to Julie instead of you? So, you try to get our attention by fooling around with a winter wizard? I have bigger concerns."

Nathan felt shaky—either from fury or dehydration. Probably both. "No," Nathan said. He should say more about why everything his father had said had been so wrong, but he couldn't find the words.

His father examined the handcuffs and snickered. "Look what you did to yourself. This is crude magic. You have to go for the lock."

"I can't do that."

His father put his thumb on the lock and after a moment, Nathan heard a click, and the handcuffs clattered to the ground. His father examined his hands in that annoying clinical way only a doctor could.

"So, when you found out I was seeing her, you burned

down their house?"

Dad slapped him in the face. The sunburn made the slap hurt much more than usual.

"How dare you," he said. "I'm no monster. They're the villains. Not us."

"Then who did it?"

"Doesn't matter. I'm sure they deserved it."

"I'm sure they didn't."

Dad had the flame in his yellowish-green eyes that made Nathan think he might hit him again. But instead he just shook his head.

"You're an idiot," he said, with a tone that implied hitting him wasn't worth his time. "I think maybe we should have you dated again. I would swear you're a spring wizard."

"I need water."

"We're going back to the forest. Your mother ran off and I think she went out there. And we're picking up your brother. It's your job to keep an eye on him and you're not."

"He's fine."

"Just get in the car."

Patrick hated sneaking out with Mom passed out asleep, but he had to. They couldn't wait any longer. Xavier had this strange, unstable quality to his energy, like he would soon either explode or fade away. Patrick didn't feel like waiting around to see which way he went. He hoped looking for Evangeline would keep him focused and present.

They went to the gas station where Evangeline had disappeared. They got out of the car, and Patrick thought he could sense the summer wizards from a distance. But it was hard to tell. The temperature gauge in the car said 109 degrees, which made it the hottest day of the year so far. Summer wizards around or not, summer itself had attacked mercilessly. The heat made it hard for Patrick to breathe. The blinding sun made it hard for him to open his eyes. They couldn't search out here for long.

Patrick suggested they go inside the convenience store to buy water, and he picked out a couple of two-liter bottles. Xavier drifted toward the potato chips, and Patrick grabbed his arm. Xavier jerked back and looked ready to strike, as he always did when someone touched him.

"Stay where I can see you," Patrick said.

"I'm not a child."

"Come on, you know why."

Xavier grumbled something and took the water Patrick handed to him. Patrick didn't think that Xavier would get caught in the snare, but the possibility scared the crap out of him. Emmy bringing Evangeline here and losing her, and then Patrick bringing Xavier here and losing him, was too stupid and horrible to consider.

Xavier did as Patrick asked him, and stayed close as they bought their water and went back outside. At least, he stayed as close as he ever would to another human being.

"They're here," Xavier said.

"Summer wizards?" Patrick asked.

"Yeah."

"I thought so."

"How many do you think?"

"I'm not sure. Not that many." Xavier pointed toward the woods. "They're not far."

"Well, I'm not going to go home with my tail between my legs because summer wizards are here," Patrick said.

"Fuck, no. Of course not."

"Alright then."

Patrick followed Xavier into the woods. The thick pine trees provided shade, but somehow it felt hotter here. He could see the heat distorting the air. He hoped this meant a winter witch as cold as Evangeline would stand out in contrast.

"Do you sense her?" Patrick asked. "Evangeline?"

Xavier stopped and listened for something, or *felt* for something. "Yeah, I do." He whispered the words with reverence, like a prayer.

"Good. Then, she's alive, right? We'll find her."

Xavier nodded. "I think she's alive, but…I don't know. Something's not right."

Patrick didn't want to hear what wasn't right. He could guess well enough. He hoped Evangeline frightened her captors and much as she frightened him. But he knew if she could have overpowered them with magic, she would have already come home.

They both froze. They heard footsteps crunching the dry leaves on the ground. Patrick knew if they could sense the summer wizards, then it worked both ways. They couldn't hide from each other for long.

"Xavier, I'll distract them," Patrick said. "You stay hidden, and then keep looking."

"What? No."

"You're a winter wizard. They might try to hurt you. I have a better chance."

"Dammit, Patrick," Xavier whispered, while Patrick headed straight towards the footsteps.

The summer wizards caught sight of Patrick emerging from the trees and aimed guns at him. With as much as Patrick had recently learned about "good" wizards, he had not expected the guns. At closer inspection, the guns looked like hunting rifles, meant for deer and not people, but still deadly.

Patrick put his hands up. "I'm unarmed," he said.

The two boys looked close to his age, although the taller one might be older. They looked similar. They both had bronze-colored hair and yellowish-green eyes. Their skin glowed, subtle enough that someone could mistake it for no more than good health and time spent in the sun, but Patrick knew better.

"Who are you?" the younger boy demanded.

By the look in their eyes, they didn't recognize him. That nagged at Patrick. He wanted to know if they had set the fire. His rage needed somewhere to go, but he wanted to know for sure. He wanted revenge. He didn't know how he would get it, especially since they had the guns. And unlike him, they knew how to practice magic. But he needed to know.

Of course, they could not recognize him and still be the arsonists. Summer wizards wouldn't care about their names and faces. Dark wizards should burn.

"Oh, my God," whispered the older boy. He looked at Patrick with so much awe and fear that Patrick had the instinct to look behind him to see who he really looked at. "Luke, stay back."

"What?" asked Luke.

The older boy lunged toward Patrick. But when he came close, he lowered his gun and surprised Patrick by reaching out and grabbing his arm. Patrick didn't have a chance to resist. The touch gave him a nervous feeling in the pit of his stomach, and not just because it was a strange thing to do. But he dropped his arm after a second or two.

"God, no..." he said.

Luke had moved closer, but still had his gun aimed at Patrick's head. "Nathan, what is it? Is he...another one?"

"It's not possible. It couldn't be...but I think so."

"I'm another what?" Patrick asked.

"Why are you here?" Nathan asked. He asked the question with complete incredulity, as if Patrick walking out of the woods was as unlikely and strange as if the tooth fairy popped out in front of them.

"For the same reason you are, I assume. I'm looking for my little sister."

They glanced at each other. "You mean, Evangeline Vandergraff is your sister?" asked Nathan.

"How did you know that? How do you know her name?"

"It was on the news, bro," Luke said. "Calm down."

"What's your name?" Nathan asked.

"Patrick Vandergraff."

"But Evangeline is not *really* your sister, right?" Nathan said. "Not by blood."

"Uh, yeah, she's *really* my sister. We have different mothers, but the same father. It's none of your business, anyway."

"Vandergraff had two of them?" Nathan said. "What are the chances?"

"Two of *what?*" Patrick asked, his voice dripping with venom and impatience.

"You *sure* you have the same father?" Luke asked. He didn't snicker, but he might as well have. The implication dripped all over his tone.

Of all the ways this interaction could go, he didn't know how the hell they had gotten here.

"Yeah, I'm sure, asshole. You better watch what you say about my mother."

Luke laughed. "Right, because winter wizards never cheat."

"That's right, they don't." Patrick didn't know why he said it—something so untrue, but he couldn't abide these random strangers insulting his family out of nowhere.

"Well," Luke said, "He may be only half dark, but can lie as well as the rest of him. At least, he knows how to lie to himself."

What the fuck was the matter with this guy?

"You want to hear something true?" Patrick asked. "I don't know about the cheating and lying, but yeah, my family is *dangerous.* And we stick together. I don't know what you plan on doing with those little toys you got in your stocking from Santa, but if you hurt me, or if you have or will hurt anyone else in my family, you will invoke a wrath you can't even imagine.”

"I don't doubt it," Nathan said. *"Listen to me."* His voice pulled at him like gravity. "Nothing we have said or nothing you have said up to this point matters at all. Don't let it distract you. The only important thing is what I am about to say right now—*you need to leave this place now and do not come back.* You are in serious danger here."

Patrick thought he might catapult out of the forest. He backed up automatically.

Patrick heard a stick crack behind him. *Xavier, no. No. No.* He pleaded with him in his mind. *Let me handle it. Don't make it worse.*

Patrick turned and didn't see anyone.

"I knew someone was out here with you," Luke said. "I can sense them. Who is it? One of your supposed siblings? If they're going to be cowards and stay in the shadows, maybe we should give them a little incentive. *Burn* them out."

The word *burn* made Patrick's mouth dry up. Arsonists or not, that worked as an admission of guilt. He felt magic building in him, sliding up his spine. But he didn't know what to do with it. However, things happened so fast, he didn't have much chance.

"Luke, don't you dare," Nathan said.

"Oh, are you afraid it's your girlfriend? I'd love to meet her," Luke said.

"I swear, if you…"

Nathan didn't get a chance to finish his threat. Luke dropped his gun on the ground, as if it was nothing more than a ridiculous plaything. Luke had this look his in eyes—pain— as if he himself burned from the inside out. Then with a flash, Luke thrust the burning outward. Patrick felt an intense thirst. And his skin felt so dry that it might flake right off. The heat came with a sense of impending doom. As if it would never rain again. It meant drought. Famine. Death. Apocalypse. A sense of burning so deep it could cover the whole world.

Luke released this feeling from inside himself. As much as Patrick despised Luke, he would never think of summer wizards the same way again. Winter might be dark and cold, but man, summer was a nasty bitch too.

Patrick feared to open his eyes. He felt certain his eyeballs would dry up and turn to glass, but he felt his arms and found that they weren't on fire. To some extent, it had to all be in his head. He opened his eyes, and saw that although the impending doom might be in his head, the fire was very real.

The dry, drought-ridden land around them began to smoke. Then, piles of leaves and branches erupted into flames all around him, as if the air itself had ignited them.

"Why don't you come on out now, you frigid bitch?" Luke said.

Patrick heard Xavier cough and wheeze from not far away. As he feared, he hadn't run, and now he would burn. Patrick picked up the gun Luke had discarded and pointed it at him. Nathan pointed his gun back at Patrick.

"Don't even think about it," Nathan said.

Luke didn't care about the stand-off. He headed toward the coughing, with that same pain in his eyes as if he prepared to release another blast.

The radiant heat in the air made the guns crack and sizzle. Patrick knew the gun would fire on its own or explode in his hands, so he dropped it. The same thing must have happened to Nathan because he dropped his too.

Patrick turned to tackle Luke. This might cause him to spontaneously combust, but he had to do something. If the heat felt horrible to Patrick, a September, it had to be agonizing for Xavier. Besides, Luke could cause a full-on wildfire. The dry trees lapped up the flames eagerly. It was possible none of them would make it out alive.

But Patrick didn't have the chance to grab Luke. He heard this cracking, splitting sound, as if the air itself had cleaved in two. Xavier had come out of the forest to face Luke...or at least, Patrick assumed it was Xavier. Whatever Luke did to project the light, Xavier did the same thing to project his darkness. The darkness obscured his features. Against the blaring heat, he appeared as a black hole shaped like a boy. Patrick couldn't say what felt worse, the heat coming off Luke or the absence coming off Xavier. "Absence" was the only word for it. More than cold. More than darkness. You could experience cold and darkness. This was oblivion, the absence of all experience, of all vision, and sound, and feeling. If Luke could set the world on fire, Xavier could erase it from existence.

Darkness had lurked close to him his whole life, and people he loved had done terrible things, but he had never seen the darkness so clearly, so raw. The black hole that *was* his brother was not just dark, it could be evil itself. Or, fear itself.

Nathan touched Patrick's arm, and Patrick turned, ready to swing. But something in Nathan's sad eyes stopped him.

"We have to go," Nathan said. "Now."

"You don't understand." He gestured toward the demonic figure. "That's my little brother."

"Yeah, and the fireball is mine. It doesn't matter. Like I said. It's all distractions. It's all part of the spell. The magic wants us to stay...or *you* to stay. But their fight is not important. The only important thing is getting you out of here."

"How could you say that? You're okay with leaving our brothers to kill each other."

Nathan didn't answer. He grabbed Patrick's face so he could look at him in the eyes. "*You're leaving this place. Now.*"

Patrick felt a lurch in his abdomen, like the steep fall on a roller coaster. And then he ran, with Nathan on his heels. Running was so easy. Too easy. He wanted to think he ran because of Nathan's magical command, but that felt more like a shove to get him started. He wanted to run. He wanted to get as far away from the emptiness that was Xavier. That shell of a boy who had disguised all of that darkness. That darkness that slept feet away from him. He wanted to go back to the place where he thought that dark wizards couldn't be that bad. They were people after all. Humans. His family.

Before he knew it, Patrick had his hands on his knees on the side of the road. He coughed until his throat and lungs burned. The flames hadn't moved too close yet, but the sky had turned from gray to black. A wildfire had erupted. In the drought conditions, the fire could decimate hundreds of acres in no time. And Xavier was in there. And somewhere, Evangeline was too.

Tears streamed down his face but he didn't know if they came from the smoke or were just tears. Emmy came to this forest with Evangeline and came home without her. Now, Patrick would come home without Xavier, just as he had feared.

"I hate you," Patrick wheezed toward Nathan. "You'll regret this."

Nathan kneeled near him, also wheezing. By the supplicant way he kneeled on the cracked earth, Patrick thought he already regretted it.

"There was nothing we could have done anyway."

"Fuck you, you coward."

He didn't know if he spoke to Nathan or to himself.

"They probably won't hurt each other, you know. They're too oppositional. Their magic will cancel each other out. They're all flash and smoke anyway. Sure, their magic is dangerous. But it's nothing compared to what you can do."

"What? I'm barely a wizard."

"You don't know what you are, do you?"

Patrick didn't say anything. He had put together the pieces and come to a conclusion, but it seemed ridiculous. If he said it out loud, Nathan would laugh at him.

But Nathan said it for him. "You're the equinox. A *perfect* equinox wizard, standing directly at the sunset on the autumnal equinox. Extremely rare. Extremely powerful. A master of both light and dark in equal measure."

It seemed absurd, but it had to be true. In any case, an issue for a different time. The wildfire beat out all magical concerns. Humans burn. Wizards burn. Everything burns. Everything dies. Magic or not.

Patrick tried to run back in for Xavier, but his legs wouldn't move.

"I don't think so," Nathan said.

Patrick didn't understand how Nathan could call Patrick extremely powerful and then subdue him a minute later. He had never felt so useless. He couldn't stop Jude from raping Samantha. He couldn't stop Evangeline from being kidnapped. Now, he couldn't save Xavier. If he was an equinox wizard, then that made it worse. He had no excuse. He had the power he needed, but too cowardly or too stupid to use it.

Nathan lunged toward Patrick and grabbed his face again and this time Patrick shut his eyes tight.

"That's not going to do anything," Nathan said. "You're going to get in your car and drive home, right now."

Patrick felt the pull again. He pulled his keys out his pocket.

Nathan released his grip and spoke to him in a more normal fashion. "As powerful as you are, I can tell you have no idea what you're doing. But I do. I'll go back. I'll bring them *both* out."

Patrick nodded. He wanted to trust him. He had to trust him, because this was the moment. He hoped he could resist Nathan's command for long enough for it to wear off. He put one hand on his pocket and felt the bizarre warmth there. Julie's bracelet. He couldn't say why, but at the last minute, he had the overwhelming instinct to take it with him. And now, he would bring it to her.

CHAPTER TWENTY-SIX

Jude saw her for the first time last May, the same weekend he would have graduated if he hadn't dropped out. He would have already committed to a college football team. All of which now, seemed odd. He couldn't remember why he had cared so much about football, and SATs, and Mundane girls. Ever since he had given himself to magic, the unmagical world had become gray, flat, and tasteless. And so much of the world lacked magic—just billions of Mundanes, living their pointless, disappointing lives. He hated all of it.

So when he caught a glimpse of her at the college party he had crashed for the free beer, he decided to follow her. She stood out, the colorful Oz against black and white Kansas. He found he could follow her without seeing her. Once he recognized her energy, he could just find her, whenever he wanted to see color. Everyone else just saw her as another pretty blonde college girl. They might as well have been blind. He had never sensed any energy like hers. Not from any wizard. And although wizards were rare, he did see them around town from time to time. They seemed more common in Austin than they had been in Houston.

But no, she was different. Beyond magical. Something greater. And more unique. He couldn't classify her magic. Not hot or cold, or anything in between. Beyond classification. Beyond the seasons. The hottest heat and the coldest cold at once.

So he followed her. Maybe because he wanted to understand her unusual energy. Or maybe just because she was a pretty witch. Or, perhaps for something to do other than wade in an endless sea of gray. He had considered talking to her, but for some reason he held back. She was more than a pretty girl. She was something frightening and exotic he didn't understand. He felt as if he hunted a mythical beast, not a girl. And so he knew to approach with caution.

When he walked around campus, he donned a simple disguise of a baseball cap, T-shirt, khaki shorts, flip-flops, and a laptop case…empty, of course. He felt like he wore a disguise, but as an eighteen-year-old white boy from Houston, he couldn't stand out on the UT campus if he tried. The Mundanes didn't give him a second thought, but he knew that the witch did. Even if he didn't shine with an overwhelming and mysterious energy as she did, she could tell a dark wizard stalked her. And she didn't seem frightened, nor did she seem to care at all. And that intrigued him more.

Before finals, she spent a lot of time in the library studying. And he tracked her to one of the larger libraries on campus. Once he got close, he could follow her easily. Her energy moved and breathed as if alive, beckoning him, whispering in his ear. He felt a pull upwards and took the stairs to the second floor.

The first floor of the library had no books at all, just computers. But books filled the second floor. The shelves made this floor feel less open than the first. She could be anywhere. The strength of her magic made her easy to track from a distance. But once he got close, her energy overwhelmed him and he couldn't pinpoint the source. She was *everywhere*. The magic felt so strong, he could hear it hum. In the middle of the floor, he found a large section filled with desks and couches. Students occupied every open spot. Laptop cords strewn everywhere. He could smell the caffeine sweating from everyone's pores.

"Are you looking for something?"

No one else looked up, as if only he had heard the voice. He shuddered, first thinking it had come from a disembodied speaker, but then he saw her, her face peeking out from behind her laptop screen. She smiled at him.

She gestured him over with a nod of her head. He didn't know how he'd make his way through all the people to get to her, let alone sit next to her. As if she read his thoughts, he heard shuffling around him as all the other people in the section got up to leave. Except for the fact they all happened to leave at the same time, it looked normal. They packed up their backpacks and computer cases, and said goodbyes to each other.

It took a minute or two for them all to wrap up their cords and chargers, but it was still quick, and dramatic. And none of them looked the least bit concerned by the fact they suddenly had decided to leave. They did so cheerfully, as if a silent school bell had dismissed them.

Jude put his empty laptop case on the desk next to her and sat. "Wow," he said.

"Thank you."

She was prettier up close. And it wasn't the long tanned legs and breast-hugging T-shirt. She sparkled. Her hair and skin and eyes and teeth had been sewn from a mixture of fire and flesh. However, he knew everyone else saw a boring, vapid sorority girl. But she had made this her own secret joke. On her T-shirt he had two Greek letters. Alpha and Omega. He had a feeling that wasn't a real sorority.

"I was tired of waiting for you to talk to me," she said.

"You weren't bothered by the fact that a dark wizard was following you around?"

She laughed a sparkling laugh. "Well, I'm not frightened of

you, if that's what you mean. It's a common mistake dark wizards make. The big bad wolf thinks nobody can be bigger or badder than himself. He ignores Little Red Riding Hood. It's a dangerous habit."

"Okay. I'll keep that in mind."

"And if big bad wolves didn't occasionally try to eat me, life would be boring. It makes for a good study break."

"Do you really go to school here?"

"What? Witches can't get a college education?"

"I didn't mean that."

"Yes, I go to school here."

"What do you study?"

"I'm in the Honors Program in Mathematics."

"Math?"

"Yes, *math*. The language of Gods. Perhaps the most misunderstood form of magic."

Jude stared at her.

She smiled. "I would say it's a shame the cute ones always have to be so stupid…but that would be a lie. That's how I like my men, cute and stupid."

"I'm not stupid."

"I didn't mean offense. You're probably not stupid, just stupid compared to me," she said, as if that would weaken the insult.

Jude scrunched his nose at her.

"I'm sorry. Don't leave," she said. "I sometimes get out of the habit of talking to people. I don't do it much."

"Me neither."

"Yeah, I gathered as much while I've been watching you," she said.

"I thought I was the one watching you."

"No. That's why you *think* you ended up here, in that chair, across from me, at this moment, but it's not."

"Then why am I here?"

"You're here because I want you to be."

"Is that so?"

"You're here because you're a function in the big, beautiful equation. The one so many wizards play a part in, but so few understand."

Jude scoffed. "And what function do I serve?"

"I'm not sure yet. I don't always understand how my own spells work. But I'm glad you're here. If anything, to keep me company. It takes a while for these things to unfold. Quite boring."

Jude laughed.

"You don't believe I called you here?"

"I don't know."

"How about this. If you were the one stalking me, and not the other way around, how come I know everything about you, and you know nothing about me?"

"What makes you think you know everything about me?"

"Well, maybe not everything. But a lot. Your name is Jude Michael Vandergraff. You were born on April 5, 1996 to David and Amanda Vandergraff. Your parents now live at 634 Tremont Street in Houston, with your siblings Patrick and Emmy, and your half-siblings, Xavier and Evangeline. Although of course, you'll have to take my word for it on the last part because you haven't spoken to anyone in your family since you left your uncle's house on New Year's Eve. Since then, you've been crashing on couches, but basically homeless, unemployed, usually drunk, and utterly pathetic in every way. Did I get that all right?"

Jude's mouth parted in speechlessness, and she giggled. "Okay, then your turn, what do you know about me?"

"Nothing. You're right. Just that you're different. Special."

She smiled and held out her hand. "I'm Caroline Prescott. And we have a lot in common. Well, except for the last part about being pathetic."

Jude laughed. "All right, then. It's nice to meet you Caroline."

CHAPTER TWENTY-SEVEN

After Nathan ran back toward the smoke, Patrick found himself alone. He wanted to follow, to find Xavier, and drag him out, kicking and screaming if need be. But he had to let himself trust the summer wizard to save Xavier, too. Patrick's gut said Nathan would do his best, as he'd said he would. Patrick had to hope that as a wizard, and apparently a powerful one, his "gut" might know what it was talking about.

Both Julie and Evangeline had disappeared alone, the moment that their sibling looked away. His chance had arrived.

He couldn't think about it. He just had to go, and hope the fire hadn't destroyed the snare, or portal, or whatever would suck him up. But the fire hadn't reached this part of the forest, and the girls had both disappeared right along the fringes. Patrick ran back into the trees, deep enough to make sure no one could see him from the road. Nothing happened. He didn't fall through a portal. So, he race-walked parallel to the road, waiting for the invisible monster to grab him. He had simulated the situation perfectly. He had even arrived with a sibling, who had moved out sight. If this didn't work, he had no idea what else to try.

But then, when he looked back towards the road, he

couldn't see it anymore. He had been less than twenty feet away, and now, it wasn't there. He only saw more forest.

Holy fuck.

He wouldn't fall into an obvious portal or rabbit hole. At some point in his frantic race-walking, he just went through it. As he looked around himself, he noticed strange things. The brown pine needles caught on the branches hung at odd directions. He reached for one that hung straight up, and at his touch it fell again as gravity would have it fall. Patrick's heart raced. No one in his family had any real magical training, so he couldn't say for sure, but he couldn't imagine any of them doing anything this dramatic.

Although his heart raced with nerves, another sensation pushed its way through, as if it came from outside him. He felt a pleasant sensation that he couldn't describe at first. Maybe pride—seeing yourself at your very best. Feeling on top of the world.

Then, he noticed something else wrong with his surroundings. It felt nice. Not blazing hot, but a fresh cool. The air smelled of smoke, but it had a different quality, more like a campfire. Everything about the scene reminded him of camping with his family. They had gone to Garner State Park every fall…except for the last one. Away from electronics and all the other distractions of the world, they were happy, relaxed. They would cook steaks and marshmallows over the open fire. He could hear the crackling fire. The sound of talking, and laughter. The cool air. The fall leaves in the trees, a blaze with red and orange.

Then it made sense. He felt Fall. Autumn. The best parts of it. He guessed that's why it reminded him of the best parts of himself.

Since pine trees look the same in every season, he hadn't noticed it right away. But the forest around him had changed. He had walked right out of summer into fall. He could see the changing leaves on the oaks and maples scattered between the pines. He could feel the cool air. Water droplets hung from pine needles, from a fall rain that hadn't happened.

So, whatever magic had brought him here had recognized him, as Nathan said. The Autumnal Equinox. And the magic had heralded his arrival with a tribute to Fall.

Patrick had to wonder if Evangeline had stepped into winter. If all the plants died in front of her, and the air became frigid. Perhaps ice hung from the pines. And Julie, well, since it was summer, maybe nothing changed. Maybe she just felt it. The best parts of summer. Watermelon, fireworks, and swimming pools.

The magic felt so welcoming, as if the forest honored him, worshiped him. But he stayed vigilant. Whether the forest honored him or not, he knew from his visions of Julie that whoever called him here had no intention to honor him at all.

As quickly as the glorious autumn feeling had hit him, it passed. He felt the heat encroaching, and the smell of burning…and not the campfire kind. The destructive kind. The overwhelming kind. He noticed a strange flutter of white that looked like snow, and then realized it was ash. Whatever illusion had made it fall had faded away, and he had returned to the real world, but this didn't feel like the same world he had been in with Nathan at the road.

Something odd caught his eye through the trees. An armchair. Light blue, and ripped and stained. The chair faced away from him, and he could see the top of *something* sitting in the chair. Matted, dirty, brown hair. He approached the chair, and with his heart beating in his throat, he looked to see what sat there. A large Teddy bear. Like the chair, it was dirty, and damaged. One eye was missing. Garbage. That had to be all this was. A dumping ground for people who didn't want to drive to the landfill. In the normal world, that's what this would be. But now he'd passed through the portal, he couldn't say for sure.

He heard a sound that made his hairs stand up on end.

Music. A specific kind of music—the kind you hear from an ice cream truck. The happy, carnival-esque sound wafting across the breeze. But it didn't make him feel happy. The music had a sinister note.

Sure enough, he passed through a clearing, and found an ice cream truck. The brightly-colored menu had faded, and brown pine needles carpeted the roof of the truck. The truck appeared empty, but he had no desire to double check. The truck had a dark and dangerous feel. One he couldn't explain, but he knew it was wrong. Misplaced.

He continued walking, and found more lost vehicles. An empty, battered school bus that might have sat on the bottom of a lake for a decade. An ambulance. Old cars with broken windows and gutted engines. He couldn't imagine why they would be here. He could feel the wrongness. Fear. His fear, or a fear that came from the air itself, it permeated everything.

He decided to pray then. He didn't know what to say, so the prayer became wordless. An acknowledgment of God. He knew God didn't need words to hear him anyway. He knew what went on. He knew what would happen. And He knew what Patrick should do. Patrick wanted to pray for safety, but he didn't know if that was God's plan. Maybe Patrick needed to be in danger to save the girls, even die. So, no matter how scared he felt, he wouldn't pray for safety.

He felt her presence before he saw her. A woman, waiting by a rusted tow truck. She walked toward him and smiled. He should have found her beautiful, because by all visible signs, she was. Tall, and graceful, and glowing with life. But she didn't seem beautiful to him. She seemed wrong, broken, repellant.

"Julie?" Even as he asked it, he knew she wasn't Julie. She looked similar, with reddish blonde hair and green eyes, but five or six years older than Julie. And although they looked similar, this didn't look like the girl from the photo.

She shook her head, still smiling. "No," she said.

"What are you?" For some reason, "what" came out instead of "who."

"I am *everything.*"

When Patrick didn't reply, she went on.

"You see, you are one thing. You are the perfect version of that one thing, I admit. But still one thing. One brief, fleeting moment in time. And no matter how perfect that moment might be, we all know perfect moments don't last. They may linger as memories, but time ravages them all. You are one perfect moment, but I am every moment, of every day, of every year, for all eternity."

"Where are Julie and Evangeline?"

She laughed. "I see. You're here to save them. Am I right?"

Her twinkling laughter made him feel nauseous. "Yeah, that's right."

"Aww, aren't you sweet? And handsome. I think, even more handsome than your brother. Especially, when you have a few more years on you. Too bad I won't get to see that. Follow me."

Patrick didn't move.

She cocked her eyebrow. "Well, you could go back the way you came. But that wouldn't be very heroic, would it?"

Patrick followed her. A house loomed between the trees, as misplaced and broken as the rest of the refuse.

CHAPTER TWENTY-EIGHT

David headed toward the place that made the most sense. The gas station where Julie and Evangeline had disappeared. If something horrible had happened to one of his sons, it happened in that damn forest.

"We're being followed," James said.

"I know."

David glanced in his rearview mirror. A royal blue Prius had followed them for some time now, a royal blue Prius containing Thea Prescott. He couldn't get a good look at her from the mirror, but he could feel her magic and could make a guess. He didn't see anyone else in the car with her.

"Who does she think she is?" James asked. "Stalking two dark wizards all by herself?"

"Maybe just she's headed to the same place we are."

James scoffed. "I don't know."

"Normally I wouldn't be concerned about a lone, middle-aged woman, but I know better. If she does plan on attacking us, what do you think she will do?"

"Hard to say. If it was hand to hand combat, she'd use some kind of fire or heat. But there are plenty of other ways to attack. More indirect ways. She could cause us to be in a car accident, for example."

"How do we stop that?"

"Don't worry. I got it under control. You drive."

"What are you going to do?"

"I'm already doing it. I have been since I sensed her close by. Using a repellant spell. Her magic probably can't penetrate the shield."

"What do you mean, 'probably?' "

"If she's a better wizard than me, she could find a way around the spell. I doubt she can. But I've learned not to underestimate people. Especially, petite kindergarten teachers driving a Prius. She's got danger written all over her."

David didn't know if James joked or not. They had gotten closer now, and David spotted a plume of black smoke on the horizon. His throat and stomach constricted at once. He feared he was too late. At least *something* already burned. He promised himself—if any summer wizard had harmed any of his kids, he wouldn't worry about misdirection spells anymore. He would murder John and Thea Prescott, and anyone else who threatened them.

"Smoke," James said. *Like David couldn't fucking see it.* David thought he could smell it seeping in through the air conditioner vents. David's hands shook on the steering wheel and he hoped James didn't notice. He had to drive. He had to be active. He couldn't stand sitting even if the car hurtled forward at ninety. He needed his own foot on the gas.

A car coming from the other direction slammed on its brakes and did a squealing high speed U-turn on the highway. David thought he recognized it as the Prescott's Honda Pilot. Before he could react, the SUV sped up and rammed him. He heard the bumper crunch and the glass break before he registered what had happened. His brother's car skidded into oncoming traffic and an eighteen wheeler was seconds away from pulverizing them when the car rushed forward at unnatural speed and off the road. The airbags inflated as the front bumper wrapped around a pine tree.

David's heart hammered and his head hurt. He felt blood trickle from his temple.

"James?" David asked.

James had flecks of blood on his forehead and face as well, but could still crawl out of the broken passenger side window with the unnatural strength and flexibility of a giant spider.

Once he got out, he looked back at David. "You stay, I'll go."

David tried to open his own door, but it stuck. David pulled at the handle and shoved his weight against the door, but he couldn't budge it, and he didn't know why. He thought James's protective spell had pushed them out of the way of the eighteen wheeler. Maybe the protective power of the spell had lingered.

David heard two gunshots.

In response to the sound, David crawled out of his own window with a lot less grace. He put deep cuts in his hands and legs in his rush to see where the shots had come from.

Then it felt like a dream. It had all happened so fast. In one moment, he sat next his little brother in the truck. And now, he looked at him lying face down, blood soaking the parched earth around this head. This couldn't be real. He had wandered into a nightmare, that was all.

Thea, also on the ground for some reason, reached a shaking hand toward James's body.

"John, no," she said.

"He went after you. He was going to hurt you."

David knew he should pay attention to the man with the gun. He should look up. He should move. He should fight. He should run. But he could only watch the stain of blood around his brother's head grow larger. Lying there dead, he transcended time. He was the little boy David had once tried so hard to protect. He was the grown man who had stepped out of the car first, this time to protect David. And he was the old man he would never become. The one that should have grown old with the man he loved.

David finally looked at John. He still held the gun. His hands shook and he looked pale. He had been staring at James's body too, until he felt David's glare on him.

"He attacked you," John said in a wavering voice. "I had to." David assumed John spoke to Thea, but he kept his eyes on David.

John pursed his lips and squared his shoulders, steeling himself. David didn't fear being shot. He didn't fear anything. He felt numb. He felt gone. It wouldn't surprise him if he saw his own body bleeding on the ground.

John stood several yards away. Despite his lack of training, perhaps David could find a way to attack with magic, but he knew a bullet would be much more…decisive.

"John. No," Thea said.

David felt a rush of heat. The heat rippled the air like an invisible explosion. He thought his eyelashes might have seared off. When the heat passed, John was on the ground and Thea stood over her husband. She had his gun, but held it limply at her side.

Thea tossed the gun in David's direction. David looked at the gun sitting in the straw-like grass, feet from him. The numbness had started to pass, and his hands trembled. He felt grief saturating his body. Thea's actions made no sense, but he didn't care. He moved toward his brother and felt like he had floated there, hovering above him as a ghost.

He wanted to touch the body. He wanted to feel the heat of his brother's body before it left forever. The warm blood soaked the knees of his jeans as he kneeled next to him. He pressed his head into his brother's shoulder.

Then, Thea grabbed him by the hair and pulled his head up. She pressed the gun into his unwilling hands.

"What do you want?" David's voice sounded thick, as if he spoke under water. He could barely speak, let alone understand why she handed him a gun. He looked over at John still passed out on the ground. The man should die. David should kill him right now. Was that what she wanted? He didn't want to leave his brother's side. Grief had surpassed rage. He wanted to wait for the warmth to pass, for the bleeding to stop. He had missed out on so much of James's life. He wanted to be there beside him for every moment of his death, even though could tell from the gaping hole in his skull that James's life had ended as soon as the bullet hit.

"I'm tired of you not fighting back," Thea said. "There is no sport in it." Her tone didn't match her words. She sounded as if she held back tears of her own. "I'm tired of not getting credit," she continued. "I've done so much to you, and you don't even see it. *I* was the one who burned down your housing development in Tangled Woods." She laughed a shaky laugh that sounded more desperate than evil. "I ruined your business. You lost your house, your money, and your dignity. And I did it all just to spite you."

David stood to face her, the muscles in his body spasming in strange places, like his forearm and his jaw.

"But that wasn't enough," she continued. "I wanted to hurt you more. So, I set your house on fire, with you and everyone you love inside. I wanted you and your children to burn. I wanted them to scream. First afraid…fearing death. Then, begging for death to stop the pain. I wanted my fire to rip the flesh from their bodies, and leave them nothing but charred bone and ash. I wanted to send you and your babies to Hell where they belong. *Hell*…where your little brother is now burning."

She glanced at the gun in David's hands. "So, knowing this, there is only one thing to do. You will kill me. You, *David Vandergraff*, will kill me, *Thea Prescott*. And then, the prophecy will be fulfilled."

This last part sounded too formal, too specific. It reminded him of the spell Rachel Colter had cast. The one that destroyed the talisman of protection over her brother. Thea wanted to cast some kind of spell.

David dropped the gun and grabbed Thea by the neck and throttled her. "Why do you want me to kill you?"

"No…" she said between gasps as he restricted her air supply. "The gun….blood…there must be blood."

"Why do you want me to kill you?" he asked again. His mind swirled with darkness. He wanted to kill her. She deserved to die. She had to die. But he didn't trust her. Some of what she had said had been true, but some of it had been a lie. But his senses had become clouded, so he couldn't sort it out. The hate and rage inside him erupted from his hands around her neck. He could feel her going cold.

"No…" she spluttered. "Blood…please, blood."

David could feel death spilling from his own hands. Not by repressed oxygen, but from something deeper. Just pure death, coming from inside him, and saturating the little woman's body. Her eyes rolled back and he noticed white flecks in her eyelashes. Ashes.

He released her and she crumbled to the ground, but he could still see her chest rising and falling. He hadn't taken her life. He looked up to see that the fire had eaten its way through the drought-ridden forest quickly, igniting the dry trees with vigor. The smoke had taken over the whole sky, and the black cloud rising over the forest reminded him of a massive thunderhead. It blotted out the sun. He heard sirens.

Thea grabbed him by the ankle. "Kill me," she said again, in a strangled whisper. "With the gun."

He shook her off. He turned back to his brother and squeezed his hand one last time. He left the gun on the ground and ran towards the flames. Thea could have shot him in the back, but he knew she wouldn't. He could read people. And she had the most complicated intentions and motives of anyone he had ever met. He had no clue why she had attacked her husband, and then begged him to kill her. But he knew she wouldn't kill him.

He had to get to his kids. He ran along the road, limping. He hadn't realized he had hurt his leg in the accident until he started to run. He wouldn't get to the fire fast enough this way. Thea's Prius sat by the side of the road, with its royal blue paint untouched by the accident.

Hating having to move backwards when his body wanted to fly towards the smoke, he limp-ran back toward Thea. He wished he could fly. Wizards in movies could fly.

Thea cowered when he ran back at her, still on the ground, but she looked at the gun and looked back at him hopefully. Maybe she thought he had changed his mind.

"Give me your keys."

"You'll have to kill me for them."

David lunged at her. She didn't have a purse, so he hoped she had the keys in her pocket. Despite wanting him to kill her, she fought back, kicking and scratching at him as he tried to get to her pockets. A lot more vicious than her little body would suggest. He tried to subdue her with magic, but she was better. She resisted his dark magic violently, trusting another wave of toxic heat toward him. She reminded him of a frightened animal shooting poison at a predator.

David had to scuttle away, but only for a moment. He turned toward her again. "Give me the damn keys. All I want is the keys. We don't have time for this. It's a distraction. Distraction. Distraction." He chanted the word a few times and knew he sounded crazy. *Distraction* was the only word that could get him to leave his brother's body. He needed to find his sons.

David turned and looked at the smoke again, and when he looked back at Thea, her eyes were on the sky too.

"My babies are in there," she said.

As soon as John roused, his head burst with pain. His whole body felt dried out, and he half expected to see leathery claws instead of hands. He never knew what she planned to do anymore. He'd had his eyes on the dark wizard, and never thought to defend himself against her.

He smacked his lips, trying to generate saliva. It took him a moment to remember what he had done. It didn't fully hit him until he saw him lying there. Face down, in a pool of his own blood. John might have vomited if he any fluid left in his body. He trembled instead, the pain in his head intensifying.

This was her fault. He did this for her. Because of her.

Only official vehicles remained on the road. Perhaps they had closed the road because of the approaching wildfire. He had cast a concealment spell around them when they approached the dark wizards so nosy Mundanes wouldn't bother them. The spell continued to work, and cars sped by as if he and the dead man were invisible. He knew the spell would make it so no one would look over, or if they did, they wouldn't care about what they saw. It would slip in and out of their mind with no lasting effect. He didn't want anyone to see what he had done, but he could hardly remember ever feeling so lonely. His entire world had shifted to the point that the sky above him might shatter. But no one cared. No one noticed.

He hadn't realized how vividly he still remembered that night. But when he saw the dark wizard knock Thea to the ground, the images flashed through his head again.

John and Thea had travelled the world together. They had visited countries few others would. Countries torn apart by war and poverty. Dangerous places. Places where women were still treated like property. Places where Westerners could be killed just by taking a step in the wrong direction. But they had been brave. They had been careful. They were there to do good. To give vaccinations. To teach the children. That goodness protected them, or he'd thought it had.

The true danger lurked closer to home, and found them on

June 21st, 1993. The summer solstice. He knew that wasn't a coincidence. That had been part of the fun. Part of the joke.

John and Thea had gone to the grocery store. They bought food to bring to a solstice gathering later that night. Thea had planned on making strawberry pie. He remembered this because when the attack happened, the strawberries scattered all over the floor. The strawberries never made it into pie. Instead, they grew blue fuzzy mold. After the attack, he would find them everywhere, serving as a constant reminder. A moldy strawberry under the couch. A dried strawberry tucked under a rug. Smashed strawberries would never come out of the damn carpet.

They had left the door of their apartment ajar as they brought in the groceries. Five winter wizards took their chance. Burst in without warning.

They beat him. They raped her.

For no other reason than because they existed. Beauty and life and happiness and the light of angels filled Thea to the brim. And they hated her for it. They wanted to take it away.

And he failed to do anything to stop it.

But John believed they failed to take their light. They had hurt them in a way that would never be fully repaired, and had managed to leave a mark of their evil that would last—in the form of a baby girl named Caroline. But they hadn't taken their light. They hadn't won. Until now.

It had taken twenty years, but they got what they wanted. They had turned them into villains.

CHAPTER TWENTY-NINE

Patrick followed Caroline toward the house. The sky had a strange quality. Orange and blue and gray. A place with no season. No time. He could feel the absence in the air. It felt empty. Dead.

He didn't know what any of this meant, but he knew this witch was powerful. He knew he didn't have much skill himself, but he had never seen a wizard create anything close to this. A repelling spell maybe, but she had created her own universe inside the real one. He didn't know much about the magical world, but he knew that was unusual. That was the stuff for fantasy novels and movies, not real magic.

He felt compelled to follow her, as if he'd walked in this direction for long time, and only now knew where he had meant to go.

They didn't enter the house, She led him around the side, and pointed to a single wooden dining chair.

"Have a seat," she said.

Patrick couldn't deny her, so he sat.

"Where are they? Inside?" he asked.

She nodded.

"Who the hell do you think you are?"

"I told you. I'm everything."

Nothing visible bound him to the chair, but he couldn't move. His arms stuck to his sides and his ankles couldn't uncross, as if invisible ropes bound him. Jude had done something similar the last time Patrick had seen him. He paralyzed him with magic, but only for a moment, just enough to throw him off while he ran out of the house forever. But it had been a passing stumble compared to this.

"Do you know what prax potentia is?" Caroline asked.

"No."

Her shoulders slumped, as if she had hoped for a different reaction.

"Well, then I guess I'll have to teach you." She walked closer to him and leaned down, close enough he could tell she smelled of strawberries, but not in a pleasant way. It had a vile sweetness about it, like rotten fruit.

"It's a fun game, because everyone is different. Summer wizards are so easy. Getting power from them is like squeezing juice out of a big ripe grapefruit." She said it with relish and Patrick winced, thinking of Julie.

"But the winter witch is harder," she continued. "Working with her is like trying to squeeze juice from an apple with my bare hands. She bears the marks of previous spells. Perhaps there is a limit to how much can be taken from one person, and she's been sucked dry. Or, perhaps, she's become practiced at shielding herself. Or, considering she's a winter solstice witch, maybe she's too dark. Has no soul to take."

"How could you torture your own little sister?" He didn't know their relation for sure, but he thought it was a safe bet.

"I'm going to teach you something about magic. It may not be what you want to hear, but it's true. The most powerful wizards are good at seeing the big picture. They think long-term. End result. The main thing that keeps most wizards from reaching their full potential is distraction. Most wizards are easily distracted by the details. And Julie is a detail."

"She's not a detail. She's your sister."

"The world's most powerful wizards, even the ones who excel at their craft, are still missing out on the true potential of magic. In truth, wizards today are pretty pathetic. If wizards realized their abilities as a group, we would be extremely successful. Wealthy, powerful, and living unnaturally long lives in blissful happiness. But it's the opposite. As a group, we're pathetic humans beings. On the whole, less successful than the Mundanes. How sick is that? Wizards today either repress their magic or destroy themselves. It's tragic. It's a terrible waste. We could be living better lives, but also making the world a better place. So many would give anything for just a taste of power beyond human, and we burn through it without a second thought.

"And I can tell you why this has happened. It's because wizards are too polarized. Even the best wizards in the world only excel at *their* type of magic. We're so keen on classifying ourselves and focusing on one specialty. And that's extremely foolish. Magic has four seasons. And using any less than all four is like driving a car without all its wheels. However, only focusing on one season has become the norm. Because of this, wizard magic is unbalanced, imprecise, ineffective, and dangerous.

"Absorbing the magic from each solstice is a start. That's what gives me the power. With the equinoxes, I get the precision. Even without spring, I can use you to moderate and focus the winter and summer. Everything is going to change from here on out. With each one I collect, I get stronger, and calling the rest gets easier, faster. So, now it won't be much longer until spring comes too. Which is good, because the siren spell I cast to get you all here was taking way…too…long."

She cocked her head at him and examined him like a science project. "The basic theory behind prax potentia is simple, but it can be complicated. It's both a science and an art. Every subject is different. You have to find the right way to make them hurt. It takes perception and subtlety."

Patrick scoffed.

"What?"

"I've seen what you've been doing to Julie, at least I've seen the effects. You've been burning her with a wire hanger or something. That's what you mean by a science and an art? Any idiot can cause pain. It doesn't take any skill at all. You only need to be a disgusting and worthless human being. Which you are. Congratulations."

"You've seen it? Jesus. That's impressive, Patrick. I think I'm going to like practicing on you. I'm not sure what will work, but I have some ideas I'm looking forward to trying out."

Caroline took his hand, and he couldn't resist. She pressed the soft skin between his fingers and his hand erupted in pain. All the nerves in his hand and arm spasmed. White fog floated in his vision. He thought he might pass out. He wanted to pass out. The pain surpassed anything he had ever experienced. The whole world disappeared and nothing existed but pain. Nothing mattered other than getting it to stop.

Caroline released his hand. His vision remained cloudy, but the pain receded. Just the absence of the pain was a beautiful feeling.

"Please...don't..." he said. He noticed his eyes were wet with tears and he hated himself for it.

Caroline laughed lightly, as if she where chatting with girlfriends at Happy Hour.

"Awww...Patrick. I suspected as much. The only person who would talk about physical pain in such a dismissive way is someone who had never experienced it. You don't know shit about pain, Patrick. You've lived a cushy little life. And in response to your claim from before, no I did not burn her with a wire hanger. I'm a motherfucking witch. And I can make people hurt in ways you can't imagine."

The pain had passed, but the fear of its return was torture in itself. *I'm a motherfucking wizard, too*, he thought. He should at least try to counter her. He thought maybe if he concentrated hard enough, he could get her to stop. Or, he could hurt her. He could do something.

But before he could form a singular spell, she hit him again. She placed her fingers on either side of his knee now, and activated the nerves up and down his leg, from his toes to his groin, but the pain felt bigger than that. It was everywhere.

"No…no…no," he managed to grunt, thinking maybe he could use some magic against her, but he couldn't. He screamed. A horrible, pathetic sound.

She let go of him again. His body had tensed against the pain, so his muscles still ached.

"What do you want from me?" he asked. *That is how these things work, right?* Torture. She needed some kind of information, or something. Without knowing what she wanted, he felt desperate to give it to her. He would tell her anything. Do anything. And he hated himself so much for it. He had always assumed he was a better man. The heroes in the movies who would die for a cause. Suffer pain gladly if it was the right thing to do. But he couldn't stand a few minutes of torture. Pathetic. An embarrassment.

"Wow, it's already working," Caroline said. "This is going to be so easy. It's kind of disappointing. I had hoped more from one of my kind. I've met so few. I thought you would be better. More like me."

Patrick looked up at her, but didn't respond.

"Well, what kind of wizard did you think I was, anyway?" She rolled her eyes. "Winter, maybe, because I'm so *bad?* Or summer, because I'm from a family of summer wizards? Nope. I'm fall, like you. It's why I'm so good at what I do. I have a keen sense of cause and effect. How to manipulate multiple factors toward a goal. I'm sure you've noticed, most summer and winter wizards are idiots playing with fire. Just seeing who can make the biggest bang. Not us. We're ten steps ahead of them all of the time. But you're the one who is supposed to be the *equinox* wizard. You're supposed to be better than me, right? I mean, of course, not for much longer. So, how does me torturing you fit into *your* master plan?"

She laughed.

"You're going to lose," Patrick said. "I don't know how. But you will. You're right. I've seen things you can't. And Julie, Evangeline, and I…we're all going to live to suffer another day." He laughed now. A weak, crazy laugh, but a laugh. Because, he was right. They would survive this, he knew because he'd seen worse. More pain. More suffering. God hadn't finished punishing them, not by a long shot.

Caroline leaned close again, and this time put one pink manicured finger on each of his temples. His body tensed before the pain hit. He couldn't imagine pain worse than he had already experienced…until it came.

CHAPTER THIRTY

Evangeline moved toward the light. She couldn't see the light with her eyes, or feel the warmth with her flesh. But she could still find it, because she was a witch. She could see the things everyone else ignored. She had been trying to get to the light every day, but it was hard to move with her hands and legs bound. She had to crawl like an inchworm under the house where the woman kept her—locked in the hollow foundation like a lost raccoon. But she wasn't alone. There was the light.

She had known the light was a person before she heard her breathing. As Evangeline crawled closer, the person, the girl, breathed heavier. And Evangeline knew she had frightened her.

But she didn't stop. She crawled closer, her hands bound. Dirt embedding into the cuts and burns the woman had given her. She knew what the woman was trying to do. She had been part of this kind of spell before. Prax potentia. The practice of power—the easiest way to take magical power from a person. And all you had to do was hurt them. Take their power. Take their hope.

If the light was what Evangeline thought it was, then they might have hope. She might see her family again. And see all the color and the light of the world.

The light's breath caught, and she sounded like she was crying.

"It's okay," Evangeline said.

"Are you a demon?" asked the light.

"No, I'm a girl, like you."

"You can't be. You're so dark."

Evangeline knew she was. As a winter solstice witch, she was the darkest dark. And in a place so full of darkness and pain, she would blend in to the background as if invisible.

"I'm a girl," Evangeline said again.

Evangeline flinched when she felt hands. But with a steadying breath, she let the other girl touch her. Feel her arms, and her face. This girl didn't have her hands bound as Evangeline did. Maybe she was past that. Maybe she had stopped fighting.

"You are a girl," she said.

"You are Julie, right?"

"Yes, who are you?"

"My name is Evangeline."

"You are a girl like me, and that means…"

Julie's voice was lost, as if sucked away by wind.

Then she found her voice again. "You must be winter."

"Yes."

"Then she's won. She has us both. The light and the dark. It's over."

"No."

"That's good. Then, maybe she'll kill us. And it will really be over."

"I don't want to die."

"I do."

When Evangeline had walked through Caroline's concealment spell, she hadn't been afraid. She felt like Alice walking into Wonderland. Cold air had rushed from the sky and the wind whipped her hair off her sweaty neck. The cold made her feel fresh and clean. Droplets of ice crystallized on the pine needles as if the forest were dripped in stars.

Even when the winter passed, she still walked in amazement. Before this, Patrick's concealment spell had been the best she'd ever seen. This concealment spell fell into it's own category. Concealment, repulsion, illusion, display—all sorts of magic wrapped into one massive, impenetrable spell like nothing she had ever seen.

She had been thrilled to meet the wizard who had created this world within a world. She had wanted to meet the person who could push the boundaries of usual magic. She wanted to learn from them, and to honor them.

However, Caroline was just another predator…who happened to be good at magic. Evangeline tried to fight. She cast every defensive spell she could think of, but Caroline was the better witch. Once she bound her with magic, she bound her with duct tape too, just in case Evangeline broke the paralyzing spell.

Caroline talked a lot. About her plans. About how she was better than everyone. However, after Caroline started making Evangeline hurt, she talked less. Evangeline thought she could handle the pain, but Caroline could make her hurt in new ways she couldn't have imagined. All Evangeline could do was cry. She kept thinking about Xavier and her new family, but she tried to push the thoughts away. The belief she might be safe again would make it harder. Hope was dangerous.

She knew all about prax portentia. She knew Caroline wished to take her power, as her stepfather had.

She didn't think she had much left to give, but she might have been wrong. The more Caroline hurt her, the more depleted she felt. Caroline would take long pauses to simply stare at Evangeline. She had a look of concentration and annoyance. Something about Evangeline didn't sit right with Caroline. Something bothered her. So she went at her harder. Evangeline watched the skin on the arms bubble and blister even though no fire touched her. Eventually she passed out.

When she woke up, she felt different. Caroline's spell had worked. Something was missing inside her, but it might not have been what Caroline expected. Caroline had left her and the worst of the pain had passed. Evangeline felt adrenaline rushing through her body. The world felt oddly clear and silent, as if everything had moved into sharper focus. She felt clean again, like she had when the winter wind enveloped her.

Something had gone out in her, and left a pleasant absence in its wake. She felt darker, and in this darkness, she could see light more clearly. She could see Caroline a few rooms over— not her body, but her life. Evangeline could see her life, light a little light inside her. At that moment, she realized she had a power that few wizards had.

She could reach into Caroline and snuff out that light, like extinguishing a candle with her finger.

Now she only needed to figure out how.

David thought it had to be getting late, but the day went on forever. The sun refused to set until it had finished with them. Driving Thea's car felt surreal. She had given over her keys, but had gotten in with him. He didn't stop her. To stop her, he'd have to attack her again, and he didn't want to. He wouldn't do anything else to delay saving his kids. He'd already been misdirected more than enough.

So, he tried to ignore the woman sitting next to him. He tried to ignore James's blood on her knees. He tried to ignore the fact that her husband had murdered her brother. And that she had admitted to burning not only his house, but unexpectedly, the development in Tangled Forest. And he tried to ignore that everything about her—body and soul—made him want to rip the hair from his head. He kept saying to himself, *distraction, distraction, distraction.* The magic wanted his kids at the forest, and wanted him away. And the magic would do *anything* to keep him away. James couldn't be helped. Thea's fires had already burned out. But the one in the forest continued to burn.

Thea stared out the window with rapt attention. She leaned away from him and sat frozen, as if he might not see her there if she didn't move. He doubted any two people had ever driven in a car together so silently. Even though theirs was the only car other than fire trucks and police cars that headed toward the flames, no one stopped them, or noticed them at all. David wondered if he had cast a spell on accident, or perhaps Thea had cast one on purpose. But his unrelenting determination to reach his kids felt so powerful it had to be magic. Nothing would stand in his way. He wouldn't let it.

"You lied," David said.

Thea ignored him.

"I just don't know why. What you said about burning down the development was true. And what you said about starting the fire at my house was true. But when you said you wanted us dead. When you said you wanted my children to suffer and die, you were lying then. You can't lie to me. Reading people is one of my specialties. You didn't want us to die at all. If you had, you would have set the fire differently. But no. You designed a fire that was dramatic, but stayed on the surface. You put us in danger…and you're not going to get away with that. But you wanted us to make it out alive."

"No, I didn't," she said without looking at him. "If you don't kill me, I'll try again. I'll kill your whole family. And it will be your fault, because you were too weak to kill me. Because you're a coward."

"You're still lying. I just can't figure out why. If you want to die so badly, take your own life. Use the gun on yourself. Or, maybe you think God won't let you into Heaven that way? Is that it? You have to be murdered by a dark wizard to make the cut?"

"I don't want to die. But if someone has to, it will be me."

They had reached the gas station. The place had been evacuated. He pulled in by the pumps, but thought better of it. If the fire took the station, the gas pumps would be the worst place to be. He might park Thea's car there out of spite, but he had to get himself and his kids out of here somehow.

He went down the road further and parked in the middle of the road, and both of them got out of the car.

"Can you stop the fire?" Thea asked.

"Why would I be able to do that?"

"I don't know. You're winter. Maybe you can make it cold."

David would have laughed if he hadn't been so terrified. She might as well have asked him to make the sun cold. The air itself seemed to burn.

Thea examined the forest's edge, perhaps trying to find the best place to run in. If she did, she would die. He didn't need magic to know that. If the winds shifted, the fire would overcome her like a tsunami hitting a beach. Errant sparks blew through the air, and David noticed black spots on his shirt where embers had already hit him. They were too late. Maybe even to escape themselves. Their only salvation was the road. The fire would cross it eventually, but they had time. If they stayed on the road, they were safe, at least for now.

"No," Thea said. "No."

"And the girls…" David asked. "Can the fire touch them wherever they are? Are they really in the forest, or did the portal transport them somewhere else?"

"They're in the forest. The magic hiding them is a powerful concealment spell. There is no such thing as a portal."

David began to cough and couldn't stop. The smoke filled his lungs and he couldn't breathe.

When someone grabbed him, he hardly cared at first. He let them drag him away. Nothing mattered. It wasn't until he saw Thea clawing at the face of a fireman he realized they were being rescued.

"Ma'am, stop."

"No, John left our sons here. They were looking for Julie. They were here."

"A group of teenage boys? That's who you're looking for?"

David shook off the fireman leading him away and moved towards the fireman trying to calm Thea, blinking his stinging eyes.

"They're fine. We already got them," the fireman said.

His whole body could have melted with relief. He had forgotten he wasn't alone in the world. Other people, such as Mundane firefighters would risk their lives, not for their own children, but for strangers. And it wouldn't matter if they were wizards or Mundanes, summer or winter, they would save their lives for no other reason than that they needed saving.

"Yeah," the fireman continued. "Three teenage boys."

Thea looked at David, probably doing the same horrible math David had done. Thea had said sons with an "s." So both of her sons must have been in the forest. And that meant the firemen had left with one too few.

"What were their names?" Thea demanded.

"I'm afraid I don't know Ma'am. We need to get you out of here."

"What were their names?" David shouted at the man. "I'm not going anywhere until you tell me their names."

"I said I don't know," the fireman said. "I only saw them. Two with sandy brown hair, looked like brothers. And one with dark hair. Weird, quiet little kid. Looks like you," he said to David. *Xavier.*

That brief moment of relief passed. The missing fourth was his. Of course it was his. *Patrick.*

Emmy rushed into the Sugar Land ER—the exact same one she had been in four days ago—and Mom didn't have trouble keeping up with her. They didn't have to ask anyone where he was. They could find him by his energy. A nurse stood in the way, but Mom pushed by her.

"That's my son," she said.

Xavier looked up at them from where he sat on an ER bed. He held his head as if it weighed a hundred pounds.

"No. He's not here," Xavier said, so quietly Emmy thought she might have imagined it.

"I meant you," Mom said.

"Oh," he said.

"Are you alright?" Mom asked.

He looked at her as if she spoke German, and she might as well have. She had asked a stupid question. He had lost Evangeline, and now Patrick. Nobody was all right now. Emmy wasn't. And she knew Mom wasn't.

"Are you hurt?" Mom asked now, revising her question. Xavier had a bandage on his arm, and an oxygen machine by the bed, but he breathed on his own now. He didn't reply.

"Your father is fine. He'll be here soon."

After an awkward silence, Xavier said, "What about Patrick?"

He said it so quietly this time, Emmy thought Mom didn't hear him. She looked around, perhaps seeking out someone to discharge him.

"We don't know," Emmy said. "What happened?" Her heart thumped erratically. She could never remember being so scared. She looked into the eyes of her only remaining sibling out of four.

Xavier expelled a breath as if he meant to say something, but nothing came out. He shook his head.

"Patrick is smart. He'll be okay." Emmy wanted to believe it, but she knew it made no sense. You couldn't outsmart fire.

CHAPTER THIRTY-ONE

Patrick could sense his presence before he spoke. When you spent your whole life living one room over from a wizard, even if you didn't know you were wizards for most of the time, you got a sense of their magic, their energy.

Jude.

Even though he had spent so much time and energy hating him ever since he had raped Samantha, his first reaction to Jude's presence was relief. His big brother had come to save him. He would protect him. Something about the pain had stripped away a lot of his anger. He wanted to go home. To get far away from Caroline. He wanted his brother to take him home.

"No," Caroline said. "What are you doing here? I told you to stay home."

"You know, you can't expect me to bend to your will like that. If you wanted a man like that, you should have dated a Mundane."

"I love you, but you don't have the stomach for this."

Patrick's own stomach turned. They were dating. This horrible creature was his brother's girlfriend. At least he could say these assholes deserved each other. But he had the sick feeling from the way they spoke to each other that they didn't treat each other as they treated everyone else in the world. They made each other happy. And they *really* didn't deserve that. But whenever Caroline lost—he knew she would—perhaps she would die. Or, at least go to prison. And if Jude loved her that would punish him too, making the victory sweeter.

"No, I do," Jude said. "It's fine. They gave my mom six months. We can't waste time. I'll help anyway I can."

"Well then, I have good news. We're closer than ever. Maybe close enough to cast the spell to save her."

"We are?"

"I have the third."

Patrick knew it was bad Jude hadn't sensed him there right away. It meant his magic had already grown weak, what little magic he had in the first place. Patrick could hardly move, due to the lingering effects of the paralyzing spell and the way his whole body still ached with pain. But he hated Jude seeing him lying there in a hopeless heap. With a grunt, he pushed himself up and turned away from the wall.

Jude stared at him when he turned around. Caroline stood behind him, looking scared for the first time since Patrick had seen her. She watched Jude's reaction with her brow furrowed, lips pursed. She looked afraid he would be angry with her, or disappointed, or leave her maybe. The look made her look human, and Patrick hated it. She didn't get to be a human and a monster at the same time.

Jude's face turned pale, but Patrick couldn't read his expression. He looked better than Patrick would have expected. He looked normal. Clean. Well-dressed.

"Why?" Jude finally said.

"He's the third," Caroline said.

Jude didn't take his eyes off him. Patrick tried to compose his stiff, aching face into a look that showed he simultaneously despised Jude, but also barely recognized him, as if he wasn't important enough to remember.

"I don't think so," Jude said.

"I don't make mistakes like that, and you know it. I know you're not experienced with wizard datings, but I'm sure if you took the time to really consider his magic, you'd see it too."

"He's not powerful," Jude said. "There is no point to this."

"Traditional solstice arrogance. You think he's not powerful because he doesn't make the biggest bang. All that flash means little."

Jude scoffed. "That may be true for you. But I know him. He can't do much."

"He's an equinox wizard, Jude. You can argue it all you want. It won't make it less true." She squeezed his hand. "I'm sorry. I honestly didn't know it would be him. But this is why you shouldn't be here."

Jude stopped looking at Patrick, and stared at something invisible on the floor. He stayed quiet for long enough Caroline tugged him arm.

"Are you okay?" she asked.

"Yes," Jude said. "It's fine."

"You don't love him," Caroline said. "You think you should. Because you share DNA. And you've been conditioned by society that you're supposed to love your brother. But that doesn't mean you do. He certainly doesn't love you."

Jude stared at Patrick for a long time, then he turned to Caroline. "My family turned their backs on me," he said. "But not you. You saved me. I'm on your side, Caroline."

She smiled and threw herself into his arms, and kissed him.

Disgusted, Patrick turned back toward the wall, and decided if he got the chance, he would kill his brother in a heartbeat.

CHAPTER THIRTY-TWO

Emmy knew Nathan was at the hospital. When the firemen called Mom, they said Nathan had saved Xavier from the fire. Xavier had passed out from the smoke, and after Nathan brought his brother out to the road, Nathan went back in for Xavier. And the firemen couldn't stop him. Of course they couldn't. Nathan probably commanded them to stay.

And she could feel him. His energy. She could feel the energy of other summer wizards too. But she didn't care.

While Mom filled out paperwork, Emmy followed the energy to the other side of the ER. The Mundane doctors seemed to instinctively know that the summer wizards and winter wizards needed rooms as far apart as possible. Or perhaps they had tried to kill each other on the way over here in the ambulance.

Emmy pushed the curtain away in an over-dramatic fashion. She hadn't meant it to be, but she was nervous. They both stared at her as if they had expected her arrival, which they probably had.

Luke, Nathan's brother Emmy had never met, stood by Nathan's bed. Luke had a hospital bracelet on, but looked okay. Nathan looked less okay. He had his shirt off and a large bandage on his back. If wands existed, he would have his pointed at her. Instead, he had to settle for a deadly glare.

"Go away," Luke said.

"You go away," Emmy said.

"I said, get the fuck out," Luke said.

"You can't tell me what to do."

Nathan half groaned, half growled in a way that told Emmy he was in pain. "Stop it," he said. "Luke, give us a minute."

"You've got to me kidding me," Luke said. "You're kicking me out?"

"If you don't go, you know I can make you. But I'm tired, so I'd prefer it if you did as I asked. Stay close though."

Luke took a wide berth around Emmy, glaring at her the whole way.

"What happened to you?" Emmy asked. "Are you okay?"

"I got hit with some flaming debris. I'll be alright."

With his shirt off, Emmy could see more of his old burn marks. He had them all over. They had too much of a pattern, too much symmetry. It reminded Emmy of Evangeline's tick marks.

"Is that how you got your scars? Saving people from fires?"

"I'm afraid not."

"You didn't have anything to do with the fire at my house, did you?"

"No."

"I feel bad about what I did to you."

"I don't feel great about it either."

"I'm sorry."

Nathan nodded. He sat up in bed, but hunched, as if moving hurt.

"Can I get you anything?" The question sounded stupid. What would she get him? Water? A sandwich? How helpful would that be? She hated seeing him in pain. She wanted to do something to take it away.

"No, thank you."

Emmy put her hand on his. He looked up at her and she leaned into him, resting her forehead on his.

"Patrick," Emmy said.

"I know."

"Not Patrick."

Nathan pulled her closer and she cried into his shoulder.

Patrick looked at the sky. Night had fallen, but the sky stayed orange. It looked as if the entire world were burning. But Caroline's cloaking spell had managed to protect them. The air continued to have that still, empty, seasonless quality. The fire couldn't burn them, but it could light up the night. Keep the day burning on forever.

"Pretty cool, huh?"

Patrick flinched at the sound of his brother's voice. The fire had distracted them, and Patrick had a moment of peace. He sat on the ground, leaning up against the side of the house.

Patrick didn't respond, so Jude kneeled in front of him.

"That's because of you, you know," Jude said, and he gestured toward the sky. "If you hadn't shown up, we all would have died in the fire. But with your magic, Caroline is even stronger now. The concealment spell was powerful before, but not like this. Right now she's working on strengthening the perimeter, but it looks like it's going to hold. It's fucking incredible. Did you know a large wildfire can cause hurricane force winds?"

"That's fascinating. Did your girlfriend tell you that?"

"She did, actually."

Patrick's mouth felt dry and it tasted of dirt. He needed water, but he refused to ask his brother for it.

"She's amazing," Jude said. "If she can stop a wildfire, with three out of four of the events. With spring, she'll be able to do anything. Absolutely anything."

Jude smiled at him with perfect white teeth. He hardly looked familiar. Something about him had shifted. He'd always been evil. He'd always been crazy. But now he seemed happy, which made him seem more evil and crazy than ever.

"Oh, yeah. She's amazing. I *really* like her. Can I please be best man at your wedding?"

"I know you're being sarcastic. But I would love it if you would be best man at my wedding."

"Do you not understand what's happening here? You and your girlfriend have kidnapped and tortured three people. You are not going to live happily ever after, you are going to *go to jail*. And that's if you're lucky. I'd like to see you both avoid getting murdered. Because you've pissed off a lot of powerful wizards."

"Well, we've managed to avoid getting murdered so far. These so-called powerful wizards are doing a terrible, *terrible* job at taking down one witch."

"You gave Mom cancer. Or, was it Caroline's spell? A distraction so she could take Evangeline."

Jude's face darkened, or maybe his eyes sparkled less. He stood back.

"That was an accident. It's wasn't Caroline. She wouldn't do that."

"Oh, sure. What was I thinking? Caroline wouldn't hurt a fly."

"Caroline is going to save Mom's life. That's better than anything you can do for her."

"What?"

"With the power of all the seasons, she can do anything. *Anything.* And saving Mom is the first thing she's going to do."

"Is that how she explained all this to you? I mean, I know you're a horrible person, but some part of you had to be at least a little annoyed when you found out your girlfriend had taken your sister and brother as her personal playthings and didn't even tell you about it. So, that's what she said right? Oh, no, Jude, it's okay. I'm only doing it to save your Mommy."

Jude kicked him in the chest. After going through the worst pain of his life, Patrick could handle the pain of the kick. But he hated the way it took his breath and rattled his heart in his ribs. He coughed until his coughing turned into a strange wheezy laughter that didn't sound like him.

"That is what she said, isn't it?" Patrick asked with a hoarse voice. "That's exactly what happened. She is so good at playing you, isn't she?"

"I don't have to defend my relationship to you."

Patrick laughed again. He didn't know why he laughed, and he knew he sounded crazy. He probably *had* gone crazy.

"That's fine," Jude said. "Enjoy yourself now, because Caroline will be back soon."

CHAPTER THIRTY-THREE

Evangeline kicked at the wooden panels along the side of the foundation. She had tried magic too, and it would have worked if Caroline had been a Mundane, or even a lesser witch, but she must have cast a spell to keep them here. She needed to get closer to try a killing spell. Since she'd never done it before, she needed proximity, concentration, and minimal distractions—and she didn't know how she would manage that. But now she had a new reason to fight.

Evangeline gave up on the trap door and crawled over to Julie. She just lay there. Evangeline touched her arm and she shuddered. Like Evangeline, Julie had old scars. She knew nothing other than a life of being tortured by her sister. And Evangeline knew how that felt. The person seemed so big. They were the whole world, and there was nothing before or after them. Just them. And just pain.

"It's just me," Evangeline said. "I need you to help me. Did you hear that?"

Julie didn't respond. It was too dark to see much of her face. But she glowed less, which meant Caroline glowed more.

"Did you hear it?" Evangeline asked again. "I can't tell if it's in my mind, or if it's real."

"What?"

"Screaming. Someone screaming."

"Yes. I think it's me." She had really lost it.

"No, no, it's not you," she said patiently. "It's a guy." Evangeline had the sick feeling she knew him, she recognized his energy, but she couldn't tell for sure. She was too far away.

"I know," Julie said. "Not me. But I'm with him. He has a piece of me."

"Please, Julie, you have to focus. It's important. If someone else it out there, then she's found another one. An equinox wizard. That's really bad…I'm scared I know who it is."

"Who?"

Evangeline didn't want to say it out loud. That would make it more true. "I don't know…What did you mean, when you said he had a piece of you?"

Julie didn't respond.

Evangeline grabbed her and shook her. "You said it. What did you mean?"

"I don't know. I'm sorry. It just feels like that."

"Maybe he does." Evangeline touched the spot in her pocket where her rock should have been. Caroline had taken it from her. "Your talisman. The bracelet."

"How did you know about my talisman?" Julie sounded more lucid now. She sat up. In the dim light, Evangeline thought she saw her rub her wrist where the bracelet should be.

"My sister found it. We have it."

Julie sniffed. "I thought I had lost it forever. You have it?"

"Maybe…maybe, now it's here. Maybe my brother brought it with him."

"You think it's your brother, the one screaming?" She paused. "I'm sorry."

"I know we've already tried different spells together and it hasn't worked, but if we had Patrick too…"

"But we don't."

"He's not that far. We can still give him our magic."

"You know him. You can lock on to his energy. I can't."

"He has your talisman. That's not his energy, it's yours. Can you find that?"

Julie grew quiet. Evangeline couldn't see her face well enough to see any expression.

"Maybe," she said.

"All we have to do is try. If it doesn't work, we won't be any worse off."

"I'm too weak."

"You're not weak. *You're the light herself.*" Evangeline said, spitting the words at her. She wanted to shake her again.

Julie expelled a breath that sounded like either a laugh or a sob.

"I know that's not how you feel," Evangeline said before Julie could say anything else. "But it's a trick. Caroline made you feel small. And you can believe it if you want, but it doesn't make it true. She's some random fall witch. You're the *sun*. Caroline wants to watch you burn. Well, why don't you let her? Show her how you can burn."

Julie stayed quiet, so Evangeline continued, "He can use our magic. I've seen him use mine. If he had the power of light and dark at once, he could use it. He could make the forces work together in ways we can't. We're too much. Too dark. Too light. We need him. I promise our spells will work better if he wields them."

Evangeline knew she lied. Well, not lied exactly, but she didn't feel as certain as she sounded. The only time she'd tried to give him her magic, it had overcome him. She believed he could do it, but he had no idea how to do it, and had no one to teach him. And right now, he probably felt weaker than ever.

"I want to see him. I can do it if I see him."

"We have already tried everything to get out of here."

"We've tried to get our bodies out," Julie said. "We've

been thinking too three-dimensionally."

"You know a spell? Something that could make us see him?"

"If you have light, you can see."

Evangeline would have to trust her vague statement, because this must be summer magic. She had no idea how to see through walls.

"Help me with the spell," Julie said.

"I don't know it."

"Please, I can't do it on my own."

"Okay." Evangeline took Julie's hand. She was bluffing. She didn't know the spell. She couldn't cast it. But maybe if Julie thought she had help she would be more confident.

One way or another, it worked. Evangeline had the unsettling sensation of being two places at once. Like when each eye was seeing something different. The scene started at a super close up, and panned out, as if Julie started at the talisman and worked her way out. She saw Patrick's legs first, and then his whole body, bound with magic to a chair. The whites of his eyes had red patches, and his lips looked too white. Whatever Caroline had done to him, he couldn't take much more.

The scene expanded, and she could tell Julie was gaining the strength needed to bring more light to the scene. Evangeline almost dropped her hand when she saw Jude, standing next to Caroline. They both studied Patrick, consulting in whispers, as if determining their next move. *How the hell did he get there?* No wonder Caroline's prax potentia worked so well on Patrick. Nothing sucked your power faster than being hurt by someone you loved—especially someone who was supposed to protect you.

"When?" Julie whispered. "He doesn't look ready."

A major understatement. "I know."

"You're sure he'll know what to do?"

"No...but we have to do it anyway. Look at him. He's

losing."

"I've never tried anything like this."

"I did. Once. Give him your magic. It's like anything else. If you want him to have it, he will."

"So, shall we?"

Evangeline hesitated. "Now."

They had given Patrick a moment of reprieve. Not out of kindness, but to discuss their next plan of attack. He didn't know why they kept going. They had won. They had taken every last drop of his power. He would give them anything to make them stop. Anything. He could no longer remember why he was here in the first place. Or, where he would rather be. He wanted to be in a place without pain. He didn't care where. He didn't care if that meant death. As long as the pain stopped.

So, when he felt the pain coming, he tensed, perhaps more than he had before, because he didn't understand it. Caroline spoke to Jude, and they both faced away from him. He had at least grown a minor sense of comfort knowing when pain would come, and when it wouldn't. It would only come if she touched him. This made no sense. And that terrified him.

The pain didn't run down his nerves as when Caroline touched him. It started at his core and worked its way out. If his soul existed, then that's where the pain centered. A cold, darkness that blotted out the light behind his eyes. His skin burned all over. But he realized relief could come. The darkness would take him away and make him numb. It would take his soul. Take his life. And then there would be nothing. He welcomed it, willing his body to stop fighting against it, despite the powerful instinct for survival. The darkness would come, and when it did, they could never hurt him again.

But then, as if the darkness realized it comforted him, a

new sensation rushed in. A horrible, horrible heat. A fire burned him from the inside out, and filled him with the life he wanted to escape. A life that burned far too hot. He couldn't stop himself from crying out.

The rush of pain made it hard to see, but he sensed Jude and Caroline coming closer.

"What are you doing to him?" Jude asked.

"Nothing."

"What do you mean, 'nothing?' "

"I'm really not, Jude."

Patrick had the urge to run, to fight, to do anything to get the fiery monster off of him. And in his panic to flee, he flew out of the chair, breaking the magical bonds that held him there.

But he couldn't stand for long. He tasted blood in his mouth, and crumpled to the floor.

"Oh no," Julie said. "No. No. No. We're killing him. We have to stop."

Evangeline felt the same way. She hated seeing Patrick suffer, especially knowing she caused the pain. But she had to be the tough one. Julie was way too soft.

"Wait. Please, wait. Look, he broke the paralyzing spell already. Don't stop."

"He's not moving."

"Please, Julie. Don't stop. Of course, it hurts him. How do you think it would feel to have pure summer and winter magic blasted into you at once? Just wait."

Evangeline thought maybe he *was* dying. She could sense his light fading. But the light was still there. Even if he didn't realize it, he had so much power right now, he didn't need training. He could take them down with a look. But he still didn't move. He had his face pressed against the ground, and Evangeline thought she could see blood trickling from the corners of his mouth.

Jude kneeled next to Patrick. Evangeline could see the scene but she couldn't hear it, however, it looked like Jude shouted something at Caroline.

"He's no use to me dead, Jude," Caroline said. "Why would I kill him? I'm not doing this."

"Then what the fuck is happening?"

"I don't know. I keep telling you, I don't know."

"Shouldn't you though? Aren't you supposed to be the omnipotent genius?"

"Stop talking and let me think."

"I can still feel his pulse."

Then Patrick realized Jude touched him. Jude had his hand on his wrist. His touch jolted him back into reality. He hated Jude. He hated him and he loved him at once. And that made him so, so angry. He wanted Jude to stop touching him. He wanted him away.

Patrick felt a surge of magic leave him and enter Jude at the point where their skin made contact. He had no idea where the magic had come from.

"Jude?" Patrick heard Caroline's voice, but the light behind his eyes was so bright, he couldn't see anything around him. He blinked until he could focus. He saw Jude lying near him, Caroline kneeled beside him, shaking him.

Patrick pulled himself up. His body felt so weak, but he found that he didn't need his muscles. He wanted to stand, and so he rose, powered by magic alone. And he hovered over Caroline. She turned and looked up at him.

Her eyes looked red, as if she had started to cry, but she

still smiled up at him. "I'm glad it's you. The fall."

He hit her with a spell. He didn't take much time to think it through and had no idea what he hit her with. He wanted her down. He wanted her to be no longer a threat. He only needed to want it, and it happened. She crumpled, her head falling on Jude's back.

Patrick must have blacked out, because he didn't remember anything else until he saw Evangeline and Julie hovering over him. His sight went in and out, his eyes burning with light and then covered in dark. He knew if the girls kneeled over him, then they must have won. It was over. But he still felt so much pain. His heart raced, and skipped irregularly. He knew his body couldn't handle any more.

"Are you okay?" Julie asked.

"No," Patrick said.

"You did good," Evangeline said.

"What?" Patrick asked.

"We should stay back," Julie said. "He's confused. And still all filled with magic. He could curse us too."

"Are you going to curse me?" Evangeline asked.

"No."

"I know you're in pain, Patrick. But I promise. It's over. They're gone."

Patrick felt heat. He sat up and looked around. Pain shot up his arms and legs as he moved. Summer had returned. Early summer morning, the light in the sky still a cool purple, and the heat still bearable. The perfect moment between light and dark.

"Caroline's spell, it's gone? We can walk out."

Smoke still darkened the horizon, but it had dissipated since yesterday, which meant the fire had burned down.

"Yeah, they're gone," Evangeline said.

"Gone? As in…dead?" Patrick asked.

"No. Just gone." Evangeline cast her eyes down as if this disappointed her. "If you had wanted them dead, they would be dead. But that must not be the spell you cast. They got knocked out, but by the time we made it out, they were gone. And all the spells cast around this place went away."

"Where did they go?"

"I don't know. Where did you send them?"

"It wasn't like that. I didn't know what I was doing. I wanted it to stop. I wanted them away."

"Well, then that's what happened. If you wanted them away, they are *way* away. Probably on their way to China. They'd be going to the moon if it was possible."

"How?"

"I told you. I saw it in the park. You can use other wizard's magic. And you can use it well. Decisively. More than what the wizard alone could do. We gave you ours. Me and Julie."

"You did that. That…pain. I thought I was going to die."

"I'm sorry," Evangeline said. "But you're not going to die. Not today, anyway."

"I'm sorry, too," Julie said. She smiled at him tentatively. She looked different from the girl in the photo. Thinner. And much less bright. But alive. And she could go home now.

Patrick reached into his pocket, took out her charm bracelet, and held it out to her. He could swear she already glowed brighter. At least, she smiled bigger when she put the bracelet on.

"Thank you," she said.

"Okay. I want a cheeseburger. And a chocolate shake," Patrick said. "Let's go."

And so they walked out. Slowly. Patrick still hurt everywhere. His muscles spasmed with every move. The girls wandered like lost ghosts, tired and weak. But they walked.

When they came through a patch of trees, they all stopped

in their tracks. The trees dropped off suddenly. They had reached the edge of Caroline's spell, and found a perfect line, obliterated by fire on one side, and untouched forest on the other. The wildfire side still smoldered, but they could see the road through the black carpet of ground and field of black sticks that used to be trees.

Patrick felt another surge of unease seeing the power of Caroline's spell. And she was still out there. Probably looking for the spring equinox to round herself out.

"How do you think the Mundanes are going to explain this?" Patrick asked.

"Aliens?" Julie suggested.

"Come on," Patrick said and they padded their way across the charred earth toward the road.

CHAPTER THIRTY-FOUR

Patrick and Evangeline had been admitted to the hospital for "observation," which meant anyone could see something was wrong with them, but the doctors didn't know what, other than dehydration and some cuts and bruises. Patrick also had two broken ribs from where Jude had kicked him. And his blood pressure was too high, which the doctors found strange for someone young and in good health. But Patrick knew his body had been pushed to the limit.

Surely, Julie had been admitted to the hospital too, but Patrick didn't know. As soon as the firefighters brought them to the hospital, she disappeared back into her summer world. Maybe her parents had her moved to a different hospital, far, far away from the Vandergraffs.

Dad came in with a pizza. It hurt to eat, but Patrick didn't care. He wanted to do it anyway.

"Good, you're awake," Dad said. "You can have dinner with me. Evangeline wanted sushi, so Emmy and Amanda went to get that. But I'm not interested in sushi and I figured you wouldn't be either."

"No. Thanks."

Dad pulled out plates and sodas. Things still sucked a lot. But Patrick had to admit, it was all relative. Being alive. Not being in pain. Eating pizza with his Dad. It was all pretty freaking fantastic.

"I would say it's nice you're all staying here with me and Evangeline…but you don't have a house, so…"

Dad chuckled. "Eh. Details."

"What am I supposed to tell the police?" Patrick asked. "So far, I've just been saying I don't want to talk about it. That's not going to work for much longer."

"Tell them as much of the truth as you can."

"Even about Jude?"

"He's done nothing to deserve your loyalty."

Patrick nodded.

"Try not to be too upset when they don't believe you," Dad said.

"What do you mean?"

"I've already talked with the police. We've talked and talked in circles. They say no one named Caroline Prescott exists. I'm thinking she has some spells up to hide her identity, which is why I had trouble finding her." Then Dad's eyes seemed to darken. "And the police don't believe for a second John Prescott shot your Uncle James. They instinctively trust the Prescotts and presume them to be good. I'll keep trying. He doesn't get to just walk away…" Dad trailed off, glaring at the bubbles popping in his Dr. Pepper.

"If they don't believe Caroline or John are guilty, what do they think? That we all just ran away from home?"

"They found Jude's fingerprints at the house. And he's in the system. They believe *he* exists. And he fits their idea of a criminal. It's an easy answer and they all seem to like it. They think that's why I'm fabricating things about the Prescotts, to try and cover up my son's crimes."

"So, they'll arrest him? He'll go to jail?"

"I suppose that's up to Caroline."

"What do you mean?"

"She managed to hide several acres of land from the

police. She can hide one man if she wants to."

"Right." Patrick rubbed the skin around his IV. His hands shook. "So, then, there will be punishment for them at all? No justice?"

"I didn't say that. I'm saying the justice won't come from the Mundane police."

"Are you disappointed in me?"

"Why in the hell would I be disappointed in you?"

"I didn't save your brother. I didn't forsee him dying. I don't know…I guess I didn't know him well enough to have a vision about him. I'm sorry."

"Son, you're not responsible for preventing every bad thing that ever happens. I don't expect that of you. No one does."

"I never actually saw it. The vision I had of Julie being tortured. I never saw the same image I saw in my head. What does that mean?"

"I don't know."

"Does that mean it was a trick? That the siren spell made me see it, so I would come to the forest?"

"Perhaps. Or maybe it means your power is more complicated than you realize. You knew Julie was being tortured, and you were right. You may have been taking the vision too literally. You assumed you would have to see it as you did in order for the vision to make sense. But maybe you just knew."

"Maybe."

"Even if you didn't understand why, you were right. You were right that Julie was being tortured. You were right that you could walk through the concealment spell. And you were right that you could save Julie and Evangeline. I hate to say it, but if fall magic is anything like other types of magic, it involves a lot of guesswork. But in the end, you were right."

"Being right is overrated."

"I wouldn't know. You'll have to ask your mother." He

smiled slightly, and handed Patrick another slice of pizza.

EPILOGUE

Amanda opened her eyes and saw the empty chair where David had sat a moment ago.

"David?"

She had dozed off, a strange thing to do while getting chemo. She didn't care how tired she was, she couldn't sleep with chemicals being pumped into her veins. And where was David? He always stayed with her. She believed in the power of his presence more than she believed in the power of chemotherapy.

She tried to comfort herself. He could have seen she was sleeping and took the chance to go use the restroom or get a drink. But she doubted it. She could feel agitated, dirty magic polluting the room.

"Mom?"

She saw Jude, and that monster, Caroline. Jude looked stricken. He hadn't seen her since the chemo had taken her hair and all the youth left in her skin. But Caroline smiled at her, her arm looped around Jude's. If Amanda had any strength at all, she would have done her best to attack her. But she had neither physical or magical strength anymore, at least not enough to put a dent in Caroline. She had sucked magic out of three of the four events, and had to be more deadly and dangerous than ever.

"David," Amanda called.

"He'll be right back," Caroline said. "Just taking a break."

Amanda looked around and saw everyone had taken a break. The nurses. The other patients. The entire chemo room had emptied.

"Stay away from me," Amanda said.

"Mom, it's okay. She's here to help you." Jude approached her and reached for her hand.

Amanda grabbed Jude's hand and squeezed it as hard as she could, a combination of affection and attack. "You need to stay away from her."

"That's not going to happen."

"How could you? After you've seen what she did to your brother and sister? I still had faith in you. How dare you prove me wrong?" She threw his hand back at him.

Caroline put her hand on Jude's arm. "Don't worry about it," she said. "She's sick. In pain."

Caroline poked at the tubes on the chemotherapy machine curiously. "Did they give you odds?" she asked.

Amanda didn't answer. She looked around. She knew magic would do no good. So, she prayed to God instead. For David to come back. For Caroline to leave. For Jude to be okay. For her to live.

"It's important," Caroline said. "I need to know your odds. They must think you have a chance of survival, if they continue treatment. Is this right? Is there some chance? If not, I need to know."

"Tell her, Mom. What kind of odds did they give you the treatment would work?"

"Go away," she said.

"If you're terminal, then I may still be able to help," Caroline said. "But I'll have to wait until I find the spring equinox wizard. Magic from three out of four events will be enough if you have a chance of survival. But in order to reverse death, I'll need the spring."

"Reverse death? That's not something wizards can do."

Caroline smiled. "That's not something polar wizards can do. A wizard with magic from each event could do anything."

"I don't want your help," Amanda said. "I don't want any of your dirty magic touching me. I know what you did to get it."

"Please, Mom," Jude said. "You don't like her, that's fine. But that's no reason to die. Think about Dad. About Patrick and Emmy. How could you leave them knowing you didn't have to?"

"I don't want to leave them. I don't want to die."

"Of course you don't," Caroline said.

"5-10% chance of remission. Those are my odds," Amanda said.

"That should be plenty," Jude said. "Right?"

Caroline nodded. "You're going to be fine," she said.

Amanda wanted to spit in her face, but instead tears slid down her cheeks. She wanted to live. All she had wanted for the past few months was for someone to tell her she would be fine, and *really* mean it.

"It won't happen overnight, I'm afraid," Caroline said. "At least I don't think so. It means the treatment will work. You'll still have to get the chemo. Do you understand?"

"Yes."

Caroline took her hand. Amanda winced. At her touch, she felt fear. And for a moment she didn't know if Caroline had come to kill her or save her. A demon and an angel all wrapped into one.

Caroline patted Amanda's hand. "This won't hurt a bit," she said.

ACKNOWLEDGEMENTS

Authors notes 2019: Watch Me Burn was re-published in 2019 through Animus Ferrum press. The new cover was created by Kimberley Marsot and formatting was updated by Dorothy Dreyer.

In life, there haven't been too many places where I've felt like I truly "fit in." However, the community of readers and writers is different. I belong perfectly with the hard-working, big-dreaming, weirdoes and misfits that I am so pleased to call my friends, fans, and colleagues. Within this community, there are countless people who deserve thanks. If I had time, I would write a thank you note to every one of you who chooses to purchase my book, and then a big, squishy hug for everyone who takes the time to write a review or tell someone about my book in person or online. I also want to thank the talented ladies who helped make Watch Me Burn the best it could be—beta readers Vicki Keire, Gwen Gardner, and Emma Adams, acquiring editor Katie Hamstead, and my lead editor Julie Rodriguez. Also, Nikola Vukoja who found some last minute edits. All of you left your lovely and clever fingerprints in the text.

Thank you my cover artist Michelle Johnson for her breathtaking work, and to all the staff at Curiosity Quills Press who help me share my stories with the world—especially Eugene Teplitsky, Lisa Gus, Nikki Tetreault, Andrew Buckley, and Clare Dugmore. And as in all things, I want to thank my family for their unwavering support of my ridiculous dream, especially my husband and mother, who stand by and support me every day of my life...including the ones when I forget to shower. I'd also like to thank my sons, who frankly, are not supportive of Mommy's writing because they think she should play with them 24/7, but I'd still like to thank them for being super cute and for not yet spilling juice on my laptop.

ABOUT THE AUTHOR

Sharon Bayliss lives in Austin, Texas with her husband and children. She hates wearing shoes and loves jogging in the rain. She only practices magic in emergencies.

She is also the author of the young adult science fiction novel, *The Charge*.

You can connect with her at www.sharonbayliss.com, www.facebook.com/authorsharonbayliss, and @SharonBayliss on Twitter.